AN **AMERICAN GHOST** THRILLER

ROGUE

OTHER TITLES BY J. B. TURNER

Jon Reznick Series:

Hard Road

Hard Kill

Hard Wired

Hard Way

Hard Fall

J.B. TURNER

AN **AMERICAN GHOST** THRILLER

ROGUE

THOMAS & MERCER

This is a work of fiction. Names, characters, organizations, places, events, and incidents are either products of the author's imagination or are used fictitiously. Any resemblance to actual persons, living or dead, or actual events is purely coincidental.

Published by Thomas & Mercer, Seattle

www.apub.com

ISBN-13: 9781542048385
ISBN-10: 1542048389

Cover design by @blacksheep-uk.com

Printed in the United States of America

To my mother

Prologue

Nine days out

The five men around the table couldn't agree when the senator would die.

Clayton Wilson leaned back in his seat and sighed. Along with his colleagues, he'd been studying the classified file for hours. But it was time to make a final decision.

"Gentlemen," he said, "my view is that this man is a real threat to our interests."

Wilson looked across at Richard Stanton, who was still immersed in the file. Then his gaze fell on the other men around the table. "I believe the analysis we have proves this man will not go away. He is openly advocating we invoke Article 13 of NATO to withdraw. This position seems to be finding favor in some quarters of the media too. And it clearly jeopardizes the security of the whole of Europe, as well as going against American economic and political interests. He will not be silenced. Do we all agree on this?"

Nods from each of the four men.

"The speech to the Press Club sent shock waves around our allies. What the hell is going on in Washington, they wanted to know? And that's why I believe we should use the window of opportunity. We have exactly nine days to neutralize him once and for all."

Stanton pinched the bridge of his nose as he looked up. "I agree with the analysis. I just feel that carrying out the operation in a friendly country does pose logistical as well as diplomatic challenges. Isn't he due to head to China as part of a trade mission in eight months? Wouldn't that be a more opportune time?"

Wilson sighed. "The analysis is telling us that the timescale should be within the next thirty days. His popularity and ideas are gaining traction. Young people like him. Old people like him. If he'd stayed on the fringes, fine. But he's no longer on the fringes. He's mainstream. We can't allow this to develop any further."

Stanton turned and looked at the other three men in the room. Retired General Adam C. Johnson, Retired Admiral Charles Coleridge, and former director of the CIA Crawford McGovern. The only one of the group not present was Brigadier Jack Sands, a non-voting member, their point man in Scotland. "Gentlemen, I'm with Clayton," Stanton said. "But I'm concerned about giving ourselves such a tight window of opportunity on this. Adam, what are your thoughts on timing?"

Johnson looked up from the notes and peered over his half-moon spectacles. "The beauty of the option in nine days is that our latest intelligence shows that the senator is planning to spend a day outside the confines of the summit's secure zone. We need to take advantage. In addition, we already have an operative within striking distance. We know the senator's plans for this trip and have for the last three months. A whole set of problems will be presented to us if we wait. I'm with Clayton on this. We do it in nine days."

Coleridge nodded, eyes dead. "Agreed."

Wilson cleared his throat and looked across at McGovern, his mentor and predecessor at the Agency. "Crawford? Your thoughts?"

McGovern stared at Wilson. "I've followed the senator's career with interest of late. I met him once at a reception at the British embassy. Very sociable. Very bright. But what takes this guy to a different level is that he is being seriously touted as a presidential candidate. He is going to run. The opinion formers love him, both right and left. He makes good copy. And it's all increasing his visibility." McGovern sighed. "I say his visit to the security conference in the UK is perfect. And that's why, gentlemen, we must green-light this for nine days' time."

Wilson smiled across at McGovern. They were cut from the same cloth. Men who understood the military. Understood what America needed to remain preeminent on the world stage. What it took to stay number one. He knew as well as anyone that withdrawal from the world stage, isolationism, would only benefit China, Russia, and other sworn enemies—including Iran. They'd be free to extend their tentacles. And Wilson and his cohorts couldn't allow that. That was what people like Senator Crichton didn't get. An Ivy League background and prep school had prepared him for nothing but academia. And his ideas were dangerous. "We have five in the room giving the go-ahead. We have four agreed on the date. But as you all know, we need unanimous agreement to green-light this."

Stanton flicked through the briefing papers for a few moments before he looked across at Wilson. He let out a long sigh. "Our director of operations, Brigadier General McMichael, says both dates are open. But he's also saying the UK visit is the best option. This briefing was dated seventy-two hours ago. Is that still his position?"

Wilson nodded. "I spoke with McMichael before I arrived here. His words? *We're good to go. We have a guy in place. We know where he'll be and when. We can green-light this now.*"

Stanton nodded and scribbled some notes in the margins of the senator's file. He stared long and hard at the black-and-white surveillance photo of the senator clipped to the front. "Very well. Nine days it is."

One

Nathan Stone stared at his reflection in the mirror. He gazed long and hard at the strange new face. Higher cheekbones, brown eyes instead of blue, nose narrower, face less lined. He didn't recognize the man staring back at him. Would his sister even recognize him?

A knock at his door snapped him out of his reverie. Two men in navy-blue jumpsuits walked in and motioned for him to join them. They escorted him down a series of corridors to a windowless room.

Inside, a man was sitting behind a polished table, a pile of papers in front of him. Nathan noticed a mirror on the wall behind the man. A one-way mirror. Cameras in all four corners of the room. A huge plasma screen on the wall opposite the man.

The man gestured for Nathan to sit down in the seat across from him.

Stone complied, and the two escorts left the room, locking the door behind them.

The man smiled, reached into his jacket pocket, and leaned over to hand Nathan a packet of Winstons with a Zippo lighter. "Go right ahead," he said.

Stone tapped out a cigarette, lit up, and watched the blue smoke spiral to the AC unit on the ceiling.

The man leaned back in his seat. "Good morning, Nathan." His accent sounded midwestern, educated. "How are you feeling today?"

Stone dragged heavily on the cigarette. "Do I know you?"

"No. But I know all about you. Does that surprise you?"

"Who are you?"

"I'm a doctor."

"No shit."

"I'm a psychologist."

Stone said nothing and took another hard drag on the cigarette.

"Are you comfortable here?"

"What do you mean, comfortable?"

"I mean, is there anything we can get you?"

"I'm good."

The man nodded. "Do you want to talk about anything?"

Stone dragged on his cigarette and shrugged.

The man was quiet for a few moments. "Nathan, do you know where you are and why you're here?"

Stone shook his head.

"I've just been looking at your medical notes and history since you've been with us, and flashbacks are a recurrent theme."

Stone stared at the man. His voice seemed familiar.

"Do you want to talk about that?"

"Not really."

"I think it'd be very helpful."

"I'd like to talk about why I'm being kept here."

The man sighed. "We're looking after you, Nathan. Keeping you safe. We only want what's best for you. Do you believe me when I say that?"

Stone said nothing.

"I've been watching your progress, and I like what I see. The physical assessments are first-rate. You're in very good shape. We just need to work on your flashbacks."

Stone wondered what the man was getting at.

The man glanced at his notes and leaned forward, hands clasped. His gaze didn't waver. "Would it surprise you if I said I know everything there is to know about Nathan Stone?"

Stone dropped his cigarette on the wooden floor and crushed it with the sole of his sneaker. "You wanna get to the point, Doc?"

The man picked up the remote control and pressed a button. Stone turned around. The screen showed surveillance film of a middle-aged white man in a suit walking in what looked like DC, talking into his cell phone. "Can you identify this man?"

Stone studied the footage for a few moments. "Can't say that I can."

"Take a good look."

Stone focused on the footage on the screen. It showed the man hailing a cab.

"This was taken yesterday in Washington, DC. I'm going to ask you again. Do you recognize this man?"

"Same answer, Doc. Nope."

The doctor smiled as the image froze. Just as the man was about to get into the cab.

"Why are you smiling?"

The doctor looked at him long and hard. "Take a good look at this man one final time."

Stone did as he was told. He was well turned out. Professional class. "Who is he?"

"A politician."

"What else?"

"Commit that face to memory."

"Why?"

The man fixed his steely gaze on Stone and smiled. "Why?"

Stone nodded.

"Because you're going to kill him in nine days' time, that's why."

Two

Senator Brad Crichton was sitting at his desk in the upstairs study of his colonial mansion in a gated community on the outskirts of McLean, Virginia. In front of him was a pile of briefing papers for his upcoming foreign intelligence trip. He took off his glasses, leaned back in his seat, and stared at the silver-framed photo of his wife and him standing alongside their two sons in a box at a Redskins game. He smiled, remembering his sons high-fiving some of the players after the game.

He didn't see his sons as often as he used to. They were off at school. His eldest, Adam, away at Duke Law School, his youngest at Deerfield, a prestigious boarding school in Massachusetts. He was immensely proud of them both. They worked hard. And they weren't spoiled like a lot of modern rich kids. His wife had done a good job with them, raising them with solid values. Hard work, family, God, and the American way. But he'd also instilled in them the importance of being truly independent and not having the government do everything for you. Self-reliance. Sacrifice.

He joined the Marines straight out of school and served in Afghanistan. After four years, and losing countless friends, he realized America was making a terrible situation much worse. And it began to shape his political views. Crichton left the military and was accepted into Harvard Law School. His father's advice had been simple: work hard, be true to yourself, and don't be afraid to take risks. He graduated top of his class. He got recruited by a top-four New York law firm, Weiss & Weiss. This was followed by years of working long and hard. Unexpectedly, on his fortieth birthday he became a partner. The clients rolled in.

Among them was a wealthy Manhattan philanthropist, Mort Lintbourg, who began to bankroll his political ambitions. Brad had always been interested in politics. His father, a self-made man who had built a fortune importing Persian rugs into the US in the 1970s, believed strongly in free markets and personal freedom and had spoken of them often to a young Brad. He had listened intently as he soaked up his father's view of the world. But over the years he had grown more libertarian in his views: economic freedoms, social freedoms, noninterventionist foreign policy.

Crichton was elected to the Senate as a Republican in 2014. But in the intervening years he had grown increasingly strident in his views. The most eye-catching was his belief that the United States should withdraw from NATO. His popularity ratings took an initial dive, but slowly they seemed to get traction, and now his numbers were at an all-time high.

His views were popular on the left, and he had garnered numerous plaudits in the media. The fact of the matter was America was trillions in debt and couldn't afford to keep propping up a Cold War relic in NATO. He was a constitutional conservative who wanted America to start living within its means.

His star was in the ascendency, and he knew that a powerful team had been assembled by Mort in anticipation of an announcement later in the year that he was throwing his hat in the ring for the Republican presidential primary next spring.

His phone rang and he picked up after two rings.

"Senator, hope I'm not disturbing you." It was his aide Lionel Epstein.

"Not at all. What's on your mind?"

"Just a heads-up. I'm hearing there's going to be a paper, which we're still trying to get hold of, on the conference agenda talking about a five-cent real-money increase on intelligence spending over a three-year time frame. And the US is pressing for two percent of GDP as the norm for all NATO partners."

"Yeah, I heard about that last night. What's your point, Lionel? I've got to leave in a few minutes to catch a plane."

"My point is the thrust of everyone there will be to agree to this, to try and show how patriotic they are and not look weak on terrorism and all that stuff we've heard a gazillion times before. We need to be talking about the vested interests of the military-industrial complex versus the real needs of the American people."

"Yeah, I got this, Lionel."

"There's something else."

"What?"

"I'm hearing that one company, Aviotrics Software Inc., who specialize in military computer systems, has been sounding out some staffers on which politicians would want to join their board. Offering crazy inducements. Guarantee if you meet with them, within five minutes they'll be offering you the earth."

"Like I said, Lionel, I got this."

"I'm only saying, Senator. They've got a $2.4 billion cash mountain to throw around, and they've got the best lobbyists on Capitol Hill, and they're actively trying to recruit amenable politicians."

"Well, they can throw around as much as they like, I ain't interested."

A long sigh down the line.

"You OK?"

"Too much coffee and too little sleep, Senator."

"Lionel, take off for a few days. Recharge the batteries. Like I said, I got this, and I know what I'll be facing."

Downstairs his wife shouted. "Brad!"

"OK, if that's all, Lionel, I gotta go."

"Have a great trip, Senator."

Crichton ended the call. His cell phone indicated a message. He opened it up. It was from another aide, Jessica. It read, *Last night was special. Can't wait for you to return, J.* His heart skipped a beat, and he deleted it immediately. Over the last few months, she had been sending more and more personal texts to him as their relationship had become more intimate. He loved spending time with her. She made him feel happy. Young again. Carefree. As if life could still be fun instead of a grind. His mind drifted to the previous evening. A romantic meal at the Mandarin Oriental followed by a nightcap with Jessica at her apartment. She had wanted him to stay over. But that wasn't an option.

He put the papers into his briefcase and headed downstairs, where his wife was holding a mug of coffee. He pecked her on the cheek and took a sip of scalding, strong coffee. "Thanks. Gonna miss you, Madison honey."

She smiled. "Yeah, whatever. So, your case is packed. And your overnight bag too. Both in the trunk of the car."

"What would I do without you?"

"Flounder."

Crichton smiled, knowing it was true.

"Look, I'll be back before you know it. Are you all organized?"

She folded her arms. "What do you think?"

"Fair enough."

"What's the best number to reach you on?"

"Let me call you. They're five hours ahead of us, so I'll give you a call before dinner every night. That'll be around lunchtime here."

She hugged him tight. "I'm gonna miss you, Brad."

Crichton saw a sadness in her eyes. "Hey, stop worrying. I'm coming back, all right?"

Madison put on a brave smile for him. "And don't work too hard. Promise?"

Crichton pecked her a final time on the cheek. "You worry too much, you know that?"

Three

Eight days out

Nathan Stone felt sweat dripping off his nose as he did pull-ups on a horizontal steel bar fitted above the bathroom door, adjacent to his bedroom. He felt the endorphins rushing through his body. And the blood was flowing hard through his veins. His mood had begun to lighten.

He wiped himself down with a towel.

Afterward, he did an hour of yoga. It controlled the body and mind. He closed his eyes. Listened to his breathing. He felt calm again. More focused.

Stone felt a euphoria wash over him. He opened his eyes and looked at himself again in the mirror. He frowned, then smiled, then frowned again. Was he getting used to this new face?

Waves of tiredness washed over him, and he lay down on top of the bed.

He felt himself drifting away. Floating on dark waters. He thought he heard his sister's voice whispering to him. Reassuring him that it was going to be all right.

A knock at the door snapped him out of his dreamlike state. "Hey, Stone," a man's voice shouted through the intercom. "Shake a leg."

Stone got to his feet as the door was opened. He was escorted down corridors to the same windowless room. A nurse took blood samples before he underwent a series of physical tests. Cardiovascular, body fat, muscle tone, heart rate, blood pressure, and a urine sample.

When the tests were finished, Stone was handed a bottle of chilled water. He gulped it down. Then he sat on the examination table and lit up a cigarette. A knock at the door and the psychologist he'd seen the previous day walked in.

The man took a seat opposite Stone.

Stone dragged hard on his cigarette and stared across at the smiling psychologist. "What's going on, Doc?"

"You're a new person, Nathan. New face. New ID. Everyone thinks you're dead. In your line of work, that's good."

Stone dropped the empty plastic water bottle in a trash can. "My line of work."

"Yes . . . a line of work you've excelled at for many years. We needed a job done, you did it."

Stone flicked ash onto the concrete floor. He knew what he was.

"Do you remember your previous life?"

Stone nodded.

The psychologist pointed to his adjacent office, and they both walked through the doorway. Stone sat on the same seat as he had the day before.

"Nathan," the psychologist said, leaning back in his seat, "yesterday I showed you an image of this man." He pressed the remote, and images of the politician again appeared on the huge screen. "How do you feel when I show you this man's photo, Nathan?"

Stone stared across at the psychologist and then up at the screen.

"Answer the question."

"How do I feel?" Stone shrugged. "I feel nothing."

"Take a good look at his face."

Stone stared hard at the image.

The psychologist looked at his watch. "It's getting late. You need your rest. Nathan, can you do me a favor?"

Stone shrugged.

"I'd like you to go back to your room, lie down on your bed, close your eyes, and listen to any sounds you hear."

Stone nodded. He was escorted back to his room. The door was locked, and he lay back on his bed. He could hear his breathing. Deeper and deeper he felt himself falling.

Then he began to detect the softest music he'd ever heard. Gentle. Soothing. Then a man spoke.

"Nathan." The voice of the psychologist echoed around his room. "Listen to my voice. Listen to the rhythm of my voice. The tone. The texture. Are you listening, Nathan?"

Stone nodded, eyes closed.

"That's good, Nathan. That's very good. The time is getting close, Nathan. The time you live for. The time when you will be free. Do you know what I'm talking about, Nathan?"

Stone moaned his agreement.

"We've got four words for you. Do you know what they are?"

Stone shook his head.

"It's been a long time since you heard those words, isn't it?"

Stone moaned.

The psychologist began to hum a tune. A tune Stone's father had hummed whenever he'd come home drunk, crazy, and evil. An old lament. A lament for lost souls. "Can you see Daddy's face again, Nathan? Can you?"

Stone moaned.

"You know what those words were?"

Stone shook his head.

"He said, *Time to play, Nathan.*"

Stone said nothing.

"Do you remember that phrase from your past?"

"Yes, I do."

Stone opened his eyes. The voice was familiar. A voice he'd heard hundreds of times. Ingrained in his mind. In his soul. He'd never seen the man before, until now. "Yeah, I remember."

"All coming back to you now?"

Stone closed his eyes. "Oh yeah."

Four

It was late morning and Jeff Patterson was finishing a three-thousand-word article for the radical libertarian magazine *Beware the State* at his loft studio in Dupont Circle. His cell phone rang. It rang a second time. Then silence.

It's the signal.

Patterson logged off, finished his coffee, and headed out onto the broiling sidewalk. He walked the two hundred yards to the Metro station and took the Red Line to Metro Center. He arrived four short minutes later.

He changed to the Silver Line and caught a train to East Falls Church.

Patterson left the station and walked five minutes in the high humidity to the Benjamin Banneker Park. He felt the sweat trickling down his back. Through the thick summer foliage, he saw kids playing soccer. Then he saw the parking lot, his intelligence source sitting in the white Audi.

Patterson walked over as the man opened the passenger door. He slid in and shut the door. His source was a white, late-middle-aged man with closely cropped hair, piercing blue eyes, and a thick neck. He wore a white T-shirt, jeans, and sneakers.

"How you doing?" the man asked.

"Good, Charles."

The man stared at Patterson with his penetrating blue eyes. "You're not carrying a cell phone, iPad, or electronic equipment of any sort?"

"Absolutely not."

"Been reading your articles. Interesting stuff." The man glanced around as two female joggers ran past, his thick neck straining against his T-shirt in the process.

"I've been snowed under. Doing three separate investigations. I haven't heard from you for a while."

"Been out of town."

"Out of town? Do you mean out of the country?"

The source just smiled. "Let's just say I've been busy too. OK, let's get down to business. I need to know that you've got connections on Capitol Hill."

"Let me tell you, the list is getting smaller by the year. Only a handful will give me the time of day. So . . . what've you got?"

"Jeff, I trust you. You've been straight down the line. And I appreciate that."

"That's the only way, man."

"You know where I'm coming from. I'm a patriot first and foremost. But I loathe the encroachment of the state."

"Amen to that."

"OK . . . here's where I'm at, Jeff. In my line of work, we operate on a need-to-know basis. We only know so much of what's going on."

"Sure. Compartmentalized and all that, right?"

"Right. So we both know where we're coming from."

Patterson nodded but said nothing.

"I have a friend—well, actually he's a friend of a friend. And he started working as a highly paid contractor for the CIA a few months back. He's an analyst."

"What does he analyze?"

"Doesn't matter. He got talking to his coworkers over recent months, as you do. Going out for a beer, the usual socializing. So anyway, he was out, and the guy he was with, a longtime CIA guy, gets blind drunk, so my friend's friend, he drove him home."

"Sounds like a good guy."

"He is. Anyway, when he gets home, he realizes he put the drunk guy's car keys in his own jacket by mistake."

"It happens."

"That's right. So my friend thinks, OK, I'll drive on over early the following morning to drop them off. But when he looked more closely at the bunch of keys, he noticed one of them was, in fact, a flash drive."

"Interesting."

"My friend's friend is nosy I guess. What's in it? Who carries a flash drive on a key ring disguised as a key? And then he starts thinking, what if it contains classified information? So he decides to check it out for himself."

Patterson nodded, not wishing to hurry his source. "What did he find?"

"Intercepted NSA message. Highly classified stuff. Clearly, a major security breach. My friend's friend was furious."

"Did he report it?"

The man sighed. "No, he did not. He handed back the bunch of keys to his coworker the following day, saying 'You dropped these, buddy.'"

"Cool."

"But here's the thing. The information on the flash drive unsettled him."

"So what did it contain?"

The source turned and stared out of his window as a dog walker went past. "You'll find out."

"How?"

"He made a copy. I've seen the contents and decided that people need to know."

"Can I see it?"

"You will. A friend of mine has slipped it into your mailbox on the ground floor of your apartment block in DC."

Patterson flushed. "What? How do you know where I live?"

"Don't worry about it. I just wanted to ensure that it would arrive in one piece at your place."

Patterson took a few moments to digest the information. "You want to tell me what it contains?"

"It's a kill list."

"What do you mean?"

"It's a kill list of undesirables. That's what they call them. Undesirables."

"Who's on the list? Who are they?"

"Politicians. Journalists."

"What?"

"I know it's crazy."

"Stop shitting me. Journalists? Are you kidding me?"

"You don't know the half of it. Two names on the list I checked. They're already dead. One skiing accident. One suicide."

Patterson's stomach knotted. "Shit."

"There's one name on the list that jumped out at me. The reason I wanted to contact you."

Patterson shrugged. "I'm listening."

"Jeff, it's you."

"What?"

"You're on the list. You're one of the people they want to kill."

Five

Nathan Stone was drenched in sweat as he worked out alone in the facility gym. Punching bag, medicine ball, circuit training, sit-ups, ten-mile run on the treadmill, followed by weight training. When he was done after the two-hour workout, he was escorted next door to a boxing ring, where a tough-looking Hispanic kid was waiting for him. Toned muscles. Lean. Couple of gold teeth glistening under the lights before he shoved in a mouth guard.

Stone changed into his boxing gear before entering the ring. He was aware cameras were watching his every move. But he knew what was expected of him.

The bell rang.

Stone moved toward his opponent, ducking and weaving from a flurry of sharp punches. A jab to the jaw and nose. He tasted blood. He felt a switch turn on in him, and a burning anger was lit deep inside.

He led with a sharp jab and followed it up with a crushing right hook to the guy's temple. The Hispanic kid collapsed in a heap, out cold. Nathan spat blood on the canvas beside the sprawled, unconscious youngster.

In the underground gun range, he lined up a military sniper rifle. He shot from two hundred yards and five hundred yards. He hadn't lost his touch. After a shower and a light supper of scrambled eggs, toast, and strong tea, he was back in the windowless room with the psychologist. The lights were dimmed. Up on the huge TV screen was a grainy black-and-white photo of Nathan as a young boy on the Lower East Side standing on the stairs outside their hovel of a home with his sister and father. He stared at it. He remembered it had been taken by a kind teacher who thought he was bright and would benefit from extra lessons after school. He had given Nathan hardbacks of Dickens, Brontë, Hemingway, Mailer. Then he gave him encyclopedias. He learned about the Romans. Ancient Greeks. He soaked up the information. He learned about exotic lands. Foreign countries. He learned the names of capital cities. He learned their populations. He couldn't wait to tell his teacher what he learned. But then one day his father found out about the books. He found them under a pile of dirty clothes, then burned them. Burned them all. In front of Nathan and his sister. Nathan watched the paper burn as his father laughed. He felt the tears on his hot cheeks. As the paper turned to burning ash, he just stared, then sobbed.

He felt himself begin to clench his fists tight.

The psychologist leaned toward him. "Take a close look, Nathan. You remember those days? You remember that bum of a father? Alcoholic? Skid row thug? He beat you a lot, didn't he, Nathan?"

Stone didn't answer.

"It made you the man you are today. For better or worse."

Stone shrugged.

"I've read your file, Nathan. I know all about you. I know all about what happened to your sister. Your father."

"You don't know nothing about me."

"Oh but I do. I know everything there is to know about Nathan Stone, deceased."

Stone looked away from the screen.

"Why do you think your sister killed your father with kitchen scissors?"

"He was drunk. He was beating on me. She was defending me."

"Admirable."

"She's not crazy."

"I know that. But . . . they've got to put her somewhere."

Stone sighed.

"When was the last time you saw her, Nathan?"

"It's been a while."

The psychologist nodded.

Stone flashed back to a blazing-hot summer day in New York only a few months before she killed their father. He was with Helen at the huge Hamilton Fish Park outdoor pool. She was making him laugh by pretending to trip headfirst into the turquoise water. Scores of neighborhood kids from around the Lower East Side cooling off, doing laps, having fun. He remembered she was the one who had taught him to swim when he was seven.

"How is she?"

"She's good. We ensure she's well looked after at all times."

"I'd like to see her again."

The psychologist shrugged. "That can be arranged."

"Where is she?"

"Still in Florida."

Stone thought back to his sister smiling in the mental hospital in Miami. Her soft hands. The artwork she did as part of her therapy. He remembered that she had wanted to be an artist since she was a girl. Maybe an art teacher. That was her dream. She loved sketching. Drawing. She hid all her drawings from their father. He hated art. Anything to do with self-expression he viewed as odd. He mocked her dreams. Staring down at her with glazed, drunken-idiot eyes. She stammered defiance. But she was only ever met with wild laughter. *You will amount to nothing,* he screamed. *You're from a long line of nothings. Nobodies.* Disparaging her with every word and look. Disdain. Helen cried herself to sleep. She once told Nathan about her wish to run away and go to Paris. She told him about the great artists who had lived and worked in the city, artists she had read about in the library. She talked about the great light in the South of France. She talked of Monet. Cezanne. He would listen as her eyes sparkled as she imagined what her life would be like. A dream that would turn to ashes. But even throughout the years of beatings and mental abuse, his sister continued to draw, finding safe places in the terrible room they called home. Under a loose wooden floorboard, where she would eventually hide the scissors with which she would kill their father, she also kept crayons, pencils, chalk, and paper. He loved when she drew. He watched her hour after hour in silence when their father was away. It made him feel calm. Happy.

"You miss her, don't you?"

"She's my sister."

"Family's important."

"I'd like to see her again."

"And you will. But first there's work to do."

"I'm ready. When do we begin?"

Six

Jessica Friel was glad to be on a shaded sidewalk out of the harsh heat as she jogged near her Capitol Hill apartment, Lana Del Rey playing in her headphones. She felt the endorphins surging through her body. She loved every tough mile. Running was her way to combat work stress. Her mind was processing all the emails and calls she'd be expecting when she got to the office. Political journalists, White House staffers, PR firms, corporations wanting to fund her boss's political aspirations. The list went on and on.

The more she thought about it, the more she realized she was drowning in work.

Friel ran harder. She felt the fierce sun beat down on her. DC was hell in the summer. She wished she'd taken off up to her sister's place in Vermont, overlooking Lake Champlain. But instead she'd insisted on covering for another staffer, who was sensibly spending two weeks in Cape Cod.

Her reasons were purely selfish. She wanted to be in DC whenever she could for Brad. She wanted to show him how committed she was, not only to her work but also to him. She missed him when he went out of the country. Missed his touch. Missed his company. He made her laugh. A lot. She could see their relationship was getting more and more serious. He was spending time with her. Evenings with her. She hadn't told a soul. She valued his love and friendship, and it wouldn't be right to divulge her personal life at this stage, even to her closest friends. The truth of the matter was she was having a full-blown affair with a US senator, her boss. If the newspapers found out, she would be hung out to dry. She would be the one at fault. She was surprised at the risks he was taking. Taking her out to upscale restaurants at night. Theater trips. Classical concerts. People had to notice. It was almost like Brad didn't care if news of their relationship got out. Then again, maybe he was just a natural risk taker. Then again, so was she.

Ten minutes later, Friel was back in her third-floor apartment with line-of-sight views to the Capitol. She felt privileged to live and work where she did. But more than anything she felt privileged to work for the senator. She gave her all for him. She believed in him. And he believed in her. In them. She felt excited for her future.

After a cooling shower, Friel put on a summer dress and poured herself an iced tea. She sat down and flicked through the *Post* and the *Economist.*

Her cell phone rang. She didn't recognize the caller ID. "Hi, Jessica speaking."

A beat. "Jessica, you don't know me . . . but I need to talk to you."

"I'm sorry. You don't know me? So how did you get this cell phone number? Are you a journalist?"

"Yeah . . . I got it from a friend."

Friel was intrigued. "Who?"

"Rather not say. I was given it in confidence."

"Listen, I'm going to hang up."

"Don't do that, Jessica. I need to talk to you."

"What about?"

A deep sigh down the line. "Your boss."

"Not possible."

"Look, it's vital I speak to him."

Friel sighed. "Buddy, whoever you are, this is not how it works."

"I have information about your boss. I want to warn him, but I can't get through to him on his cell."

"He changed his number a couple of days ago."

"Shit."

Friel sensed the guy was genuine but couldn't tell for sure.

"I need to get something to you or him *right fucking now*. Do you understand?"

"Look, I'm going to hang up and call the cops."

"I want to warn you. Your boss is on a fucking kill list. People want to kill him. Do you understand that?"

"You crossed the line, pal. Don't ever call me again."

Seven

Seven days out

The cold morning sun peeked over the horizon as Nathan Stone looked through the window in his room. He took a drag on his cigarette, filling his lungs with smoke, and watched the clouds flit across the endless sky.

A sharp knock at his door, and the same two men, keys jangling from their belts, came in. They escorted him again to the windowless room with the one-way mirror.

The psychologist was scribbling notes and yawning. "Take a seat, Nathan," he said without looking up.

"Early start," Stone said, crushing his cigarette in an ashtray.

The psychologist nodded and smiled.

"What?"

"I just wanted to start by saying that we are delighted with your progress."

"You got a thing for me, Doc, is that it?"

The psychologist laughed. "As I said, we are pleased with your progress."

Stone felt an anger building inside him. "Don't bullshit me, Doc. You know this is like a holiday camp for me."

"Your physical tests show that you're in remarkable shape."

Stone didn't respond.

"My colleagues have asked about nicotine patches for you. How do you feel about that?"

"Not an option, Doc. I like my smokes."

"Fair enough."

Stone said, "I want to know where I am."

The psychologist sipped his coffee and stared at Stone. "At this moment in time, you don't have to know that."

"This is an American facility, right?"

"It is an American facility."

"What's the big secret about the location?"

"Nathan, you'll know better than anyone that we all only know a small part of the big picture."

"It gets light early here. Are we in Alaska?"

The psychologist gave a wry smile. "No. We're a long way from Alaska. But you will know sooner rather than later."

"Guaranteed?"

"That's a promise."

Stone sensed the psychologist was building up to something.

"Nathan, we know all about you. Your motivations, background, what gets you going—you understand what I'm saying?"

"You wanna get to the point?"

"The point is we have been monitoring you to see if you still have the skill set required to do a particular job. It's high level. Classified. But we believe you are equipped and ready to do this again."

"You know what I can do."

"You're a valuable asset. You don't have compunction about who lives and dies. And that's a very valuable commodity in our line of work."

Stone shifted in his seat.

The psychologist sighed. "We believe in you. And we want to see you out there again . . . My question is, are you really ready to take that first step?"

"What do you want me to do?"

The psychologist smiled. "You see, that's why we like you, Nathan. It's not about what you want. It's you thinking about how you can offer your services. We respect that. Admire that."

"You want me to kill someone to prove myself?"

The psychologist leaned forward, hands clasped. "We're looking for you to show you've still got it."

"I'm listening."

The psychologist looked at his watch. "It's 5:49 a.m. I'd like you to take the elevator down to subbasement Level F."

"F?"

"Right."

"Then what?"

"When you get off the elevator, turn right and head down to the door at the farthest end, which leads through to a TV room. A young man is in there just now, drinking tea, watching a rerun of a Cardinals game."

Stone nodded.

"We want you to go in and make yourself a coffee from the machine, make small talk. And then at 0600 hours precisely, kill the man."

"Kill the man?"

"Correct. Afterwards, you will get back in the elevator and get off at Level C. You will then be escorted to your room. Is that clear?"

"What about the body?"

"What about it?"

"Do you want it disposed of?"

The psychologist shook his head. "That's not your problem."

Stone took a few moments to digest what he'd been told. "Who is he?"

"He's someone we want taken care of."

Stone cleared his throat. "Very well."

"You good?"

Stone took a moment to answer. "Oh yeah."

A minute later, Nathan Stone was escorted from the windowless room and walked to the elevator. The doors opened and he stepped inside and punched the button for Level F. The guards stared at him as the doors shut. He descended several levels in the steel box elevator before it came to a juddering halt.

A ping sounded and the doors opened. Heart beating hard, he turned right and headed down a poorly lit corridor. Stone pushed through the door at the end of the hallway and looked around. An open-plan TV room. Large screen, football playing as he had been told.

Stone saw the back of the black man's shaved head. He walked over to the adjacent kitchenette and fixed himself a coffee. The man turned around and nodded.

"Who's winning, bro?" Stone asked.

The man winced. "Cardinals are destroying the Chiefs," the man drawled.

Stone took a sip of his coffee as he moved closer to the screen. His mind was racing as he considered how he was going to kill the man. He saw a clock on the wall, the red second hand turning relentlessly. Three minutes and twenty-four seconds to go.

"Pull up a seat," the man said. "Where you from?"

"Originally New York."

"Where'bouts?"

"Down around the Bowery."

"Tough part of town."

"Used to be. It's all hipster bullshit these days. What about you?"

The man fixed his gaze on the game. "What about me?"

"Where you from?"

"Tampa."

"Florida boy, huh?"

Stone noticed a camera high up in a far corner of the room, red light on. He was being watched. Were they watching right now? In real time? He glanced at the clock. One minute forty-eight seconds to go. "Used to work down in Miami. Miss the weather."

"Hell yeah."

Stone lit a cigarette and breathed smoke out of his nose. "You smoke?"

The man shook his head. "No, thanks. Gave up years ago."

Stone dragged hard on the cigarette, filling his lungs with the smoke. "Smart. What part of Tampa you from?"

The man turned around. "What's that?"

"I said what part of Tampa you from?"

"You wouldn't know it."

Stone dragged on his cigarette and dropped it on the concrete floor, crushing it with his foot. "Try me. I've worked all over Florida."

"Ybor. South of Seventh. You heard of it?"

"Can't say I have."

The man focused back on the game. "Fuckin' dump, man."

Stone looked again at the clock. Less than a minute. The second hand moving. Past the five. Then ten. *Not long now.* He got up from his seat and began to walk back to the kitchenette but doubled back to position himself behind the man. He took off his thick leather belt. "Hell of a game."

"Yeah."

Stone stepped forward and wrapped the belt around the man's throat. He pulled tight. The man kicked out, knocking over a footrest and spilling his tea on the floor. His arms flying, the man arched his face up as Stone stared down. He saw the same terror he'd come to know so well. He pulled harder and harder until there was no give. The leather bit down into the man's throat, crushing out the air. Mouth agape, eyes bloodshot. The man struggled for nearly a minute. Then Stone saw the life drain out of the guy. No movement. Dead.

Stone held the belt tight for another ten seconds just to make sure. Then he let go, the dead man slumping motionless back in his seat.

He unwrapped the belt from the man's neck and put it back on his jeans.

Stone turned and looked up at the clock. It showed 0601 hours precisely. He headed out through the doors. He took the elevator back to Level C as instructed. Waiting for him were the two guys in uniform.

He was escorted back to his room.

Stone lay back down on his bed as they locked his door. Then he gazed up at the flaking white paint on the ceiling, affording himself a smile.

Eight

It wasn't even five in the morning and Clayton Wilson had already completed thirty of his sixty daily laps in the empty Ritz-Carlton pool, close to the Pentagon. He had never been a late riser. He couldn't abide not getting a start on the day. It was the way he'd been since he was a boy. And this day was no different.

Wilson's mind drifted to the task at hand. He was in charge of the operation to kill the senator. The Commission trusted him to oversee each and every targeted assassination.

His purpose was to ensure the military-industrial complex of the United States of America flourished. He was a patriot. And he knew the interests of his beloved country went way beyond the boundaries of what had been laid down by fickle politicians.

The beauty of the Commission was that they didn't exist. Not officially. A back channel with the Pentagon ensured that only a select few were in the loop.

Wilson had a meeting with the back channel—the vice chair of the Joint Chiefs of Staff, now a four-star general Wilson had himself promoted fifteen years earlier. At 8:00 a.m. Wilson would secretly update him on preparations.

Wilson was on his final lap. His mind was beginning to feel sharper. Clear despite the three single-malt whiskies he'd enjoyed the previous evening in the bar. He was sixty-two years old but felt as fit as he had when he was fifty. He'd retired from the CIA at sixty. But still he was serving his country. And would do so until the day they put him in the ground.

Wilson thought back to his grueling old life. The punishing hours. The foreign postings. The eternal meetings. The interagency rivalries. The politics. The secret wars. The intelligence disasters. The overthrowing of regimes. The installing of regimes.

He realized the importance of the measures America was forced to take to ensure its own liberty and that of its allies around the world. He thought of his part in the overthrow of the Chilean government. He knew there had been some internal dissent within the CIA on that one. But mainly those in the know knew Allende would have to go. He saw better than most the creeping influence of communism in all its guises. Whether through peasant struggles against landowners or student occupations of universities. He saw the hand of the Reds at work. They were smart. They wanted to undermine a country on America's doorstep. Same with Central America. Sandinistas in Nicaragua were just a bunch of Soviet-backed Marxists out to overthrow a stable country.

Wilson finished his customary swim by 5:25 a.m. He put on his white Ritz-Carlton terry robe and Nike flip-flops and took the elevator back to his fifteenth-floor suite. He picked up his copy of the *Post* left outside his room. Then he showered, shaved, and ordered himself a pot of black coffee, freshly squeezed apple juice, and scrambled eggs and toast from room service.

He got dressed in a dark-navy suit and white shirt, put on his maroon silk tie, and his black leather oxfords. He read the paper and watched Fox News talking about the existential threat from the Islamic State across the Middle East.

A soft knock at the door.

The room service waiter served his breakfast at the huge dining room table in his suite.

He ate alone, Fox down low. After he'd eaten, he opened the drapes. In the distance, across the freeway, the lights were on in the Pentagon.

Wilson finished his first coffee of the day and poured a second. He then checked his emails on his iPhone. One from his son, who was working for a hedge fund in Manhattan, one from his wife, on vacation with her mother in Florida, and one he'd been anticipating.

He switched on his MacBook Pro and opened up the encrypted email program. He clicked twice on the link he'd been waiting for. It asked for his date of birth, place of birth, his mother's maiden name, then his new password, which he'd memorized earlier that week. He entered all the details, and the encrypted email opened. It contained only two words.

Looking good.

It also contained an attachment.

Wilson clicked on the attachment and watched the silent footage of the man entering the room, then pouring himself a coffee. He stared as the man made small talk with the target. Then he watched as the victim was strangled to death with the man's belt.

Wilson was satisfied. He closed the file and used an advanced piece of software to erase all traces of the clip and the email from his laptop and iPhone. He gulped down the rest of his coffee.

His cell phone rang.

He recognized the number. Fellow Commission member Richard Stanton.

"Clayton?" Stanton asked.

"Yes."

"You get the message?"

"Indeed."

"Are we still green-lighting this?"

"Yeah, one hundred percent. This is our guy."

Nine

It was just after midday when the Gulfstream carrying Senator Brad Crichton began its descent to the military air base in the Scottish Highlands. He felt slightly nervous about the reception he would get at the upcoming conference as chair of the Senate Select Committee on Intelligence. He didn't like the hymn sheet that American politicians had been singing from since the end of the Second World War. But he would use the conference as an opportunity to outline his vision on where America should be headed in the world.

His views were increasingly popular back home. His meteoric rise and media profile had made him the darling of the Republican Party's right wing. He was getting great poll numbers with his vision for a "truly free" America. But he knew the reception at the conference would be altogether cooler.

Crichton looked out the window as the clouds dissipated and the rolling hills and mountains of Scotland came into view. He thought again of his career trajectory. He chalked it up to what his father had imbued in him. Being straight. Honest. Principled. At heart he was, like his father, an old-school libertarian. Some had called him a Jeffersonian Republican. It was true he believed in limited national government and reduced federal spending. And he was the darling of the Cato Institute. Socially liberal, fiscally conservative. But he was well aware that he was in uncharted waters and attracting serious attention from friend and foe alike.

The more he appeared on TV, the more traction he got. He talked of how US military dominance and interventions around the world and foreign wars were making America less safe. He was building a power base in the Republican Party that was growing daily. And some analysts speculated that he might even be a possible front-runner if he ran for the presidency.

It was true, he was going to run, but he was going to keep that under his hat for a few more months.

Crichton felt good as they touched down. He was escorted to a waiting car by the military attaché working out of the American Consulate in Edinburgh.

"Good journey, sir?"

"Very good, thank you."

They were driven in a three-car convoy through winding country roads until they came to an isolated country estate.

"This is the place, sir," the military attaché said. "Remember, if you make a call, it'll almost certainly be getting routed through GCHQ."

Crichton smiled. "I thought as much."

The car pulled up at the gatehouse for detailed checks to be carried out. Radios crackled to life. "American delegation at gatehouse, sir."

Eventually, they were ushered through and driven down a mile-long road until they came to a sprawling Gothic mansion, partially concealed by huge oaks and towering pine trees.

Crichton got out of the car and smiled at the military attaché in the back. "You not coming in?"

The man shook his head. "Got work to do. Have a good conference, Senator. I'll arrange for your bags to be sent up to your room."

Crichton shut the door as a young woman came down the steps and introduced herself as a British Foreign Office press officer. She showed him to his room, where he showered and changed into a fresh suit.

He headed downstairs for a series of informal meet and greets with other delegates at the secret conference. State Department officials, Pentagon analysts, neocon think tank directors, GCHQ intelligence experts, British MI6 spooks. It was an Atlantic Alliance "meeting of minds." Britain and the US. He raised a few wry smiles when he talked about the explosive growth of the military-industrial complex since the end of the Second World War. Far from making the world a safer place, it was making the world more dangerous, Crichton and those on the libertarian wing of the Republican Party believed. He could see in the faces of those with vested interests in defending multibillion-dollar budgets that his view was strictly in the minority.

To a man and woman, everyone he spoke to believed America shouldn't "settle for isolationism" but instead try to "encourage and spread democracy" throughout the world. *Diplomatic language for military intervention across the globe,* he thought.

Crichton listened patiently and occasionally tried to lighten the mood with some self-deprecating remarks about how his fondness for isolationism could probably be blamed on him having an overbearing mother. A few forced smiles greeted his jokes. He sensed it was going to be a very long week.

After dinner with an MI5 officer, a State Department number cruncher, and a geostrategist from a British think tank, he enjoyed a nightcap of a stiff malt whisky before he retired to his room.

He switched on his TV as waves of tiredness washed over him.

He turned on his cell phone and it rang almost immediately. It was his aide Jessica Friel. "Brad, can we talk?"

Crichton stifled a yawn. "Hey . . . what's happening? I'm just ready to call it a night."

"Productive day?"

"It's like banging my head against a wall. Special interest groups. Very frustrating."

"Sounds pretty much like Washington."

"Speaking of which, what's going on there?"

Friel sighed.

"You OK? You sound a bit frazzled."

"I am."

"What's going on?"

"Brad, I've had literally a dozen calls today from one guy. He writes for a libertarian magazine, but he's pretty out there."

"What's he calling about?"

"That's just the thing. He wants to talk to you. He's wondering why no one's answering your emails. He's a real pest. He's even called me at home. You believe that?"

"Called you at home?"

"Kinda creepy, huh?"

"Maybe I should talk to him to get him off your case."

"Forget it. He'll be like a barnacle. You'll never shake him. I say we let it go."

"If you're sure."

"I miss you."

Crichton closed his eyes and sighed. He couldn't believe that he'd been fooling around with his goddamn aide. She was beautiful, smart, and very clever. Her conversation was peppered with talk of international relations, political gossip, and strategic thinking. His wife, by contrast, was a homemaker who usually talked of what she had been cooking or who she'd had lunch with. He liked spending time with Jessica. He had hired her after she had done a two-month stint interning for his team the previous summer. He wondered why he had fallen for her so hard. It was true his marriage had been rocky for a couple of years. He had grown increasingly distant from his wife. She was always griping about his time spent away from her. She said she felt lonely. The harsh reality was he felt lonely too. He was working sixteen-hour days as he climbed the political ladder at an astonishing rate. His days were spent in meetings. Meeting donors. Constituents. Lunching with fellow politicians. Journalists. Briefing papers on intelligence to soak up.

He missed his sons badly. He only saw them at Thanksgiving, Christmas, and their annual two-week August sojourn in the Hamptons. He rationalized that the fresh voice and input of a beautiful young woman in such circumstances would almost inevitably lead him to stray.

Crichton didn't feel good about it. But he did enjoy his moments with Jessica. He couldn't be sure if anyone other than the two of them had any inkling. But he also knew his political ambitions would end if it got out. The conservative Christians would desert him in droves. Perhaps the libertarians would stick around. But he knew that, realistically, the extramarital relationship and a successful political career were mutually exclusive.

"It's good to hear your voice," he said. "And I appreciate the update. Now, if it's all right with you, I need to get some rest."

"I meant to ask, how's the weather?"

"Surprisingly, for Scotland, pretty benign."

"Don't get used to it. I've been looking at the forecast. You better buckle up. Storm's about to hit."

Ten

Six days out

Nathan Stone was enjoying the cold rain on his skin as he stood in the middle of an enclosed outside courtyard and smoked a cigarette. He felt the water run down his back. All the old feelings had returned. The compulsion to kill had been switched on and activated.

He was ready.

The door behind him opened and Stone turned around. He saw a man in his late fifties approach him. He had a military bearing, raincoat collar turned up.

The man walked up to Stone and smiled. “Helluva day.”

Stone thought the man’s voice sounded familiar. He looked familiar. But Stone couldn’t place him.

“How you feeling?”

“I’m good.”

The man nodded, wiping the rain from his eyes. “Nathan, you remember me?”

“Sir?”

“Take a good look.”

Stone stared at the man. It slowly dawned on him that it was the same handler who had overseen his recuperation and transformation at the Saudi hospital. "Brigadier?"

He nodded. "Welcome back. How you feeling?"

"Ready to go."

"You are now officially on active duty, Stone. Do you understand what that means, soldier?"

Stone closed his eyes as the rain washed over his face. "It means I kill to order."

"Good. The specific orders will come from me and me alone."

"You mind me asking why you've picked me for this after all this time?"

"First, I think you're ready. You're a proven killer. Second, you're great in wild terrains. Proved yourself in such environments. Besides, you were the only candidate who met all the criteria regarding tactical mountain operations, field-craft training for mountains and nighttime mountain operations."

Stone nodded.

"You rose to the top of the six-week Special Forces Senior Mountaineering Course that I supervised too. So you're a perfect candidate for us."

"Colorado was nice."

"Colorado was nice. Though it wasn't so nice for Leroy."

"Mad Dog?"

"That's right. Didn't you have to cut the rope when he was hanging on the high ledge?"

Stone nodded. "It was twisted around his fucking neck. No other option."

"Got himself so tangled up in the ropes he was going blue in the face."

"Broke both his fucking ankles. Poor bastard."

The man smiled at the memory. "He lived. Any more questions?"

Stone shook his head.

The man cocked his head. "Let's head indoors. It's getting a bit wild out here."

Stone grinned. "I like it."

"Thought you would."

They headed in out of the rain and dried off in a warm, windowless room.

The man shook the rain out of his hair and sat down.

Stone pulled up a seat opposite. "This isn't America, is it?"

The man smiled. "What makes you say that?"

"The rain tastes different. Cleaner. Way wilder, the weather. Like Seattle. Except crazier."

The man stared long and hard at Stone. "We're both a long way from home, Nathan."

"How long?"

"The Outer Hebrides, off the northwest coast of Scotland."

Stone took a few moments for the information to sink in. "You kidding me?"

The man shook his head. "This is a secure facility. Isolated. Perfect. OK, down to business."

Stone pulled the packet of cigarettes out of his pocket and tapped one. He lit it up and nodded. "I'm listening."

"You've seen a picture of the target. We want a tragic accident. Do you understand?"

"When do we begin?"

The man smiled. "You'll be picked up from your room at 0400 hours. I want you to rest up for the remainder of today."

"Cover?"

"You're an American student named Tom McMasters doing a PhD in politics and international relations at the University of Edinburgh. Your hobbies are hill walking, bird-watching, jogging, stuff like that.

A full background brief is waiting for you back in your quarters. Got any questions?"

Stone leaned back in his seat and smiled. "Feels good to be back."

"Good to have you back, soldier."

Inside his office within the facility, Brigadier Jack Sands locked the door behind him. He noticed a slight tremor in his hand. He longed for a stiff drink after speaking face-to-face with Stone. He had been his handler for the better part of a decade. Now Stone had been brought back to life. His face was different. But the menacing presence was still there.

He slumped in the seat behind his desk as his gaze fell on the case file photos in front of him. Photos of Nathan Stone as a boy. Then a mug shot of the juvenile delinquent on the Lower East Side more than twenty years ago. ID photos from his time in the army. Then a blank-eyed Stone drinking a beer at The Farm: Camp Peary, used by the CIA and Special Forces.

Stone had fit the profile they were looking for. He could compartmentalize and detach himself from a target's humanity. He could switch to kill mode more or less at will. And he was deeply dangerous.

He had come to the attention of Langley after field reports from Iraq showed him to be a fearless soldier, heading up a unit that took care of insurgents. Stone was reported by his superiors for unlawful deaths and killings. His bloody thirst for revenge against the Sunnis was too much for some, but the CIA immediately saw his potential.

Nathan Stone had felt right at home within the confines of the barbed-wire-topped chain-link fence that surrounded Camp Peary. He had been reborn. He was trained by the finest CIA operatives. Stone learned to bug phones, use dead drops, read detailed maps, and put suspects under surveillance undetected.

He was also trained in advanced killing methods. How to poison, how to administer untraceable drugs to induce a heart attack, how to garrote. Stone learned it all.

Brigadier Sands had been in charge of Camp Peary when Stone arrived. He knew all the operatives by their first names.

He knew Stone better than anyone. On the surface he appeared pleasant. Talkative. Intelligent. Thoughtful. Cogent. But in his eyes there was a terrible sadness. A smile rarely crossed his lips, as if the humanity had already been driven out of him. He seemed detached.

He didn't socialize as well as the other recruits. Sands liked that about him. It reminded him of himself as a younger man. Stone was a loner. And the CIA didn't try to fit a square peg into a round hole.

Sands became his sole handler. He directed Stone. He made sure his sister was looked after. He oversaw Stone's transition to lone-wolf assassin. They could deny his existence. He had left the army. He was a drifter. That was the cover story at any rate.

He was the only one who had contact with Stone.

He made sure Stone had whatever he wanted. He didn't interfere in his life. If Sands needed a person neutralized, he just made a call. Or sent a coded message to Stone's motel.

Sands protected his asset like a lion protects his pride. Like a father protects his son. His prodigy was fearsome. Stone did everything that was asked of him. He worked in the shadows, unhindered.

It had all nearly unraveled during a failed assassination attempt. Stone was in the back seat of a car being driven by a journalist he was about to kill. Unexpectedly, the woman, Deborah Jones, carried out a suicidal maneuver, driving the car straight into the Florida Everglades. She struggled free and escaped death. But Stone was trapped in the back seat and was found lifeless in the car after it was fully submerged underwater. He was dragged out of the water several minutes later by a passerby. It was reported in the press that he had died. But that was a lie.

On the way to the hospital, Stone was intercepted and taken away overseas, first to Dubai, then Saudi Arabia, for treatment from the finest plastic surgeons.

The recovery was slow. The months dragged into years.

Sands flashed back to Nathan's long therapy and recuperation. He remembered how Nathan had become close to a therapist from Colorado named Meg. She talked softly to him. She listened. He was happy in her presence. Sands could see that. He watched through the glass at the therapy sessions. Stone talked of how he felt as if a cloud were slowly lifting while he chatted with her. She talked of clean air. The Rockies. Aspen. She talked of nice things. Blue skies. Stone felt at peace.

Sands could see that his fearsome prodigy was imagining a new future. A future free of Sands. Free of the past. Free of his ghosts. A new future without killing. Without darkness. He contemplated what to do for days. He felt conflicted. But he realized he was just being sentimental.

The world he inhabited was not sentimental. It was bleak. Endless. Without pity. That was the way it was. That was the way it had to be.

Nathan Stone was an asset. Sands wasn't prepared for the investment—the vast investment, millions of dollars—to be squandered and cast aside. The therapist was released early from her contract. And she left. Without saying goodbye. New therapists were brought in. They began to reinforce the ghosts in Stone's head. He talked of his emptiness when Meg was gone. And anger. Rage. The darkness had begun to seep back into his soul. Day by day.

Stone was still the same inside. A cold-blooded killer. Only this time he had a new face. A new identity.

Sands was one of only a handful of people who knew Stone was still alive. He had taken him under his wing. He saw his potential. He also saw flashes of himself as a young man. The untrusting, uncertain eyes. Similar background. Dirt-poor. Brutalized by a sadistic father. Mentally scarred. Pent-up fury. He could see it all in Nathan Stone. He knew he had his secrets. His sister was still in a mental institution after killing their abusive, insane father. She thought her brother was dead too.

When Sands was approached to work for the Commission, he was the one who had insisted that Stone be part of the setup. The others agreed and paid the huge medical bills running into the millions.

Sands knew from the facility's psychologist that Stone had night terrors. Infrared cameras in his room showed him talking to imaginary people in the dead of night.

The psychologist believed it was memories of his sister, his childhood, and his father's death that still haunted him.

Sands leaned back in his seat and stared out the rain-streaked windows over the bleak cliffs to the stormy gray seas of the North Atlantic. Then he turned to look again at the photos of Nathan Stone as a boy . . . and felt nothing but sadness.

Eleven

Jeff Patterson was sitting in a corner booth of a diner. He checked his watch again. It was 11:07 a.m. And his source was seriously late. More than an hour late.

He'd already eaten a burger and fries, washed down with a coffee, and was ready to call it a day.

A waitress brushed past him and smiled. "Can I get you anything else, honey?"

Patterson pulled on his backpack. "I'm good, thanks."

"You have a nice day, honey."

Patterson headed out of the diner into the steam-bath air of DC. He pulled out his cell phone and punched in his source's unlisted number. It rang. And rang. And rang. But no one answered. Not even a voice mail. "Fuck."

His source was usually so reliable.

His mind wandered as he headed down Eighteenth Street NW due south, a straightforward twenty-minute walk to his home. He thought again of the secret program he believed was operational. An assassination program. Shit. How crazy was that? He felt sick. He was an American. A patriot. He thought of his options. He wondered if he should just go to the police. And tell them what? They would laugh. Maybe arrest him for stealing classified information. Set bail for a ridiculous amount. He might be able to crowd-fund to get a good attorney to defend him. Shit.

The more he thought of what he had learned, the more concerned he got. It seemed so outrageous. A plan to assassinate influential men and women who spoke out about the relentless growth of the shadow state. The people who raised their voices about the way the country was headed. More and more interference in family life. Stratospheric levels of military as well as public spending. America was $20 trillion in debt. Foreign wars and economic intervention in the markets had propelled the country to the edge, leaving it teetering on the brink.

But the file also contained the names of those who were privy to this information. It was a distribution list of ex-generals, Joint Chiefs of Staff, and former directors of the CIA. The men behind this organization. And their contact details. It was all there. He had checked over the names carefully.

The man at the top was Clayton Wilson. A former director of the CIA who had been an adviser on the ground when Pinochet was overthrown in a coup. According to WikiLeaks, Wilson consulted with numerous blue-chip American technology companies, who wanted his knowledge and contacts within the intelligence community to secure lucrative multimillion-dollar contracts, but his services were also retained by these companies—at $100,000 a month—to advise on global security concerns that might affect their country. It was a win-win for Wilson.

Patterson wondered why men like Wilson were pulling the strings of a shadowy organization that wanted to kill fellow Americans. How was that even possible or, for that matter, allowed to happen in America in the twenty-first century?

It even had its own code name: Sundowner Winds. Had this originated inside the Pentagon or Langley? Had this been outsourced to a private organization with no official links to the military-industrial complex?

Patterson snapped out of his reverie and began to focus on the senator. A man he had donated funds to during the last election.

His calls to the senator's office had just met a brick wall. He wondered if he should keep trying.

Patterson was feeling agitated as he walked. He took out his cell phone again and tried Jessica Friel's number. She picked up after the first ring.

"Oh come on, you have got to be kidding me!" she said.

"Jessica, this is the last time I'm going to call."

"Are you out of your mind?"

"Jessica, first, I apologize for the earlier profanity. It was unnecessary. Please believe me, it was just because of my concern, genuine concern, that I came across like an asshole."

Jessica said nothing.

"I'm begging—literally begging—you to meet me to discuss what I know."

A deep sigh. "I've alerted the police, I hope you know that."

"I wish you hadn't. I am genuine. What I say is not fake news or some other nonsense. I have information in my possession that places your boss at risk."

"Are you making this bullshit up as you go along?"

"Why would I do that?"

"I don't know, because you're crazy?"

"I believe Senator Crichton is at grave risk. He is on a list. I want to show it to you."

"Not possible, sorry."

"Jessica, we've never spoken before, and you're probably wondering if I'm some stalker nut—I get that."

"It had crossed my mind."

"I'm a serious journalist. The biography of Pat Buchanan?"

"That was written by Carol Levinson."

"Not true. I was the ghostwriter. I wrote the whole thing. Carol was the celebrity on the cover. Her input was, at best, sketchy. I've also written for the *American Conservative* and the *New Criterion*, among others. I've appeared on Fox News. I've also written extensively about WikiLeaks."

"I'm sorry, I'm not familiar with your work."

"That's fine. Not a problem."

"Jeff, look, if you have any concerns, speak to the police."

"I wanted you to pass it on. I'm concerned if I speak to the cops or the Feds, the information won't get to Senator Crichton."

"Can I be frank, Jeff?"

"Sure."

"I'm really, really busy. And this sounds kinda flaky to me. As if it was dreamed up by a conspiracy nut."

"This came from a source within the intelligence community," he said. The lights changed and he crossed the street. "A source is putting his job on the line. If it was known who had accessed the original information, my source would be in jail. But he would rather take that risk than not alert people. He is a patriot first and foremost."

"Have you ever met this source?"

"Yes, I have. He's a good man. And I've used him for many stories on intelligence matters."

"So it's stolen information?"

"Jessica, we could get into a philosophical discussion about whether this is in the public interest or not, if it's stolen or not. Then again we could talk about illegal surveillance methods infringing on our civil liberties, which I've reported on extensively."

"So are you saying this guy is a Snowden character?"

"Listen, I admire the senator. He talks sense. I know the senator has spoken out supporting Snowden. He speaks my kind of language. I believe he's genuine when he says he's all about changing the way America works. What I've learned concerns me so much."

"Let's say for a moment that I believe you."

"I need to speak to you face-to-face about this."

"I'll think about it."

"So we can meet up?"

"I said I'll think about it."

She hung up.

Patterson felt slightly heartened as he walked on. He sensed Friel was coming around. He tried his source again. But again, no answer.

Patterson unlocked his sun-drenched apartment, pleased to be home. He turned on a talk radio station and went over to the windows to close the blinds.

His gaze was drawn to a car parked farther down the street. He pressed his nose to the window. Inside the car he saw two men. One with a telephoto lens pointing straight at him.

Twelve

Nathan Stone wiped the condensation off the windows of the ferry that would take him to the Isle of Skye and stared out over the gray seas. He picked up his coffee and took a welcome drink as some kids screeched up and down the corridor. The smell of fries wafted from the dining area. He felt nauseated.

A kid approached and stood right in front of him. "Hey, mister," the boy said in a broad Scottish accent. "Where you from?"

Stone stared at the kid long and hard and smiled. He patted him on the head as his mother approached.

"Callum, that's none of your business," the woman said, scolding her son.

Stone smiled benignly at her.

"I'm so sorry," the woman said. "He's just curious."

Stone said nothing. He knew that nine times out of ten it was better to say nothing than to draw attention.

The boy stared sullenly at him. "Everyone knows where they're from."

"Callum!" his mother snapped. "Enough!"

Stone smiled again. He would rather be thought mute than engage in unnecessary conversation.

The mother pulled her son away. "Once again, I do apologize."

Stone nodded. Inwardly, he seethed. The woman took her son back to the group they were with. He saw the way she scolded him. But he could see the defiant look in the boy's eyes. Stone thought the boy was just a brat. A spoiled brat. Enjoying an island-hopping holiday with his well-off parents.

He thought back to his own childhood. A stinking one-room dive on the Bowery. Father an alcoholic. His sister psychotic. He remembered waiting for his father to return home from drinking with the rest of the panhandlers. Drunk. Unsteady on his feet. The smell of his rotten breath. The crazy dark eyes. Then the pain as he took off his belt and attacked Nathan and his sister remorselessly.

The torment lasted years. Until his sister snapped. She killed their father with a pair of scissors, stabbing him repeatedly, drenching herself in his blood. He remembered the screaming. The days, weeks, and months that followed were traumatic. He was torn away from his sister. He had no one besides her. And then she was gone. All he had were goddamn social workers, teachers. And a string of foster parents across the tristate area. They all tried their best with him. But the darkness within him had already swallowed any goodness he may once have had.

A man's voice boomed out of the speakers. "Ladies and gentlemen, five minutes until we disembark."

Stone finished his coffee. A couple of minutes later, his new iPhone rang. He checked the caller ID and saw it was his handler. He moved to a quiet alcove. "Yeah."

"A cab is waiting to pick you up once you land at Uig. The man driving the cab is one of our guys. Do not engage in conversation. He will drive you for a few miles to the parking lot of an isolated bar. You have the keys in your pocket for a BMW X5. Are you clear so far?"

"Yes, sir."

"You are then to proceed south through Skye until you come to the bridge that leads off the island to the Scottish mainland."

"Copy that."

"You will then take the A87 road and head to a small cottage. All the details are logged into the GPS of your car. We'll be in touch."

Thirteen

Just after midday, one block from the Library of Congress in DC, Jessica Friel breezed into the upscale Sonoma Restaurant. It was packed with staffers, interns, a few political hacks, and a few tourists. She immediately spotted her college friend Amy Blair sitting at a corner table.

"Oh my God," Jessica said, pecking Amy on the cheek, "you look great!"

Amy smiled and rolled her eyes as she sipped her martini. "Gimme a break, Jessica. I look like shit. That's what having two kids does to you."

Jessica sat down opposite her closest friend from Yale. "So how long has it been?"

"Too long. I feel like we never see each other."

"There aren't enough hours in the day. I feel like I'm jumping from one meeting to the next, juggling a million different things in my life."

Amy snorted. "Tell me about it. So how the hell are you?"

Jessica shrugged. "You see it all." She motioned a waiter across and ordered a couple of martinis. "Look, I'm sorry I missed your thirtieth birthday party last month. It's been crazy."

"Hey, forget about it. All that happened was I got drunk and puked in the cab on the way home."

Jessica laughed. "Well, good for you."

It was Amy's turn to laugh. "Yeah . . . not my best day by a long shot."

"How's Edward?" Jessica asked of Amy's husband.

Amy sighed long and hard before finishing her first martini. "Yeah . . ."

Jessica smiled and shrugged.

"Not so good."

"I'm sorry to hear that."

The waiter returned with two fresh martinis. Amy lifted her glass and took a sip.

"You wanna talk about it?" Jessica said.

"Yes . . . Yes, I goddamn do."

"I've got to say, I always thought you and Edward were so much fun together. You were perfect."

"Go figure. The fun seems to have gone out of things since the twins were born."

Jessica felt deflated. She'd known both since they were all in college together. "That's pretty common in relationships, though, isn't it?"

Amy nodded and gazed into her drink. "Yes, it is. Some couples can deal with it. But we're finding it very difficult."

Jessica sighed. "Do you want to order lunch now?"

"Good idea."

Jessica ordered a goat cheese salad and Amy ordered a burger and fries.

When the waiter had taken the order and was out of earshot, Amy leaned in close. "It's actually a bit more serious," she said. "We're getting divorced."

"What?"

"I know. Shocker. But there you have it."

"A divorce? Oh, Amy, no." Jessica reached across the table and touched her friend's hand.

Amy got teary and took a large gulp of her martini. "It's been a long, long time coming. A constant drip, drip of disappointments, arguments, and edginess. No one is to blame. But the end result is that he's moved out."

"I'm so sorry. That's terrible."

"Hey, shit happens, right?"

"Out of all my friends, I would have staked my life on you guys making it."

Amy knocked back the rest of her martini and ordered another round from a passing waiter. "OK, let's change the subject. I'm getting depressed. What about you?"

"What about me?"

"Are you dating anyone in Washington? There are gazillions of eligible bachelors in town."

"I'm too busy."

"Gimme a break, Jessica. Too busy?"

"I am. My work with the senator is all-consuming. It takes up all my time. The energy I have left I use for jogging."

Amy edged closer to her before lowering her voice. "You remember Annie McGowan . . ."

"Annie? Sure. Really smart girl."

"Yeah, well, get this. She's working at the *Post*."

"I heard that. Investigations or something, right?"

"We had lunch about a month ago and she mentioned some talk going around about who's putting out feelers to run for president."

Jessica nodded, knowing where the conversation was going.

"And she said your boss, the gorgeous Senator Brad Crichton, is picking up some serious interest in running. Said he's already been promised a ton of money for his campaign."

Jessica smiled but said nothing. She was sorely tempted to open up to her old friend.

"But here's the kicker. She said there are rumors about him."

"Washington is full of rumors."

Amy leaned in close and Jessica got a whiff of the martinis on her breath. "I know. But Annie was talking about rumors swirling around DC saying he gambles and chases women."

Jessica felt herself flush. "He's a good man. And I can vouch for him. He's a great American. I think everyone can see that."

Amy narrowed her eyes mischievously. "Jessica? You're hiding something from me."

"Maybe I am," Jessica teased.

Amy stared at her openmouthed. "You have to tell me. You're killing me! You getting engaged?"

The food arrived and Jessica picked at her salad, while Amy started on her burger and fries.

Jessica shook her head. "No, I'm not getting engaged."

"So tell me," Amy said. "What's your news?"

"You can't tell a soul. And I mean a living soul."

"Trust me. Cross my heart and hope to die. Now are you going to tell me or not? I've told you my situation. You're hiding something."

Jessica felt her cheeks flush.

"I knew it. I goddamn knew it. Tell me all about it."

"Well . . . there is a guy in my life. But this is super secret. Nobody knows about it."

"Jessica, you need to tell me or I won't be able to sleep tonight. Tell me something nice."

"I'm having an affair."

Amy stared at her for what seemed like a lifetime. "What?"

"With the senator."

"Stop. Are you kidding me?"

Jessica shook her head.

Amy put her hand over her mouth. "I can't believe what I'm hearing."

"I know. I can't explain it. I love him. I can't help it."

"You're having an affair? Like, as in having sex with him?"

"Yes, we're having an affair. I know it's wrong. I know all that. But I love him. I've fallen madly, crazy in love with him. I have no way of explaining myself. And I know he has a wife."

Amy nodded. "Yes, he does. A very pretty wife."

"And a family. I know all that."

A sly grin crossed Amy's face. "You cunning little minx."

"Stop it."

"So let's start at the beginning. How did it start?"

Jessica took a sip of her martini. "His marriage was in trouble. He confided in me."

"He did?"

"Said they were trying to get along but had discussed separation."

"Oh my God. Really? So you're having a full-blown affair? I would never have known."

"Don't say a word. He says he's going to leave his wife. He's waiting for the right time."

"So he still lives with her?"

Jessica felt herself wincing. "It sounds awful when you say it like that. It's all about appearances, public perception."

Amy sipped her drink and leaned in close. "Holy cow."

"He's a public figure. This is important on different levels. He needs to work this out before he can move on. There's financial considerations for his family, his wife and all that, and that's besides the political fallout he'll have to contend with."

"I read that his poll numbers are sky-high. I like him. I like what he says and the way he says it."

Jessica nodded.

"He needs to leave his wife, though."

"That's where he's headed, thankfully. I miss him. And I don't like the fact that his life is still so entwined with hers."

Amy shook her head and sipped her drink. "So is this physical? Ideological? Is he having a midlife crisis?"

"You're not listening. He's a really sweet guy. I love him, he makes me laugh."

"My neighbor makes me laugh, but I don't want to sleep with him."

Jessica rolled her eyes. "You know, sometimes it's meant to be."

"Does your mother know?"

"No, thank God."

"If she found out—and I mean reading it in the newspapers—that wouldn't be good for her."

Jessica sighed as she began to comprehend the potential fallout when it would eventually come out in the press.

"How often do you sleep with him?"

Jessica playfully slapped the back of Amy's free hand. "Behave!"

"I need to know. He looks very athletic."

"He works out. He runs. He looks after himself."

"I can see that."

"Don't be so cynical."

Amy got a faraway look in her eyes. "Do you think Edward will find anyone? Someone younger. Prettier."

"I think you need to think of yourself, Amy. Let's focus on what you want."

"I don't know what I want. And that's the goddamn honest truth. How sad is that?"

When they'd finished their lunch, Jessica leaned closer. "We need to meet up more often. I miss you."

Amy began to dab her eyes, tears spilling down her cheeks. "Oh God, look at me. What a wreck."

Jessica walked to the other side of the table and put her arm around Amy. "Hey, you had some great years together. And you've got two beautiful kids. Edward is still a good guy."

Amy nodded, tears streaming down her face. "Look, I'm sorry about bringing you down. You're happy. And I'm glad for you. Thanks for feeling you could confide in me. I do say inappropriate things. I know that. Edward kept on reminding me of that."

"You have every right to say whatever the hell you want. This is America, right?"

"Goddamn straight."

Jessica sat down in her seat, picked up her glass, and clinked it against Amy's. "To friends."

Fourteen

It was dark outside, and the rain was pouring down as Nathan Stone waited in the cottage, a mug of strong coffee in hand. It reminded him of winter storms lashing New York when he was growing up. Staring out through the scratched glass and the gray mold as the weather tore up his city. The wilder it was, the more he loved it. His sister was always afraid. Huddled under a blanket, crying, thinking of their father coming back.

The more he thought of those days, the more he wished he'd stuck up for his sister. But he was too young, he rationalized. Far too young. A child. His father was a fearsome man. Six foot plus. With a drink inside him, he was the devil.

Stone's cell phone rang, snapping him out of his reverie.

"GPS shows you're at the base camp," his handler said.

"Safe and sound."

"It's pretty basic."

"Pretty basic is good. I don't like fancy."

"Got a bit of news for you."

"Shoot."

"We've got an advance camp ready for you."

"You want me to go right now?"

"Leave at midnight."

"Copy that."

"Your car out front has the details uploaded to it."

Stone absorbed the information.

"How you feeling?"

"Ready."

Fifteen

It was nearly midnight and Clayton Wilson was in the study of his home in an upscale gated community in Great Falls, Virginia, checking all the reports on Nathan Stone: medical, physical, psychological. The more he read, the more satisfied he was that Stone was an impeccable choice to carry out this particular assignment. He had known through his connections in the CIA that Stone had been resurrected and undergone a long rehabilitation period.

Officially, Stone was now an American student in Scotland. A new identity. A new face. A new name. But, crucially, no connection to American intelligence. A mature student. In his thirties. A loner. The background briefing was thorough.

It had been compiled by various people at the secure facility in Scotland. Away from prying eyes. Owned by a billionaire American. Isolated.

Those who got too close to the island, like nosy fishermen—which had happened twice—were disposed of at sea. A fishing accident in rough weather. And the body would wash up a few weeks later on a neighboring island.

Wilson had been paid a nice seven-figure sum each year to oversee the program since its inception three years earlier. Eight successes so far. Tragic accidents. Car accidents. Skiing accidents. Falls from balconies.

And each time the hit was carried out by a different operative.

Suddenly, his cell phone rang.

"Clayton, good time to talk?" It was Richard Stanton, his deputy at the Commission.

"You on a secure line?"

"Of course."

"Go ahead."

"I just wanted to find out how the meeting with your Pentagon guy went."

Wilson leaned back in his seat. "It went well. I told him how we were progressing and gave him the finalized date."

"What did he say?"

"Two things. 'Good.' And 'keep me in the loop.'"

"Did he have any concerns about the date and the choice?"

"None whatsoever."

"So they're happy?"

"Yeah. Richard, what can you tell me about Mr. C since his arrival?"

"Typical politician. Meeting and greeting mostly. Pressing the flesh."

"Anything of note?"

"Not surprisingly, Mr. C is well briefed. I hear he's congenial and charming. The usual horseshit. You get the reports on our deliveryman?"

Wilson sighed. "I've just finished reading them all. He's perfect. Being moved into position to await instruction."

"Good."

Wilson sensed Stanton was holding something back.

"I've . . . I've got some news of my own."

"What kind of news?"

"Clayton, we might have a problem. We believe we've pinpointed a leak from a CIA analyst."

"Shit."

"Exactly. A briefing note of our first meeting wound its way onto a CIA server. Supposed to have been deleted."

Clayton felt his stomach knot as his ulcer began to burn. "How long have you known about this?"

"Couple days."

"A couple days?"

"My sources have been firming up what happened."

"So what's happened to this guy?"

"He's been taken care of."

"Good. Anything else?"

"We think the guy made contact with an NSA contractor, and there are numerous encrypted searches for a guy called Jeff Patterson."

"Name rings a bell."

"He's a conspiracy nut. Writes for some libertarian journals."

"I see."

"Don't worry about it. I've drawn up a plan to put out this fire."

"This is not the sort of stuff I want to hear at the eleventh hour, Richard."

"This crept up on us. But we're on top of it."

Wilson felt his ulcer burn again and he winced at the pain. "I don't want any fuck-ups. Do what has to be done. Am I clear?"

"Leave it to me."

"Goddamn!" Wilson yelled as he ended the call, slamming the phone on the table.

Sixteen

Five days out

Senator Brad Crichton was enjoying an early-morning walk alone in the grounds of the isolated Scottish country estate. His head was swimming with facts and figures after he'd risen early and digested a classified NATO intelligence briefing on security threats around the world.

But it felt good to get out in the open. He breathed in the cool, pine-scented air as he walked, his mind drifting back to discussions he'd had the previous evening. Most of the talk was about Syria. And Iran. And then back to Syria. What he found unbelievable was that there was unanimity in wanting to free the Syrian people through regime change. The talk was emotional hogwash. It had nothing to do with the Syrian people. No one around the table gave a rat's ass about Syria, its people, or the wretched state the country was in. Assad and his regime were vile, sure. But everyone was either unwilling or unable to talk about how America and the West had allowed the destruction of the country by jihadists, financed by Saudi Arabia.

When he had raised the thorny question of whether America was planning any moves against the House of Saud, you could have heard a pin drop. They didn't like it. He was pointing out their double standards. Their games. America needed to uphold democratic values, not cozy up to a vile regime like Saudi Arabia. He wanted nothing to do with it.

He walked deeper into the woods, fringing the venue.

His cell phone rang, interrupting his train of thought.

"Senator Crichton?" a man's voice asked.

Crichton wondered who it was. The man sounded educated. "Who's this? I don't recognize your number."

"Sir, you don't know me."

"If I don't know you, how the hell did you get my number?"

"Don't worry about that. I need two minutes of your time."

"Who is this? Is this some sort of joke?"

"Sir, I believe your life might be in danger."

Crichton stopped in his tracks. "What?"

"My name is Jeff Patterson. I've been trying to contact you."

Crichton suddenly remembered. "My office told me about you."

"Sir, listen to me. I'm a bone fide journalist, investigative journalist—"

"You're a conspiracy theorist, and I don't have time for your crazy theories."

"I'm deadly serious. I'm a big fan of yours. Listen to me, I've seen documentation detailing names."

"Names? What the hell are you talking about?"

"People have died in suspicious circumstances in the last six months."

"Listen, I'm going to hang up because—"

"Edward Francis Molloy, a wealthy conservative in the Hamptons, collapsed and drowned in his bath. Debbie Falconer drowned on vacation in Hawaii."

Crichton sighed, phone pressed tight to his ear. He wondered whether he should just hang up. But something about the journalist's tone of voice kept him on the line. "I'm listening."

"Both were on this list. Molloy funded a think tank advocating small government. Falconer investigated the military-industrial complex and the hundreds of thousands of government jobs in and around DC and Virginia. Put a few noses out of joint. She criticized the stupendous spending levels of the American military. The NSA. The Pentagon. The contractors. Consultancies. Multibillion-dollar businesses reliant on government military spending. Very damning."

Crichton sighed. "Look, I have no doubt you're sincere, but I've never been one for believing in conspiracy theories, and—"

"Sir, yours is the third name on a list of ten. I've spoken to Jessica Friel about it. But I don't know if she appreciates the nature of this threat."

"Listen to me. If you have information, you take it to the police. The FBI. Whatever you think. That's the correct course of action. If you're in DC, take it straight to the FBI."

"Senator Crichton, do you want me to spell it out? I think they're going to kill you next. They don't like what you have to say. And they are going to neutralize you."

"That's enough!"

"Sir, please listen to me. I have proof. I have the names of the men behind this. This is treason, sir. They're going to bring you down. You need to believe me."

"I think I've heard enough."

"For the love of God, why aren't you listening to me?"

"I'm hanging up now. I think you need help."

Seventeen

Nathan Stone had only spent a day in the cottage before he was on the move again. It was dark when he locked up and slung his gear into the trunk. He turned on the ignition and the engine purred to life. Then he flicked a switch and the car's headlights illuminated the front of the isolated stone cottage.

The young woman's voice on the GPS said, "Drive for one hundred yards, turn right, and head northeast on the A85."

He pulled away, negotiating the narrow lanes until he got onto the main road to his destination.

The windshield wipers whisked the rain away as he pressed on into the night. He drove for a couple of hours solid. He stopped off at a roadside food truck for fish and chips washed down with a Coke. When he finished, he drove the last twenty-five miles to his destination, along winding roads, climbing higher into the mountains, past isolated villages and hamlets and farms, huge electricity transmission towers illuminated as lightning tore across the sky.

Stone yawned as he drove the last few miles along a single-track road to another cottage. A light was on inside. This was it. He pulled up, switched off the headlights, and turned off the engine. He pulled his bag out of the trunk and opened the front door.

A lamp was on in the hall. He locked the front door and scoped out the rest of the house. It was neat. Functional.

He checked the windows and made sure the house was secure.

Then he put his bag in his room.

He saw a floor hatch in the kitchen and pulled it up, the cellar light coming on as he did. He climbed down and spotted the old fireplace. He pulled back the iron grate. Behind the fireplace was a black leather overnight bag. He unzipped it. Inside was a 9mm Glock, a silencer, parts of a military-grade scope rifle, $1,000 in cash, a couple of credit cards under his false name, and a pack of amphetamine-laced steroid pills.

Stone grinned. He opened up the pack, popped a couple of capsules, and swallowed. They'd kick in before long.

He carefully put the iron grate back in place.

Then he grabbed the bag and headed up the cellar stairway and locked the hatch.

Stone shut the curtains and sat down. He pulled out his iPad and opened up his encrypted emails. There was only one. From a man called Jacob, his handler's code name. He double-clicked on the email and a screen asked for his place of birth (New York), his favorite city (Miami), and third question, what is your least favorite sport? The answer, *bowling*.

The email opened up with a color photo of a beaming white man in a dark suit signing autographs. The same face he'd been shown at the facility.

Stone studied the photograph for a few minutes. His cell rang.

"You settled in yet?"

"Just arrived ten minutes ago."

"You got the email?"

"Looking at it now. Is this him?"

"Yes, it is."

"What else do I need to know about him?"

"Just that he's a real and present threat to American national security. Any further questions?"

"How long?"

"Still to be finalized. But assume a matter of days. Not long now, Nathan."

Brigadier Jack Sands put down the phone in his office and leaned back in his seat. He closed his eyes for a few moments as the monotone voice of Stone lingered in his mind. He sounded wired. Uptight. Coiled. But he knew that was good. That was very good.

He was chomping at the bit.

His cell rang and it was a number he didn't recognize. "Jack, you OK to talk?"

The voice was that of the project chair and his former boss, Clayton Wilson. A man he admired and feared in equal measure. A man who should not be crossed. "Go right ahead, sir."

"This is a secure line, just in case you're wondering."

"Very wise."

"Jack, me and you go way back, right?"

"Sir?"

"I mean, all the way back. Nineteen seventies. And before. Before it got a little too complicated."

Sands knew he was talking about the Church Committee, which spilled the beans on how the CIA was operating above and beyond the law. It hadn't stopped them from being part of the fallout from the Contragate debacle. But they'd both been moved sideways in the agency, until Wilson had left and set up his own consultancy. "Go on, sir."

"Jack, I'm hearing from a senior psychologist at the facility where Stone's sister is—he does consultancy work for us—and he's reported back that Stone's sister mentioned to him in confidence that Nathan is still alive. This came straight out of the blue a couple hours ago during a one-on-one session. And I've only now been told about it."

"That's impossible. She was told he was dead."

"She said her brother spoke to her."

Sands shook his head and leaned back in his seat. "She must've been imagining it. He has no phone access."

Wilson said, "He told her he just wanted to hear her voice."

"That would mean he had access to a phone. He doesn't have that. We check his unit twice a day when he's in the gym or jogging in the grounds."

"Whatever. It concerns me."

"Sir, I'm telling you, it must be in her head."

"What if it's not?"

Sands stared at the photos again. "Are you saying we should abort?"

"No."

"What are you saying, sir, if I can be blunt?"

"You believe he can do this again?"

"No question. The guy's a machine."

"I agree. But this information concerns me. I like certainty."

"In this business, sir, as you know, certainty is a luxury we don't have. Wing and a prayer, and a high probability of success, are the best we can do."

A silence stretched over the line.

"Sir, tell you what, let me think about this and I'll get back to you."

Eighteen

Jeff Patterson was staring out of his apartment window onto the dark streets below when his cell phone vibrated in his shirt pocket. He pulled it out.

"Jeff?" It was his source.

"Yeah, where the hell you been?"

"Forget about that. Got something more for you."

"About?"

"Listen to me. I want you to go to the Colonial Garage at 1818 North Street NW. You know it?"

"Sure I know it. Used it many times."

"Good. Go to Level 2, and you'll see a crappy yellow Mazda. In the passenger seat is a teddy bear. The keys are under the carpet in the rear seat, behind the passenger seat."

Patterson wondered why on earth his source was going to such extraordinary lengths. "Mazda?"

"Right. Then head across to Arlington. The Quincy Street parking lot."

Patterson made a mental note of the instructions. "Go on. I'm with you so far."

"Level D, the fourth level. Park, and I'll find you."

"When?"

"Now."

"Now? Right this second?"

"Right goddamn now."

Patterson did as he was told. He got the Mazda and drove it across the Key Bridge into Virginia. The GPS guided him to the Quincy Street parking lot, and he headed up to Level D. Deserted. Not one car apart from his.

Patterson wondered how long his source would be. He was reliable to a fault. But the elaborate ploy of using someone else's car seemed to indicate his source had been spooked by something.

The more he thought about it, the more he wondered if his source was just paranoid. Then again, did his source have reason to be? In light of what was happening, it was probably a prudent move. A better-safe-than-sorry approach suited Patterson just fine.

His mind drifted and he switched on the radio at a low volume. A preprogrammed jazz station playing John Coltrane. The music reminded him of his ex-girlfriend, who had played Coltrane's albums nearly all the time. He loved it. But even for him, a jazz lover, it became slightly trying when she didn't listen to anything else.

His cell rang.

"Jeff, where are you?" It was his best friend from college, Ronnie Bryant.

"Oh shit, man, I totally forgot."

"It's poker night. The guys are all here."

"Damn. Listen, I'm kinda tied up just now."

"Man, that's bullshit. Since you've been single, you've turned into a goddamn recluse. That's not the way it works. You're supposed to get out there and live a little."

"Listen, I'm sorry. I've got work to do. I'm meeting up with someone. It's pretty important. Totally forgot."

A long sigh answered him. "Jeff, this is not cool. Come on, I get that you love your job, but man, just leaving us standing here without calling? That's bullshit."

Patterson shook his head. Out of the corner of his eye a police cruiser came into view. "Look, I gotta go. We'll talk later." Jeff hung up.

The cop car pulled up behind him, blocking him in.

What the hell was this?

Patterson watched out of his rearview mirror as two police officers got out. Heavyset. The smaller of the two stepped forward and tapped on his window.

"Get out of your car, sir," he said.

Patterson wondered what the hell they wanted. He opened his door. "What's the problem, Officer?"

The cop said, "You mind explaining what you're doing, sir?"

"Waiting for a friend. Is that a problem?"

"ID, please."

Patterson pulled out his wallet and handed over his driver's license. "Satisfied?"

The cop scanned his ID as the police radio crackled into life, a woman's voice talking of suspicious activity.

"You mind explaining who you're supposed to be meeting?"

"A friend."

"Has this friend got a name?"

Patterson cleared his throat. "I'm a journalist. I'm meeting someone about a story."

"A journalist, huh? You do drugs?"

"What?"

"I asked if you do drugs."

"Drugs? No . . . What the hell kind of question is that?"

"Are you hiding any drugs or drug paraphernalia in the car?"

"Gimme a break."

The radio crackled again, giving the name of the car's owner. A name he didn't recognize. "This isn't your car, is it?"

Patterson felt himself flush. "It's . . . Look, this is kinda complicated."

"So you're in a car that doesn't belong to you, waiting for a friend?"

"I know it sounds a bit strange . . . but it's the truth."

"You mind if we look in this car?"

Patterson sighed. "Look, it's not mine . . . but I don't see why not."

The second cop, with a bull neck and a hard face, got a flashlight from the patrol car and searched the vehicle, pulling up carpets and everything he could. "Clean."

Patterson said, "Of course it's clean."

The smaller cop walked around to the rear of the small yellow car. "You won't mind opening the trunk, will you?"

Patterson said, "Look, this is getting a bit silly. I want to know which precinct you guys work out of. Who your superiors are."

"Open the trunk!"

"What is this? I've done nothing wrong. I don't get this."

"Sir, I'm going to ask you a second time—you wanna open the trunk?"

"This isn't my car."

"Just open it."

Patterson shook his head and sighed. He could see he wasn't going to win this particular argument. He took the key out of the ignition and popped open the trunk. Inside was the naked, dead body of his source.

Face blue gray, marks around his neck.

Jeff felt himself go into shock, legs nearly giving way.

Then he was violently sick.

The cold metal of a gun was pressed to the back of his head.

"Not a fucking move!" the cop snarled.

Patterson's mind was in free fall. "Oh Christ, what the hell is happening, man?" He dry-heaved, retched, and began to cry. He slumped down cross-legged on the asphalt, his back against the cop car, head in his hands. "Jesus Christ. I don't understand. This is crazy. I don't know anything about this. What the fuck is going on?"

The cops radioed in for backup as a black SUV pulled in behind the cruiser.

Four big guys with dark suits, white shirts, and tightly knotted ties emerged. The oldest stepped forward and flashed his card at the cop. "FBI," he said.

The cop said, "Sir, this is now a crime scene."

The Fed stared long and hard into the trunk. "Jesus H. Christ. That's the guy we were investigating. We had him under surveillance. Shit."

The cop said nothing.

The Fed pointed at Patterson. "And who is this?"

The cop said, "He was in the car. Journalist, he says. But it's not his vehicle."

Two Feds pushed past the cops and hustled Patterson into the back of the SUV.

"Hey, what's this?" Patterson said as the Feds strapped him into the back of the SUV.

The cop said, "Hey, this is our jurisdiction, motherfucker. You goddamn know it!"

"Not anymore. We're leading on this. Now fuck off."

"Bullshit."

The Fed stepped up to the cop and eyeballed him. "You gotta problem with the FBI, Officer?"

The cop said nothing, clearly seething.

The Fed stared at him. "Get it taped up. And call in backup, will you?" He turned and slammed the rear door shut. Then he climbed into the front passenger seat.

The SUV sped off with Patterson in the back. He was quickly handcuffed by a Fed sitting in the back seat. "I swear to God, sir," he said, "I know nothing about what happened."

"Do you know that man in the trunk?"

Patterson sighed. "I know him. As a source. That's all."

The Fed up front turned and faced Patterson. "This is national security, son. I imagine you know what that entails."

Patterson began to shake.

"You're in deep trouble, son. You got a lot of questions to answer. And we're going to get those answers, do you hear me?"

Patterson's heart sank. He stared out of the tinted windows as a Fed in the back seat pulled out his cell phone and gave details of the found body. He felt numb. What the fuck was this? What the fuck was happening? It felt like he was in the middle of a nightmare and was about to wake up. But every second he was in the car crawling through the dark streets, he knew this was real . . . Horribly real.

"What do you know?" the Fed in the front snarled.

"Listen to me, I don't know what the fuck happened. I just spoke to him about half an hour ago. Maybe an hour, I don't know. This is all crazy, man. I have no idea what's going on."

"And your phone records will confirm that?"

"Of course they will. But I swear to God, this has nothing to do with me."

The Fed was silent as they negotiated the near-empty DC streets.

"Where are you taking me? Hoover Building?"

"You'll know soon enough."

Patterson felt a growing sense of apprehension. He sensed something was amiss. His gut was telling him this was not just an ordinary crew of FBI guys. They looked and acted differently than the Feds he had known over the years. He shifted in his seat as the car headed south on the freeway. "You never answered my question."

"What question?"

"Where are you taking me?"

"A facility. A safe facility."

"A safe facility? What in God's name is a safe facility?"

"Shut the fuck up."

The initial apprehension turned into real fear as they headed away from DC. They drove on south, first along the freeway and then down some country roads. Through a manned checkpoint and to an underground garage. Patterson was hustled inside. Down harshly lit corridors, antiseptic white walls reflecting the glare.

Patterson felt his insides move. "Hey, are you guys playing some kind of prank? Because if you are, it really isn't funny. This doesn't look like an FBI field office."

The Fed beside him said, "Relax, son, this is just a national security precaution."

"So where are we?"

"First, we're going to interview you. Do you have any medical conditions? Are you on any meds?"

"Yeah, I'm on meds. I'm a diabetic."

"How long since you took your insulin?"

Patterson racked his brain. "I can't remember . . . I'm a couple of hours overdue. So, yeah, need to get some in me."

"OK, we've got an FBI physician available right now. And then after he sorts you out, we'll get your photograph, fingerprints, then we'll interview you."

"This is nuts. I need to speak to my lawyer. I've got rights. I'm an American. I know my goddamn rights."

The Fed opened a door and Patterson was ushered inside. A doctor with a white coat was there. "Doc, we need our guy in ten minutes. He's diabetic, or so he says."

The doctor leaned forward and placed the stethoscope to Patterson's chest. He listened for a few moments. "Your heart rate is very fast. Do you have anxiety problems?"

"Are you kidding me? Yeah, as a matter of fact I do. And this place sure as hell is not helping."

The doctor nodded. "Do you take anything for it?"

"Xanax mostly."

"And you're on insulin shots?"

"Yeah, of course."

The doctor took out a penlight and shone it in Patterson's eyes. "Xanax, huh?" He looked across at the detective. "How would you feel if I prescribed some Xanax so we can reduce any anxiety during the interview?"

The detective shook his head. "Not just now."

The doctor cleared his throat as he felt the pulse in Patterson's neck. "Certainly raised heart rate. Afraid Xanax is out of the question. But I assume an insulin shot would be OK."

Patterson closed his eyes, close to tears. "Yes, thank you."

The doctor turned to the detective. "Apart from heightened anxiety, he appears to be in good physical health. But he needs this insulin shot."

The Fed nodded. "Sure."

The doctor went to a cupboard and ripped open a plastic pack with a syringe inside. Then he jabbed it into a small insulin container, extracting the drug that would keep Patterson conscious. "Where do you usually get it?"

"I usually do it into my thigh."

"Upper left arm OK today?"

Patterson nodded. He felt a jab as the drug was injected.

"You're good for twenty-four hours."

The Fed said, "Appreciate your help, Doc." Then he grabbed Patterson up from the seat and hustled him to a side room with a Coke machine at the far end.

"Take a load off, kid," the Fed said. "I'm Special Agent Larry Greer. I've been assigned to a special unit set up to investigate the theft of classified materials from the NSA."

Patterson sat down. "Would the person you were investigating be the guy in the trunk?"

The Fed shook his head. "No. But we believe this man knew a certain CIA operative very well. They both served in Iraq. Military. Our CIA guy was an intelligence expert and computer whiz. Like Snowden. Maybe even worse, if you can imagine that."

Patterson said nothing.

"Tell me about this guy in the trunk. You've met him before."

"I want to see a lawyer. Right fucking now."

The Fed said, "You're up to your neck in this, son. You're in no position to issue instructions. As it stands, you'll be held on suspicion of murder."

Patterson shook his head. "I don't know what the fuck is going on. That wasn't me. Don't you fucking understand that? This is bullshit. I've been set up."

"Set up by who?"

Patterson looked at the mirror at the far end of the room. "Is this being filmed?"

The Fed nodded. "For your security."

"How many times do I have to say it? It wasn't me."

The Fed leaned against a wall. "You seem very agitated, Jeff. Why is that?"

"Why? Because there was a body in the trunk. A source of mine. And then I'm taken to this fucking place in the middle of nowhere."

"This is used for special operations. Classified."

Patterson lowered his head and closed his eyes. His head was beginning to feel fuzzy.

"It's a secure holding facility."

Patterson felt waves of exhaustion wash over him. "Why am I not in a DC police precinct?"

"Are you refusing to answer questions?"

"No, I fucking am not."

The Fed turned around and headed over to the Coke machine. He punched a button and two Cokes came out. He handed one to Patterson. "Here, take it," he said.

Patterson opened the can and took three or four large gulps. It tasted good. "Thanks."

The Fed sat down in the seat opposite. "We're here to find out what happened, Jeff. Can you understand that?"

"Sure I can understand it." Patterson felt his eyes getting heavier as the room began to move. "I don't feel too good." Swirling colors and walls caving in on him.

"What's wrong? Cat got your tongue?"

Then everything went black.

Patterson sensed he was in darkness, trussed up. There was a jolt and engine noise. He realized he was in the trunk of a car. Unable to open his eyes. The voices of men in the background. He felt himself fighting to stay conscious. Then the voices got louder.

"Warehouse ready?"

"Middle of nowhere. Nearest place is some fucking quarry ten miles away."

"Perfect."

Patterson felt a sense of foreboding like he'd never felt before. He willed himself to move. But he was paralyzed. Drugged. That's what it was.

His mind flashed back to the doctor. In his mind's eye, he saw the man in a different light. While before he had seen a man looking after his medical condition, now he realized the doctor had been instrumental in taking him out. And then he wondered, what if they'd already known about his medical condition? Was that possible?

The Feds seemed to be on the scene at the same time as the cops. Surely, if they had been monitoring his source, they would have known what had happened to him.

But then again, were those guys actually Feds?

The more he thought about it, the more scared he became. A feeling of dread was burrowing deep within him. He was scared to breathe. But he was also scared to try and hold on, despite the drug's paralyzing effects.

The car bumped over a pothole and Patterson's body was jerked against what felt like a body. Was someone else with him? Were they incapacitated too?

A few sharp turns, then over what felt like rough, uneven ground.

The vehicle began to reverse hard and fast. A few voices outside of the vehicle. The trunk was opened.

Patterson felt a jab in his arm, and he was swallowed up again by the darkness.

When he came to he was lying on a cold, concrete floor, staring up at a cracked ceiling. Out of the corner of his eye, he saw a naked black woman covered in blood, a needle in her arm. He wanted to scream. To move. But he couldn't.

Voices in the distance. Getting closer.

Footsteps.

He sensed people were watching him.

A masked man loomed into view, towering over him.

Then a gun was pressed to his head. "I could kill you."

Patterson tried to move. To say something. But nothing came.

"But I don't have to. You're about to be neutralized. Draw your last breath."

Patterson felt tears spill out of his eyes.

"When they see you and this filthy hooker, they will make assumptions. America is very quick at jumping to assumptions. Good night, Jeff."

Patterson strained to stay conscious . . . felt his eyes get heavy before they began to close.

Nineteen

Four days out

Nathan Stone had passed his five-hundredth push-up of the morning inside the new cottage, blinds drawn. The only sound was his breathing and rain battering off the slate roof. He drove himself hard. Heart pumping fast. Muscles firm. Mind clear. Endorphins kicking in. He got up and did some shadowboxing for ten minutes. Then he lay down and crunched out two hundred sit-ups.

He felt himself transported to a place of contentment in his mind. His soul felt calm.

Stone did some breathing exercises and sat himself down for an hour-long yoga session. He began to stretch. Move. Breathe. Deeper and deeper into the zone. The world of clear thinking. Hard choices.

He listened to his heartbeat for a few minutes. Controlled.

He got up and went into the bathroom and stared at his new face in the mirror. A face he could barely discern from the old one. He touched his left cheek. His skin was warm. Was this really him? But it was. They had created a new shell for him. A new identity.

He didn't exist. He never had. And that was good.

Stone felt exhilaration wash through his body. It was good to be back out in the world. Free. But it felt strange. Out of the compound. The facility.

He wasn't too sure how long he'd been in there for.

He'd been out of the game for quite a while. But he still had what it took. The way he had taken out the stranger in the TV room had told them that.

He had no qualms. Never had.

After a warm shower, he got dressed and switched on the radio. Classical music was playing low. It reminded him of his sister, her love of Bach and Beethoven. She would often drift off to sleep for an hour or so with the stolen transistor radio, listening to her music, before their father would return in a drunken rage. Nathan would stroke her hair.

His father wouldn't allow them to leave the house. They were prisoners. Just children. He would watch from the scratched, grimy windows for their father to return. For hours he'd stare down their Lower East Side street. A few longhairs. Black guys selling weed. Some Bowery bums.

Sometimes—very rarely—he headed up to Fifth Avenue to beg for money. He got loose change as he tried to avoid getting caught by cops. He remembered one cold winter's day, fingers freezing, he managed to get ten dollars in change. He went to Katz's Delicatessen and bought a pastrami sandwich and hot matzo ball soup. Nathan ran home with it in a bag and shared it with his grateful sister, half-starved, having not eaten for days.

His cell phone rang.

"Nathan." The voice of his handler. "We've got a real-time feed into the target's bedroom. Turn on your TV. We'll stream it for you."

Stone picked up the remote control and switched on the TV. "Just some game-show stuff."

"Switch to Channel 898."

Stone punched in the numbers on the remote. The screen switched to high-definition footage showing the senator adjusting his cuff links, humming a tune. Stone watched, transfixed. The strong jawline. The handsome features. The impeccable suit.

"You got it, Nathan?"

"Yeah, I'm watching him."

"You're on the clock now. We're watching this remotely too. But study him closely."

"You mind telling me when I'm going to neutralize this fuck and how?"

A long sigh. "Patience, Nathan. All in good time."

Twenty

A tangerine sun peeked over the Washington skyline, flooding light onto the Lincoln Memorial as Jessica Friel pounded the path circling the National Mall. She picked up her speed and felt adrenaline surge through her body. She ran her usual seven miles. It was long enough to challenge her, but not so much as to leave her exhausted.

Just over an hour later, she was back in her apartment, showered and finishing her orange juice, coffee, and cereal. She switched on the TV and channel-surfed until she got to Fox News. The screen showed a yellow-taped-off police cordon with an inset picture of an overweight white guy with a beard and a mug shot of a young black woman.

She stared at the image long and hard.

Her cell rang.

"Morning, honey." It was her mother's ever-cheerful voice.

Friel was glued to the TV. "Mom, how're things?"

"Pancakes, maple syrup, and sweet white coffee."

Friel focused on the screen as the Fox reporter spoke to eyewitnesses. "Mom, what did I say? How're you ever gonna lose weight if you're stuffing two thousand calories into your body first thing in the morning?"

The TV showed a medical examiner's van leaving an abandoned warehouse on an isolated part of the Potomac.

"Gimme a break, honey. When you get to my age, it all looks different. Besides, you have a high metabolism."

"Helped by exercise. Jogging. Running. Are you still swimming on Tuesdays and Fridays?"

A long sigh. "I try, Lord knows I do. But it's not easy. You know what the Michigan weather is like. All I want to do eight months of the year is eat carbs. Everyone does."

Friel picked up the remote control and turned up the sound slightly. She felt herself being pulled to the gruesome story.

"How's work?"

"Busy, busy. Crazy busy, actually."

"You need to relax, honey."

"I work. I exercise. That's how I relax. Besides, I need to work twelve- to fourteen-hour days just to keep my head above water. I'm drowning under a mountain of paperwork, emails I haven't answered . . ."

"Saw the senator on C-SPAN. Talks real good. Talks a lot of sense. Small government. It's the American way. At least it should be."

Fox showed a close-up of the dead man's home. Then his name flashed up on the screen: *Drug-induced death of libertarian writer and blogger Jeff Patterson.*

"Mom, gotta go. Talk soon."

Friel hung up and stared at the screen. Before she had time to process the information, her cell rang.

"Jessica, are you watching Fox?" It was Derek Forgan, one of Senator Crichton's political advisers.

Friel stared at the TV as if in a trance. "I know."

"Is that the guy who . . . ?"

"Yeah, that's the guy. Jeff Patterson."

"Fuck."

Friel went numb with shock. "What do we do?"

"This is the guy who said something was going to happen to Brad? Said he was going to be killed?"

"I've got to check if it's the same one. But there can't be too many libertarian bloggers in DC called Jeff Patterson, what do you think?"

"Tell no one. Not a soul. Am I clear?"

"Right. Of course, yeah. What about the senator?"

"What about him?"

"He needs to know."

Silence.

Friel said, "You want me to tell him?"

"Probably best."

She blew out her cheeks. "This is bad."

"This is worse than bad. If the press got wind that this Patterson guy's been in touch with us and the senator, saying he was on some sort of hit list, the Washington press corps would have a meltdown."

"We have to let the senator know ASAP."

"Deal with it. Then we'll talk again. Remember, not a soul."

He hung up and her apartment buzzer rang. "Goddamn."

Friel picked up the intercom. "Yeah."

"UPS Express Critical parcel delivery."

"From who?"

"Legal firm in DC. Frenton Associates."

"I don't know any Frenton Associates."

"Well, they've sent you a parcel via UPS, ma'am. You need to sign for it."

Friel sighed. "I'll be right down."

Twenty-One

Three days out

Nathan Stone was on his third coffee of the morning at the isolated cottage when he received a text. *Go for a run down the wooded trail behind the rear wall of the cottage. At least an hour. More to follow.*

He pulled on a navy hooded tracksuit and sneakers, then headed out the back door, down the garden path, climbed over the wall, and jumped to the other side. A dirt trail through the woods. He did a five-minute warm-up, breath turning to vapor in the cold. He turned left and ran and ran, picking up speed, pumping his arms hard. Through the forest, the smell of sodden leaves and tree bark and moss lingered in the air.

His heart was pounding. Deeper and deeper into the woods. The harder he ran, the more focused he felt. The foliage was dense and dark.

He checked his watch. Just over thirty minutes, so he took a short breather. Then he turned around and jogged all the way back, with a heightened sense of excitement for the operation ahead.

The more he thought about it, the crazier he felt. He didn't just get a thrill out of his work. He needed the work to make him feel vital. Strong. Charged. Without it, the tension and adrenaline rush, he was just a shell.

Just over an hour after he left, he was back in the cottage.

His cell rang immediately. "Nathan, look out the front window."

Stone did as he was told. Instead of the SUV there was a VW Golf. Metallic blue.

"Yeah, I see it."

"Your new set of wheels."

Stone knew the logic of changing vehicles.

"Go upstairs and look inside the wardrobe. At the very bottom."

Stone walked upstairs and checked the base of the wardrobe. "What am I supposed to be looking for?"

"You tell me."

Stone looked closer. He saw that the wood grain here was slightly different than on the other shelves. "I see. This isn't the bottom of the wardrobe."

"Clever boy."

Stone went downstairs and got a knife from the kitchen and prized open the wooden base. He pulled back the wood and revealed a sealed plastic bag stuffed with clothes. He pulled the bag out of the hole and ripped it open. Inside was a full set of hiking gear: waterproofs, hiking boots, a huge backpack with a compass, flares, Nikon camera, and maps of northwest Scotland. "OK, I see what we've got. Where am I going now?"

"Tomorrow you're going to be checking on the target."

"Recon?"

"Precisely. GPS coordinates to follow. Early night, Nathan."

Twenty-Two

The Gulfstream carrying Clayton Wilson touched down at a landing strip on a private island off Florida's Gulf Coast. He was picked up in a duck-egg-blue Bentley and whisked straight to the huge colonial house overlooking the ocean. He was escorted into the library and greeted by reclusive multibillionaire John Fisk Jr., a third-generation Texas oilman. Fisk had approached Wilson five years earlier about setting up the Commission. He had grown increasingly concerned, as had Wilson, that America was withdrawing from large-scale military interventions overseas to protect national political and economic interests. They both saw the dangers in the lack of political will to confront American enemies at home and abroad. Wilson had undertaken due diligence on Fisk before he decided to get involved. Fisk and his family controlled a web of shell companies to hide their true wealth, mostly based in the Caymans, although Fisk Oil still operated across the Gulf, the North Sea, the Middle East, and the Indian Ocean.

His connections to politicians were legendary. Men of power often sought him out. Mostly for donations to their campaign funds. Sometimes for their private foundations. Educational, faith-based, whatever.

Fisk didn't give a damn. He handed over hundreds of millions every year. He lined the pockets of powerful lobbyists working exclusively for his companies. But also American politicians, both Democrat and Republican, who had an interventionist mind-set. Fisk wasn't shy about getting his people to set up influential lawmakers with offshore bank accounts, getting jobs for their kids at one of the blue-chip companies he owned or was a majority shareholder in. Offering the use of his Manhattan penthouses to impress people. He loaned them all out. He didn't charge a dime. Never. But no one was in any doubt that if he asked a favor, it would have to be reciprocated. Even a small favor.

He golfed with presidents past and present. His financial muscle was useful in Hollywood. He was a link between the American government and the world of commerce. But his contacts within the State Department and Pentagon were extensive.

Fisk didn't visit anyone. They visited him.

It was the way he liked it.

Wilson smiled as the pale-skinned man wearing a light-blue shirt, rumpled chinos, and boaters stepped forward, cigar in hand. "Sir, it's a pleasure to meet you at last."

Fisk used his cigar to point to a claret-colored sofa as a warm breeze blew through the silk drapes.

Wilson sat down as Fisk pulled up a seat opposite him.

Fisk sat quietly for a few moments before he spoke. "I'm glad I could finally see you in person. I've barely had a moment to myself in weeks. Back-to-back meetings with God-knows-who about God-knows-what. You know how it is."

Wilson nodded. "How's your family?"

"They're good. I think. I haven't been home in nearly a week. Ironing things out."

Wilson smiled.

"And your family?" Fisk asked.

Wilson crossed his legs. "My wife has taken them off to Naples for a week."

"You like the Gulf Coast?"

"My brother owns a house in the Pelican Bay community. Overlooking the nature reserve."

Fisk stared at him long and hard. "That's very nice. Safe."

"How long have you lived here, if you don't mind me asking?"

Fisk blew out his cheeks. "Thirty years. No one bothers me. I see only those I want to see."

"Helluva place."

Fisk's eyes were hooded. He was unimpressed by platitudes and bullshit talk. "You hungry?"

"Sure."

"Good. Let's have lunch."

Fisk got up and Wilson followed him through to an adjacent oak-paneled dining room, fan whirring fast overhead. Staff wearing white gloves served steak, fries, and some greens, washed down with a perfect glass of chilled Chablis. They made small talk for over an hour.

The weather. The Yankees. Fisk's love of his new iPhone. Baseball. Softball. Soccer. On and on.

Fisk was an impeccable host. He allowed silences to open up when they should. But he wasn't averse to being more expansive when and if he wanted. He was very intuitive, as if he knew when to speak and when to shut the hell up.

He talked about the opening of a new gallery in Miami his wife had attended. Then he went off on a tangent and spoke in conspiratorial tones of a cocaine-addicted Democratic senator who was recuperating at his ranch in Montana after a drug bust that had been hushed up.

Wilson listened intently as he sipped his wine and smiled as the conversation flowed. Fisk never once broached the subject of his visit. And neither did Wilson.

Wilson knew that if Fisk wanted to ask any questions, he could ask them. But he wasn't going to volunteer information unless he was prompted.

Wilson was a guarded man. His decades of service in the military had ingrained that in his psyche. Even close friends never got too close. It was just the way it was.

After lunch they retired to a game room. They played snooker, smoked great cigars, drank brandy, but still didn't talk shop.

Just after four, Fisk looked across the table at Wilson.

"Let's head down to the beach, why don't we?"

The sand was fine and white, the turquoise waters lapping up onto the shoreline. Fisk took off his boaters and walked barefoot. Wilson kept his shoes on as they strolled, the sun warming his skin nicely after the long lunch.

Fisk stared off into the middle distance, his face hardening. "OK, I believe things are under way."

"Yes, sir."

"I understand that I don't get to know every last detail of what is and isn't going on, but I'd appreciate a few tidbits on where we are."

"There was a unanimous vote in favor, as you may have heard, and we got a finalized date."

Fisk nodded but said nothing.

"There are some complications. I think it's only fair to be up-front."

"What kind of complications?"

"A journalist. A blogger of sorts, libertarian, has become aware of a list of targets. A list that was on some backup CIA server, which should have been permanently deleted."

Fisk said nothing.

"We're trying to establish through back channels with the CIA and the NSA how this came about."

"And?"

"Some CIA contractor apparently took a log of names from the previously assumed deleted files, and this somehow got into the hands of the blogger."

"Where is the blogger?"

"He's been taken care of."

Fisk turned his face toward the sun and closed his eyes. "Is that the end of the matter?"

"We hope so. My only concern is if the Feds start sniffing around."

"So we're in the clear?"

"I believe so. There's no trace to you, me, or the Commission."

"Tell me about Brad Crichton."

"As I said, we're good to go. We have a team working on this."

"Point man?"

"Brigadier Sands is on the ground in Scotland."

"Good man."

"He's got us an asset who will carry out the task. But who is also disposable."

"Do I need to know any more about this asset?"

"CIA operative at one time. He was believed to have died a few years back during an operation."

"Believed to have died?"

"He was deemed to have died in the Everglades. But an exfiltration team on standby, posing as a federal medical team, took the lead from the cops and dragged his body away in a chopper."

Fisk nodded. "So officially he's already dead?"

"Precisely."

"Great cover. Good thinking."

"Thank you. But we're now on the clock."

Fisk sighed and stared at the ocean. "No more fuck-ups, Clayton. Am I clear?"

Twenty-Three

Senator Brad Crichton was sitting at the bar of the country house, enjoying a glass of whisky and chatting about economic liberalism and globalization with a World Bank suit, when his cell phone rang.

"Excuse me, Pierre," he said, "gotta take this."

Pierre Bordin smiled and sipped his white wine. "Of course."

Crichton slipped away to a quiet alcove. Satisfied he was out of earshot of the other delegates, he spoke. "Yeah, Jessica, what's happening?"

She sighed. "Senator, we've got a real problem."

Crichton's heart sank. "What kind of problem?"

"The guy who was calling you."

"What guy?"

"The libertarian."

"Oh him. What the hell does he want now?"

It seemed like an eternity before she answered. "Senator, his name is Jeff Patterson. He was found dead this morning at an abandoned warehouse, needle in his arm, dead hooker no more than five yards from him."

Crichton took a few moments to digest the information. He felt his throat go dry. He knocked back the rest of the whisky, put down his glass on a bookshelf. "My God."

"Here's the thing: that in itself is tragic and terrible. But bearing in mind that he contacted you, we're concerned you could get dragged into this as the investigation gathers pace. We have to think about this. We have to think strategically. We have to think about your career. And close down any links."

Crichton closed his eyes. "Jesus."

"There's one final aspect of this we need to consider."

"Which is?"

"What if Jeff Patterson was genuine? What if he was telling the truth?"

"I don't follow."

"What if he wasn't on drugs?"

"Jessica, he was delusional."

A long silence. "Perhaps."

Crichton turned his back slightly as a waiter came within earshot. "Why the skepticism?"

"Listen to me. There's no way he was a heroin addict. But if he was, he did a good job concealing it."

"Oh come on, Jessica, nobody knows what a man—or woman for that matter—is really like. You only have to look at us. No one knows about the true nature of our relationship other than us."

"I'm not buying it. Patterson was very specific. He said you were on a list. A list where others had died in mysterious circumstances."

"You don't know what demons he had. Was he a paranoid wreck? If he was using heroin or some opiate, he could have imagined any sort of delusional conspiracy."

"What I do know is he was desperate to tell us you were on a hit list. And then he's found dead. Coincidence?"

Crichton thought about that for a few moments. "He spoke to me too."

"Are you kidding me?"

"No. He managed to get my number, this number."

"When? Why didn't you tell me?"

"I didn't want to get bogged down in this. It happened . . . just over twenty-four hours ago. Maybe a bit more. He mentioned the deaths of two other people. Said I was next."

"This is not good, Brad. We need to really focus on this."

Crichton sighed. "Look, I'm really busy just now . . ."

"Brad, we'll take care of it. We're going to work out your options and strategy over the next few hours. And I'll give you a call tomorrow to talk things through. How does that sound?"

Crichton blew out his cheeks. "OK, I suppose."

"Are you OK?"

"No, I'm not OK. This is not the sort of news I want to hear."

"We'll sort it out, don't worry. Tell me about the conference."

"I'm surrounded by really smart people. But unfortunately they're all saying the same thing. They want bigger and bigger budgets, more intervention, more spending, more of everything. And now this news about this goddamn blogger. So no, I most certainly am not OK, now that you ask."

"That's natural." A beat. "I also just want to say . . . I miss you . . . I mean, having you around . . . You know what I mean?"

Crichton felt his neck flush. "I do. I miss you too, Jessica."

"I love being with you. I love being around you."

Crichton rubbed his tired eyes. "Sure."

"And that's why this concerns me so much. I'm worried."

"I appreciate that."

"I want us to be happy. Us. You do too, don't you?"

"Absolutely."

"You sound distant."

"Lot on my mind."

"You're the only thing on my mind, Brad."

"Jessica, I have to get back."

"OK. Don't worry about this. We'll make sure there's no fallout from Patterson's death."

Crichton was distracted for the rest of the evening. He picked at his food as he tried to make conversation with the other delegates. But they could see he was preoccupied, and he made an excuse to retire to his room early.

Almost immediately his bedside phone rang.

"Good evening, Senator, sorry for bothering you."

"What is it?"

"There's a lady in the lobby who wishes to speak to you."

"Did she give you a name?"

"She says she works for the US Embassy in London. She's been cleared by security. She says it's rather urgent she speak to you."

"Did she say what it was about?"

"Only that she needed to speak face-to-face."

Crichton groaned. He couldn't abide listening to advice from the diplomats as a rule. He wondered if she wanted to talk about the conference. But maybe it was something more urgent. The blogger perhaps. He sighed.

"Tell her I'll be there in a minute." He ended the call and headed down the stairs, where he was greeted by an attractive middle-aged woman.

"Senator," she said, extending her hand. "Sorry we haven't been introduced. Francine Carmetto, Deputy Chief of Mission, US Embassy in London. So nice to see you. I hope I haven't disturbed you."

Crichton shook his head. "Just finishing some briefing papers."

"I was sitting at an adjacent table and I saw you leave early."

"We're meeting first thing tomorrow for some plenary session, is that right?"

"Yes, I believe so. But this isn't about the session." Carmetto smiled and pointed to some lounge chairs at the far end of the lobby. "Please."

Crichton followed her, sat down, and sighed. "So what's going on?"

"A friend of mine has asked to meet you."

"A friend of yours?"

"He works out of the consulate in Edinburgh."

"Ah . . . And he wants to speak to me? Now?"

Carmetto nodded. "In person."

"Do you mind me asking what the urgency is?"

"I can't say, sir."

"So where is he?"

"He's outside, waiting for you in a car. He was attending a plenary session and thought it would be good to introduce himself."

Crichton was tongue-tied for a few moments as his stomach tightened. "Waiting for me? Why the hell doesn't he come in? We can talk here."

Carmetto sighed. "I believe he has some matters of a confidential nature he would like to discuss with you."

Crichton shrugged. "This is all very interesting. But I need to know more before I agree to such a meeting. Besides, I have some briefing papers to work my way through tonight."

"I appreciate that. But I believe we are talking about matters of a classified nature. National security, that kind of thing."

Crichton said, "I see."

Carmetto nodded and smiled back at him as if to reassure him.

"Right now?"

"I think that would be best."

Crichton sighed again. "I've got an hour. No more."

Carmetto got to her feet. "Excellent." She headed outside into the cold night air as Crichton followed. He saw a black SUV. Its engine was purring, the back door open invitingly. She guided him to the car.

Crichton looked inside and saw a rugged-looking white man wearing a gray suit, dark-blue tie, matching silk handkerchief, and white shirt. He slid in and shut the door.

They drove off and headed down the estate's long, dark driveway.

The man turned around and stared at Crichton. "Senator, appreciate your time. Apologies for the manner of our meeting. Couldn't be helped."

"Do you mind explaining what this is all about?"

"I'm Brigadier Jack Sands, military attaché, US Consulate General Edinburgh. You met my colleague, who picked you up at the airport."

Crichton nodded as he tried to assess what was coming. "Where are we going?"

"Just for a drive."

Crichton said nothing.

"How're you enjoying Scotland?"

"I had planned to get in a round or two of golf at Gleneagles, but it's wall-to-wall meetings, I'm afraid."

"Beautiful country. You ever been to Edinburgh?"

"Only passing through the airport."

"Let me tell you, if you get a chance, get down to Edinburgh. Finest city in Europe, bar none. Athens of the North."

"Brigadier, I'm sure you haven't asked to speak to me at this ungodly hour to extol the beauty of Edinburgh. You mind telling me what it is you want?"

Sands sighed and stared straight ahead. "What do you know about Jeff Patterson?"

Crichton's insides knotted tight. "What do I know about him?"

Sands nodded.

"I've heard of him."

"Have you heard he's dead?"

Crichton said nothing.

"Did you know this?"

"I was made aware of this earlier. An hour or two ago."

"Has he ever approached you?"

"Brigadier, I respect you have a job to do, but for the life of me, I don't understand what any of this has to do with me."

"Let me put it another way. Has he passed any classified documents or material to you?"

Crichton was rather taken by surprise. "I don't believe this is a matter I should be discussing with anyone."

"Let me try yet another tack. Are you leaking government security secrets?"

"Who the hell do you think you're talking to, Brigadier?"

"Answer the question."

"Absolutely not!"

"Has this guy passed you any documents?"

Crichton felt agitated at the directness of this questioning.

"Answer the goddamn question."

"No, he has not."

Sands took a few moments to digest the information. Then another few moments to answer. "I appreciate your candor. Just to give you a heads-up, there's an investigation under way into his death. And your name has come up in the conversation. Would you have any idea why that might be?"

"Brigadier, I've never met the man. I know he's a journalist."

"But we believe he was trying to contact you. And I believe he actually spoke to one of your advisers. And yourself, on the phone."

Crichton shifted in his seat.

"Can you confirm if that is the case?"

"Yes, I did speak to him."

"And would you mind telling me what it was about?"

"Brigadier, I'm drawing this conversation to a close. I think I've said enough. If you want to speak further about this, I suggest you speak to my attorney, my brother, Murray Crichton, in DC."

Sands sighed long and hard. "Of course."

The car turned around and five minutes later he was dropped off back at the floodlit country house.

Crichton opened the door and stepped out. He turned and faced Sands. "In the future, Brigadier, go through my attorney with regards to such matters."

"Enjoy the rest of your evening, Senator."

Crichton shut the door. He watched as the car pulled away, driving slowly down the dark road and into the night.

Twenty-Four

Two days out

The early-morning sun was glinting off the windows of the Scottish country house as Nathan Stone peered through military-grade binoculars with a perfect line of sight. He was hunkered down in an elevated bird blind about a mile away on the edge of woodland that fringed the ivy-covered perimeter wall of the estate. Then suddenly he spotted his prey.

Senator Brad Crichton jogging in the manicured grounds.

Moving the binoculars, he saw the security detail lurking at a safe distance, talking into radios.

Stone used the binoculars to follow Senator Brad Crichton as he pounded the dirt trail within the grounds of the country estate. He saw Crichton had earbuds in as he ran. He fixed on the politician's face. His eyes were focused on the route ahead. He appeared to be in excellent physical shape. Lean face and physique.

Stone's cell phone vibrated in his pocket, and he pressed it to his ear.

"Good morning, Nathan." The voice of his handler. "How are you this fine morning?"

"Just biding my time."

"We're in a holding pattern now, Nathan. Do you understand what I'm saying?"

"Absolutely."

"In effect, we're waiting for the pieces to fall into place before we make our move."

"You talking openings?"

"I'm talking openings . . . I'm talking a free day for delegates. But things are fluid. They seem to be changing the itinerary and schedules on a daily basis."

"Well, whatever, I'm ready. I see exactly what he looks like. Here and now. What else do I need to know?"

"He's very fit, as you can see. Wrestling champion at college. Dabbled in martial arts as part of a fitness routine. And boxing. So he can handle himself."

Stone said nothing as he stared through the binoculars at Crichton. "What about family?"

"They're back in the States."

"So we should have a clear run."

A long pause. "We don't know at this stage."

Stone sensed that his handler wasn't telling him the full story. "What do you mean?"

He let out a sigh. "His wife has spoken to a friend about perhaps surprising her husband with a visit on the final day of the conference. But we've not had confirmation. And no flights have been booked for her. Maybe something to be aware of."

Stone said nothing.

"Did you hear what I said?"

"Makes no difference to me. Whatever it takes, it takes."

"We'd like you to hunker down in the bird hide until further notice. You OK with that?"

"Got everything I need here. Flask of coffee, snacks. I'm good."

"Be in touch."

The line went dead.

Twenty-Five

Just after midday UK time, Jessica Friel's plane touched down at London's Heathrow Airport. She stepped off with her overnight bag, jet-lagged and fatigued. Her body clock was telling her it was dawn. She picked up her suitcase from baggage retrieval. Then she sat down for a complimentary coffee and some snacks in the British Airways lounge. She dialed her boss's cell phone number. It was diverted to voice mail. But then he called back.

"Jessica?"

"Hi, sorry to bother you."

"Is it about this Patterson guy?"

"Sort of."

"What do you mean?"

"Brad, I got a delivery yesterday. UPS. I opened it after we spoke."

"A UPS delivery? Not so unusual."

"It was from Jeff Patterson's attorneys."

A tense silence hung between them for a few moments. "What?"

"They had been instructed to send me a package upon their client's death."

"What kind of package?"

Friel sighed. "It was a Jo Malone perfume set."

"I'm sorry, you've lost me."

"But at the bottom of the box there was a tube of lip balm."

"What?"

"Guess what was in that."

"I have no idea."

"Brad . . . the lip balm was disguising a flash drive. A USB flash drive."

"Is this some sort of joke?"

Friel tried to block out a loudspeaker announcement of an incoming flight. "Brad, I'm in the UK."

"What?"

"I'm here, in the UK."

"The UK? You're not in DC?"

"There were instructions inside the perfume box. And they were specific. To hand it over to you in person with immediate effect."

"Why would you fly across the Atlantic to tell me that?"

"Why? Brad, after everything that's happened, I wanted you to get this."

"Oh jeez . . . Jessica, what the hell were you thinking?"

"What do you mean? I thought you'd be pleased to get a heads-up. I'm in London."

"Jessica, you should have called before you left."

"Why?"

Crichton sighed. "We don't know what it contains. What are the legal ramifications?"

"I know what it contains."

"What?"

"That's why I flew all this way. To be here with you and deliver it in person."

Crichton said nothing.

"Look, I've got to catch a flight to Inverness in the next half hour."

"You're headed to Scotland?"

"That was the plan."

Crichton groaned.

"I had to bring this to you. Patterson was right. You are on this list. Your name is on it."

"Jessica, I don't know anything about this crazy guy. But now you could be in possession of classified government secrets."

"To hell with that. This is proof that you're at risk."

"Do you know who visited me last night?"

Jessica said nothing.

"A military attaché wanted to speak to me. An American based in Edinburgh. And he wanted to know if I knew Patterson. This is already a serious issue. And the last thing I need is to be implicated in any way."

"You need to see this. Don't you understand the gravity of what I'm saying?"

Crichton sighed long and hard.

"Maybe I should have called you to talk it through."

"How long until you can get here?"

Jessica cleared her throat. "It's a ninety-minute flight to Scotland. British Airways. Half an hour till departure. I'll grab a taxi at the airport."

Crichton sighed. "No. I'll meet you at the airport. Far more discreet."

"Whatever you think, Brad. Please don't be angry with me."

"We'll talk about it later."

Crichton ended the call as Jessica fought back tears.

Twenty-Six

Nathan Stone shielded his eyes from the glare of the sun through the storm clouds as he sat parked not far from the main terminal at Inverness Airport. He took a drink of the strong black coffee he'd picked up at a roadside café en route. He had been glad to get the call from his handler to get out of the blind, even for a few hours, to keep an eye on the senator and his mistress.

He watched as a group of schoolchildren walked out of the terminal escorted by harassed-looking teachers before being greeted by their parents, bubbling with happiness. Grabbed up in the arms of mothers and fathers and smothered with kisses and laughter and hugs.

He felt nothing. It was probably true that most people would react with delight at the scene. But all he could think of was his father.

Not smothering him with affection but glaring at him before taking off his thick leather belt, wrapping it around his nicotine-stained fingers, and lashing out at Nathan, his son, just a skinny, nervous, bed-wetting boy. He still remembered the look on his father's face. Cold eyes, sneering smile, and clenched teeth. He was like a wild animal. That was what Nathan had faced. Each and every night when his father returned home from drinking.

Nathan stared at the children. He felt envious. He never knew what it was like to be treated nicely. He remembered tasting the blood in his mouth. Then closing his eyes tight as he pleaded, to no avail. The punches rained down on his face and head. Then the belt would whip through his dirty T-shirt and lash his back. If he was lucky, it would only hurt for an hour or so. But the norm was being beaten unconscious for imagined slights.

The more he thought of it, the more he didn't care. He didn't care that he was the way he was. He didn't care that he didn't feel. In fact, it meant he didn't have to worry about appearing to care.

The only thing on God's earth he cared about was his sister. She had always been nice to him. He remembered when Helen had taken him to Rockaway Beach. He thought he'd died and gone to heaven. The sun was burning hot, and the beach was packed with thousands of New Yorkers. He remembered running headlong into the cold water and screaming with delight. He remembered turning around and looking back down the beach and seeing his sister watching him, always alert. It was such an adventure and release to get out of the stinking hovel. Far, far away from the Lower East Side. He remembered closing his eyes and wishing to float away up to the fluffy white clouds in the dark-blue sky and never come down. He willed it to happen. He thought of running away. Helen talked about it with him. But they were too scared. They didn't know what to do, where to go. Their only release was their father's death. But that turned out to be a prison. They were separated. Now she languished in a psychiatric unit in Florida. Alone. Dreams had turned to dust. He hadn't visited since his near-drowning.

But she more than anything was the one who had allowed Nathan to escape his hell. She was the one who had driven the steel scissors into their father's heart. He had watched and screamed. Until he couldn't move. Struck dumb eventually.

His sister just stared down at their father's body, smearing her face in his still-warm blood.

Whenever Stone closed his eyes, he could still see that image. Like a stain that could never be removed. A ghostly memory that would haunt him till he himself was six feet under.

His cell phone rang. In the background, a loudspeaker announcement.

"The target and his aide are now together. She had one carry-on bag and a case. They'll be coming your way in a few minutes."

The minutes dragged as the London visitors filtered out to the waiting taxis. Emerging almost last from the arrivals area came Senator Crichton and a young, stunningly attractive woman, hand in hand.

Stone watched as they jumped into a taxi together. He sipped his coffee, not keen to attract undue attention.

His cell phone vibrated in his pocket.

"We're watching this on the airport's security system. Get a good look at her, Nathan."

"Yeah, I already have. Pretty."

"This wasn't in our plans."

"So?"

"So things just got a whole lot more complicated."

Stone finished his coffee and dropped the empty cup at his feet on the car's floor. "How so?"

"You're going to have to take down both of them, perhaps at the same time."

Stone started up his car. "They're on the move."

"We've got their conversation covered via electronic surveillance. But we need to know where they go, unless they play it cute and take the batteries out of their phones."

Stone pulled away. "I'm on it."

"Don't lose them."

Brigadier Jack Sands was being buffeted by gale-force winds as he walked on the high cliffs at the edge of the facility. Saltwater spray was being whipped up from an angry sea. He liked to clear his head with bracing walks. Miles and miles of walks. Hundreds of feet below the sheer face of the cliffs was a rocky shore. He stared over the gray seas in the direction of America. That was what he did it for. For his country. His blood. His soil. He thought of his family, unaware of exactly where he was and what he was doing. And then he thought of his sister-in-law, a dyed-in-the-wool Hillary Clinton supporter. He had lost count of the number of times they'd fallen out.

He couldn't abide bullshit liberals with their hand-wringing about unfair quotas and how fucking hard life was on minorities. What a bunch of bullshit.

He'd grown up in a shithole town in western Texas. But he had a stable, hardworking family. A mother and a father. His father was a handyman. Mending cars, tractors, trucks. He was good with his hands, they said. That was true. His temper was even. Sunny nature. Nothing got him down. His mother, by comparison, was cut from a different piece of cloth. She was a Southern Baptist, originally from outside Austin. She had a hot temper. Eight kids to feed and a husband who didn't bring home much.

It was hand-to-mouth.

But their Christian values were instilled at an early age. Hard work, God, country, and service.

Sands closed his eyes for a moment as he remembered the pride in his mother's eyes when he had won a Bible story contest run by his local church. His mother felt the need to tell everyone in the neighborhood. The family was proud. But he was teased mercilessly at school by some of the older boys.

He missed his mother and father. But more than anything he missed his wife. She'd died nearly twenty years earlier, from cancer.

And he'd found it tough trying to raise their kids the best he could as he flitted from army base to army base.

Four good kids. Three boys and one girl. All grown up. One still at college. One in the army. And two working for the CIA.

He couldn't be any prouder.

They were following in his footsteps.

But there was an emptiness in his life that had followed him around. It wasn't just being without his wife. It was the nature of his job. What he did. What he knew.

Sands reached the farthest point away from the facility on the island and stared out at the sea. It was in turmoil. Restless. Unpredictable. He sometimes wondered if it wasn't time to pack it all in and return to a stable life back in the States. Maybe set up a consultancy.

He turned and headed back to the warmth of the facility. He checked his watch and remembered he had a meeting with Stone's psychologist. He arrived just a minute late.

Sands dried himself off with a towel, grabbed the hot coffee handed to him, and sat down.

The psychologist was leafing through Stone's file. "I saw something interesting last night when I was looking over my notes and all the interviews I've done with Stone. I thought it was right to let you know."

"What was that?"

"I didn't think much of it at the time, but I thought I'd raise it with you."

Sands shrugged and gulped some hot coffee. "Shoot."

"The first few weeks he was here—in fact, all his time here—he said he had no memory of his family. He always said it was sketchy. But a couple of days ago, just before he left, one of the teammates looking after him found a drawing hidden in his mattress."

"In his mattress?"

"Yes, inside the mattress."

"What is it?"

"It's a doodle."

"Doodle?"

The psychologist handed him the picture.

Sands held the picture and looked at the image of a young woman gazing out of a window, cigarette in her hand. He was then shown a photo from the file of Stone's sister.

"What do you think?"

"I don't know what this proves."

"I think it's a striking likeness, don't you?"

"It's pretty basic. I don't know."

"I think it looks pretty much like her. Cigarette too. She smokes, doesn't she?"

Sands nodded.

"He remembers her."

"Which contradicts what he's said to you."

"Exactly my point, Jack."

Sands got to his feet. "Appreciate the heads-up, Doc." He headed back to his office, locked the door, and dialed the direct number for Clayton Wilson. He answered after the fourth ring. After a few pleasantries, Sands described the brief meeting with the psychologist.

Wilson spoke first. "Let's recap. First, I get information from his sister's psychologist in Florida saying that Stone was in touch. Now there's a drawing of someone with a likeness to his sister that was tucked inside his mattress."

"Yes, sir."

"You think he does remember his sister?"

"Honestly? I don't know."

Wilson said nothing.

"Is it possible, sir, that we're putting one and one together and getting three? He's a valuable asset."

"But he could well become a liability. And if that happens . . . if he's concealing far more of his memories than he's letting on . . . it's possible that Nathan Stone could become a problem."

"You think he might go rogue?"

"It's rare, I'll give you that. But he wouldn't be the first operative in my experience."

Sands sensed the matter was concerning to Wilson. He didn't like the direction the conversation was heading. "I'm at a loss to understand what you're getting at, sir, with all due respect."

"The more I think about this, the more Stone begins to worry me."

"He's one of the finest operatives we have at our disposal."

"We need people to be trustworthy. One hundred percent trustworthy, right?"

"Yes, sir."

"This is all about the mission, not the man."

Sands closed his eyes for a moment. "I guess I need to know, sir, how would you like to deal with this?"

"If we lose control of a man like Stone, on the streets, uninhibited, we're all in trouble."

"Indeed."

"I think we need to ensure that Mr. Stone sticks only to the mission."

Sands's blood ran cold. "I thought that was a given, sir."

"It should be. And I hope it will be. But we need to think of the big picture, don't we?"

Sands sensed that Wilson was talking around exactly what he wanted to say. "You want him rubbed out, is that it?"

"What I want, Jack, is to be assured that we aren't storing up problems for further down the line."

"You want him taken care of?"

Wilson said nothing.

"This might be in his sister's head."

"But what about the drawing? That wasn't in her head."

Sands sighed. "Sorry to labor the point, sir, but do you want me, in light of what we now know, to arrange plans for Nathan, sir?"

"I think it's for the best. But only once he's carried out the mission. Do what's necessary."

Sands ended the call and felt a terrible emptiness inside.

Twenty-Seven

Clayton Wilson was sitting at the head of a huge table with the other members of the Commission. He flicked through the file on Jessica Friel and stared at the grainy black-and-white photograph of the attractive political staffer. He looked across the table at Richard Stanton. "You've put this on the agenda to be discussed today, Richard. You wanna explain?"

Stanton cleared his throat and looked around the table. "We have a new problem. While Jeff Patterson is no longer a concern, electronic surveillance of this woman, as well as Senator Crichton, indicates she was contacted by Patterson only hours before he died. A search of Patterson's computer records shows he's composed a letter to his lawyer asking for documents,` unseen by his lawyer, to be sent to Ms. Friel in the event of his death. We believe these are the highly classified documents that came into his possession from a CIA contractor."

Wilson stared at the photo of Friel taken when she was out jogging near Capitol Hill. "And we're sure this is Crichton's mistress?"

"No doubt about it."

"Where is she now?"

"That's why I've put this on the agenda as an emergency item. She's now in Scotland with Senator Crichton."

"How didn't we know about this?"

"We didn't foresee Patterson having the foresight to send such documents to his lawyer."

Wilson felt his stomach tighten. "So he must have suspected he was under surveillance."

Stanton sighed. "I don't know."

Wilson looked around the table. "We're at a critical juncture here. We could abort the operation right now. Or we could continue. We need to figure out where we go from here. Gentlemen, your thoughts, please."

Crawford McGovern, former director of the CIA, was nodding. "Shit happens, right?"

Everyone nodded.

"You do stuff like this, prepare yourself for the unexpected. The unforeseen. My take on it? Dumb fucking luck. First, the CIA contractor having this goddamn flash drive with fragments of this plan, which was then handed to Patterson. Second, this Patterson, he's given himself an insurance policy by mailing the information secretly to his lawyer, only to be forwarded to Friel in the event of his death? I mean, shit, that is dumb fucking luck number two. But she now poses a real and credible threat to this operation. And sometimes, just sometimes, the end justifies the means."

A few nods among the apprehensive faces.

Wilson said, "The operative in question can take out both Crichton and Friel if the occasion arises."

Stanton nodded. "Our man on the ground assures me that the operative can deal with both. Easily."

McGovern stared long and hard at the picture of Friel. "The third option is to neutralize Crichton, but without any blood being spilled.

By that I mean, leak details of the affair, compromising photos, to *National Enquirer*. His campaign would never recover from that."

Wilson rubbed his eyes. "I think we ran through that option before on Crichton. Sure, we could tarnish his good name, drag him and his family through the mud. But we only have to look at goddamn Bill Clinton. Goes on TV with Hillary, and they get back in the race. Not only that. They go from strength to strength. No one thought it was possible. Not a soul. But he showed it can happen."

McGovern nodded. "Very true. Good point, Clayton."

Wilson breathed in deep as he contemplated what they should do. "Let's leave aside the people involved if we can for a few moments." He stared across at Stanton. "This flash drive, is it still with Friel?"

"So far," Stanton said. "But it's just a matter of time before she passes it to Senator Crichton."

Wilson shifted in his seat. "That is not good. If we leak information to the *Enquirer*, Crichton might think he has nothing to lose by releasing details on the flash drive."

McGovern nodded.

"I guess the next question is," Wilson said, "do we have someone who could retrieve the information from inside the house where Crichton is staying?"

Stanton cleared his throat. "Assuming it's kept secure in a safe and not on a person, we can do that."

"Insertion team?"

"Probably a two-man team," Stanton said. "We have uniforms already made up in case our operative needs to gain access."

"Deal with that side of things." Wilson looked around the table. "The flash drive we'll take care of. But that leaves another person who may have knowledge of its contents, in addition to the senator."

McGovern said, "Let's not sugarcoat this. We need to clarify if both Crichton and Friel are to be neutralized within the next forty-eight hours. So we need to do this on a show of hands, right?"

Wilson nodded. "Everyone who believes that Senator Brad Crichton and his aide cum mistress Jessica Friel should be dispatched in Scotland, raise your hands."

Everyone's hand went up.

Wilson leaned back in his seat. "Unanimous. From now on, I don't want to hear of any more problems. Let's get this done. Dismissed."

Twenty-Eight

Crichton put his arm around Jessica as they sat in the rear of a taxi headed back to the country house. "Look, maybe I overreacted on the phone. I'm sorry. Are you OK?"

"No, I'm not OK. I'm scared."

Crichton caught the driver watching them in his rearview mirror. He moved closer. "You wanna keep it down?" His voice was a whisper. "Listen, I'll be able to get clearance for you at the place where we're stuck for this conference. But if word got out that you were here, my wife would be asking some serious questions. Did you think of that?"

Jessica closed her eyes, tears streaming down her face.

"You didn't have to come all this way, goddammit, Jessica!" he said. "Oh shit, don't cry."

Jessica dabbed her eyes with a handkerchief. "What did you expect me to do?"

The rest of the journey was made in awkward silence.

When they arrived at the country house, Crichton signed Jessica in. She was taken to security, where she was photographed, her name and ID were checked, and her retina scanned before she was given security clearance and her passport details taken. The two of them then retired to Crichton's suite.

Crichton slumped on a sofa as Jessica reached into her handbag and pulled out the lip balm. She took off the top. Inside was a flash drive. She handed it over, along with the note from Patterson that had been sent from his legal firm.

"Strictly for Senator Brad Crichton, it says." He looked at Jessica. "And you checked to see what's on it?"

"Yes. And I'm terrified."

"What about anyone else on the team?"

"No. They don't know about it."

Crichton sighed long and hard. "I don't know . . ."

"What don't you know?"

"I don't know if this is the right way to go about this. Should I get some legal advice first?"

"I've already checked it. You're on a kill list. Half the people on it are already dead!"

"I need to think about this. It might be a really clever way to remotely access my computer, have you thought of that? It could wipe out all my private correspondence."

"Shit . . . I hadn't thought of that."

"Should I run it past the rest of the team, check the contents, and take it from there?"

Jessica dabbed her eyes as she pulled out the papers. "I don't know what you should do. What I do know is that Jeff Patterson's death is making news all over the world. Social media is going nuts. Some are saying he was no heroin user. And a lot of people are saying it looks suspicious."

Crichton seemed in a daze as he scanned the note. He looked up. "Heroin addict, you say?"

"To be fair—not that I'm expert in that area—but from the pictures I've seen of him, he sure as hell didn't look like a heroin addict. When we spoke, he was sharp, focused, and completely together, albeit obsessing about speaking to you."

"What if his motives are nefarious, Jessica? Is he using this as a ruse to get to me?"

"I think you need to speak to the Feds at the very least. This is not good."

"It might just be a coincidence. We need to be aware of that possibility."

Jessica said, "I can't understand this. It's crazy." She stared at the flash drive in Crichton's hands. She looked across at the MacBook Pro on the writing desk. "Why don't you just see what's on it? I've already seen it. Where's the harm in that?"

Crichton went quiet for a couple of minutes as he considered the best course of action. "Tell me, where did he say he got this information from?"

"Patterson? Said it was from an intelligence source."

"What else?"

"Said it was classified or something."

Crichton pinched the bridge of his nose as he felt a headache coming on.

"Brad, he came across as earnest, pretty straight down the line. Really wired, but something must've been deeply troubling him to want to speak to me and then you, then to also get his lawyer to send this beautifully concealed flash drive in case something happened to him."

Crichton began to pace the room.

"Brad, I've got to be frank. This is pretty scary territory. I mean, this is out there, way out of left field."

"You know what else is way out of left field?"

Jessica shrugged.

"The fact that an American military attaché here in Scotland wanted to see me. And all he wanted to talk about was Jeff Patterson and had he passed classified documents to me. I said he hadn't."

"Shit. This is bad."

"Tell me about it."

"So the conversation with the military attaché . . . That was all he said?"

"More or less. Probing."

Jessica got up and started pacing the room. "You need to look and see for yourself what's on the flash drive and then take it from there."

Crichton said nothing.

Jessica reached out and held his hand. "I'm sorry if I haven't handled this correctly."

"What do I always say?" Crichton kissed her on the cheek.

Jessica shrugged.

"The first call should always be my chief of staff. You should have spoken to him, Jessica."

"Don't you trust me? Is that what this is?"

"It has nothing to do with trust. It has to do with judgment."

"So you think my judgment is faulty."

"You made the wrong call. It was impetuous. OK?"

Jessica extricated her hand from his grasp.

"Think about it. I'm chair of the intelligence committee. We were warned by computer experts that we should not put any USB drives or devices into our laptops unless they come from verified sources. You were told that too, weren't you?"

Jessica nodded.

"It's easy to hack, seemingly. Besides, I've only been in this role for a matter of weeks. Classified information should stay classified. I can't just pick up anything on the say-so of some goddamn blogger."

"I think he was telling the truth."

"I'm not saying he wasn't. But I need to think of the legal consequences before I proceed. It's almost certainly encrypted anyway."

"I've checked it. I saw it with my own eyes. Why don't you believe me?"

"Jessica, if this information is, as Patterson indicated, classified, do I really want to access that without first getting legal advice? It means it must have been stolen from the US government. I need to know where that leaves me."

Jessica nodded. "You're right. You're absolutely right."

Crichton pulled out his cell phone and dialed the number for the intelligence committee's legal counsel in DC.

"What are you doing?"

"I think it's time to get a second opinion."

Twenty-Nine

It was dark when Nathan Stone finally pulled up outside the cottage. Inside, he locked the door, shut the blinds, and drew the curtains. Then he showered and took some fresh clothes hanging in the wardrobe and put them on.

He fixed himself an omelet and toast and washed it down with a cold Coke from the refrigerator.

He switched on the TV and channel-surfed until he came to a BBC documentary about the Rolling Stones. He felt himself getting aroused as he watched the Altamont footage from 1969 when some Hells Angels killed a black guy in the huge crowd. The music blared as chaos ensued. Stone watched, transfixed. Thrilled. The Angels glared at the hippies, occasionally meting out pool-cue justice. Blood spilled. Scuffles. Then more beatings.

The hippies were tripping. And the Angels were going mental. And all the time the Stones played, or tried to play. Jagger pleaded for calm as the Angels mocked him from the side of the stage.

The atmosphere was poisonous.

Stone loved the band. He had been too young to see them in their prime. And he had been too poor to see them while growing up. But he loved their music. They sounded American, despite being English.

The snarling, bluesy sound, underpinned by seductive rock riffs and tight, incessant drumming, seemed to strike a chord with him.

Stone stared at the screen as Altamont became a battleground, unlike Woodstock on the East Coast. The whole vibe had been poisoned. He loved it. Wished he'd been there.

When the documentary finished, he switched off the TV. He got up and made himself a black coffee. He switched on the radio. Classical piano music played low.

His cell phone rang.

"Nathan, good day today?" his handler said in a world-weary tone.

"Hanging out in a fucking bird hide and hanging about some goddamn airport is not my idea of fun, let me tell you."

"You getting cabin fever?"

"I want to get it on."

"All in good time, Nathan. We're moving closer to resolution."

"So the target is now accompanied by a lady friend. How does she fit into my plans?"

"That's why I called. You'll like this."

"What?"

"Turn on Channel 928 on your TV."

Stone wondered what his handler was talking about. "Huh?"

"Just turn on your TV."

Stone got up, headed through to the living room, and turned to the channel as instructed. And there it was. High-definition footage of the senator and his aide going at it. The footage was extremely precise. Stone stared at the flushed face of the libertarian politician and his mistress.

"Working hard for all Americans, right, Nathan?"

"He's working hard all right. How long now?"

"We're nearly good to go."

"But when?"

His handler sighed. "Take a good look at the senator."

Stone stared at the red-faced politician.

"You're going to be the one who wipes that smile off his fucking face. Do you hear me?"

Stone's mind flashed back to his father's eyes, leering at a young woman on a New York street. He'd never felt so crazy. It was as though his head was going to burst. "But when?"

"It's all in hand. And then you can deal with both of them."

The line went dead.

Thirty

It was early evening, and Jessica Friel was sitting up in bed while Crichton got changed after his shower. "Have you forgiven me yet?"

Crichton buttoned up his shirt and smiled. "What's done is done. You were acting in good faith. That's all I need to know. But in the future, just gimme a call."

Jessica was glad her boss-lover wasn't mad at her anymore. "Where are you going at this time of night?"

"Dinner at eight thirty, then drinks with some British diplomat. Sir Henry something or other."

"Am I invited?"

"Not this time. We've got you security clearance to be on-site. But not inside the conference itself."

"So what am I supposed to do? I'm hungry too."

"Room service."

Jessica puffed out her cheeks with a huff as Crichton put on a jacket, combed his hair, and tightened the knot in his tie. "Can I stay here tonight?"

"No. If my wife called, we'd be in deep shit, trust me."

Jessica folded her arms. "Fine."

"Listen, I've got business to attend to over the next couple of hours. But tomorrow is a free day."

"Thank the Lord."

"I have a hiking trip planned. Why don't you come with me?"

Jessica smiled. "I'd like that. But I don't have any gear."

"We'll buy some. What do you say? And we can get some fresh air, exercise, and time together."

"Sounds like heaven."

"Crack of dawn, OK?"

Jessica jumped out of bed and hugged Crichton tight. "You've got a deal, Senator."

After Jessica had showered and changed, while she was drying her hair in the bathroom, her cell phone rang. The caller ID showed it was her mother. "Jessica, where are you, honey? You said you'd be flying up for lunch today, remember?"

Jessica closed her eyes and groaned. "Mom, I'm so sorry. I've been so caught up with things here."

"But, honey, you said you'd be up for my birthday."

"Mom, what can I say? A situation came up."

"A situation . . . ? What kind of situation?"

"The senator is out of the country on business, and I had to join him for part of it. I'm sorry, but it was very last minute."

"I see. So you're not in the country."

Jessica stared at the shadows under her eyes. "That's right. Scotland to be precise."

"Oh my Lord . . . Is it a conference?"

"It's a political gathering. Diplomatic stuff. I can't say any more."

"So who else is there from the senator's team?"

"It's only me."

"Only you?"

"Yes, only me."

There was a long pause. "I see."

Jessica sighed as she adjusted her earrings. "What is it, Mom?"

"I don't follow, honey."

"I know that tone of voice, Mom. What do you mean by, *I see*?"

"Jessica, I may not know much about the workings of Capitol Hill, but I do have a mother's instincts."

"What are you getting at?"

"You don't know?"

Jessica sighed again. She'd grown used to her mother's sharp tone and insinuating comments about her private life. "No, I don't know. You mind enlightening me?"

"Jessica, I can hear it in your voice."

"Hear what?"

"You're being defensive."

"Defensive? I am not."

"Jessica Friel, I know everything there is to know about you."

Jessica stared at the reflection in the mirror, tears filling her eyes.

"You were never very good at hiding your feelings," her mother continued. "You're like me in that way."

"Mom, look, I'm kinda busy. You mind getting to the point?"

"Jessica, I'm not an idiot."

Jessica felt the tears on her cheeks. "I never said you were."

"So don't take me for one."

"Mom, honestly, I have no idea what you're getting at."

"What I'm getting at is why you're the only member of the senator's staff who's there with him thousands of miles from home."

"And what's that supposed to mean?"

"You're a junior aide to the senator. Where's his chief of staff? His secretarial support team? They're nowhere in sight. But you are. Why is that?"

"I told you . . . this is an important meeting . . ."

"That only the junior aide is invited to?"

Friel saw her cheeks flush in the mirror. "What are you insinuating?"

"Do I have to spell it out?"

"Please."

"You have a thing for the senator, don't you?"

"What? Don't be ridiculous."

"Jessica, I'm not stupid. I can see the way you talk about him, show us pictures of you and him."

"What?"

"Jessica, Senator Crichton is a married man with children. Does his wife know you're there?"

Jessica closed her eyes. "I don't have to listen to this."

"Are you having an affair with this man, Jessica?"

"No, I'm not."

"You haven't answered my question. Does the senator's wife know you're there with him?"

Jessica felt her eyes well up with tears again. "No, she doesn't."

"Jessica, he doesn't love you. Do you understand that?"

Friel said nothing.

"Nothing good will come of this."

"Mom, I think you've said enough. I gotta go."

Jessica ended the call as the tears fell.

Thirty-One

Brad was at the bar enjoying a whisky with a senior British diplomat when his cell rang. He recognized his home telephone number. "Gotta take this," he said, leaving his seat.

The diplomat smiled. "Of course."

Crichton retreated to a quiet outer room near the bar. "Honey, how are you and the kids?"

"We're good, Brad. How's Scotland?"

"Beautiful. Sadly, not seen much of it. Wall-to-wall meetings. But very rewarding."

"Oh, Hans was asking after you."

"Hans?"

"You know . . . Peter's father. The journalist from *Newsweek*."

"Oh, him. Sure. Tell him if you see him we'll have to do lunch."

"Don't worry. I already did."

"Just what my calendar needed. Another lunch with a member of the press corps."

"He's really nice."

"I don't trust him."

"Just because he doesn't like the NRA doesn't mean you have to dislike him. He's very smart."

For the first time in a long while, it felt good hearing his wife's voice again. *Absence does indeed make the heart grow fonder,* he thought. "I miss you."

"And I miss you. Look, just wanted to let you know we're good and looking forward to seeing you at the end of the week."

"Can't come too soon. We've got a day off tomorrow, so I'll get out into the great outdoors. Get some much-needed fresh air in me."

"I want to see some nice pictures to prove it!"

"You got it."

The diplomat was pointing to Crichton's empty whisky glass, and Crichton nodded in agreement. "Honey, I gotta go."

"Take care, honey. Love you."

Crichton ended the call and rejoined the diplomat for a nightcap. Afterward he headed back to his room. Jessica had already called it a night and left a note apologizing for dashing across the Atlantic. He felt bad for being so tough on her. But he also felt guilty after hearing his wife's voice, thinking about the deceit at the heart of their relationship.

He wondered if it wasn't time to end his relationship with Jessica. She was lovely. He had come to care for her. But he didn't love her the way he loved his wife. And the way he suspected Jessica had come to love him.

He fixed himself a single malt from the minibar and switched on a late-night TV program about British politics. He sipped the whisky, the amber liquid warming his stomach as the commentators talked about the rise of the right in British politics. He felt the liquor go straight to his head.

His cell phone rang and he reached for his jacket pocket.

Crichton recognized the name of the intelligence committee's legal counsel, Jack Schultz, whom he'd left a message for earlier.

"Brad, are you on a secure phone?"

"Absolutely. You?"

"Of course." Schultz sighed long and hard. "First, you did the right thing sending the encrypted files to me. There's CIA classified information on this. Highly sensitive."

"What exactly does it contain?"

A beat. "Just a moment. Brad, I need to know who's seen this."

"No one."

A long sigh. "Are you sure?"

"Positive."

"What about your aide Jessica what's-her-name?"

"Jessica Friel. She definitely did access this information."

Schultz sighed. "And she's the only one?"

"Yes."

"Would've been easier if she hadn't looked at it."

"Jack, she flew all the way over here to bring it in person. She could have easily put it in a laptop in DC and sent the contents across to me. She didn't."

"OK, fair point."

"So, what've we got?"

"Let's get back to basics. You took an oath when you joined the Permanent Select Committee on Intelligence."

"I know."

"Rules of Procedure are very clear. Rule number twelve limits the discussion of classified work with people outside the committee if the classified information was received from any source. Therefore, as Jessica Friel isn't on the committee or assigned to the committee, she should not be privy to any information of such a nature."

"With that in mind, you care to cut to the chase?"

Schultz sighed. "Brad, how long have we known each other?"

"A decade? A long time."

"Just over. Eleven years. I've known you since you arrived in DC. You served in the Marines. You served your country overseas. And I don't doubt for a minute that you've served all those you represent with distinction."

"Jack, you wanna tell me what's in the file? Jessica said I'm on a kill list."

There was a long silence. Eventually Schultz spoke. "Brad, I can't divulge what it says."

"You can't divulge it? Are you kidding me, Jack?"

"Brad, hear me out. My first duty is to serve the interests of the committee. The information on this file has been stolen from a CIA computer. And it contains details that I can't share with you."

"I can't fucking believe what I'm hearing!"

"Jack, as I said, we go back a long time. My advice to you? Get a good lawyer."

Crichton took a few moments to compose himself. "Get a good lawyer? Let me get this straight. I can't know what's on the file? Why the hell not? I don't get it."

"Brad, not only is this highly classified, it's . . ."

Crichton sensed Schultz wanted to tell him more. "Come on, Jack, it's . . . ?"

"You're correct. You're on a list."

Crichton's blood ran cold. "Patterson said as much. He even suggested it was a list of people, Americans, who were going to be neutralized. Some of whom already have been. Is that what it says?"

Schultz said nothing.

"Jack, listen to me. I have no idea what's on that file. If you say I'm on a list, I trust you. But I've got a right to know, don't I?"

"No, you don't. Under law, your obligations are to uphold the Constitution and the security of the United States of America."

Crichton closed his eyes for a moment as he tried to come to terms with the information. "You're cutting me loose?"

"Jack, do you still have the flash drive?"

"Yes, I do. It's in my room safe."

"As the counsel for the committee, I'm obliged to serve their interests first and foremost. And I have to ask you not to access the flash drive, in the interests of national security."

Crichton took a few moments to allow the words to sink in. "What do you want me to do with it?"

"Do not share it. Or lose it."

"Yeah, I get that. But what do you want me to do with it?"

"Nothing. I'm going to collect it in person."

Crichton closed his eyes for a moment as he reflected on that. It didn't make sense. "In person?"

"That's right. Also, do not make a copy."

"You want to collect this in person? That's highly irregular."

Schultz said nothing.

"Are you saying I can't see what the hell it says? Despite my aide accessing the information?"

"That's precisely what I'm saying."

"Jesus H. Christ, Jack, this doesn't make any sense."

"Brad, this Jeff Patterson, he's either stolen or been passed stolen CIA material."

"With my goddamn name on it."

"I can't comment any further on it. I've said enough. I'll be there in twenty-four hours."

"What the hell?"

"Brad, I've known you a long time. I like you. A lot. And trust me, this is for the best."

Thirty-Two

One day out

It was the dead of night and Nathan Stone was wide awake. He was lying in the dark on the wooden floor of the cottage living room, smoking a cigarette. He couldn't sleep. He took a long drag on the Winston, feeling faintly annoyed by the pale-orange glow it emitted. He closed his eyes as the smoke filled his lungs.

He felt himself begin to fall into a dark cavern. Falling. Deeper and deeper he fell. He loved the sensation of not being in control. He was exhilarated. High.

His stomach fluttered as he came to a stop.

Stone opened his eyes and adjusted to the near-total darkness. A feeling of calm washed over him.

His mind flashed back to the sessions with the facility psychologist. He knew he was being observed. His body language. His speech patterns. His eye contact. His demeanor. He was being judged. But he was also being retrained. Reprogrammed. Subtly.

Planting trigger words in his brain. He knew what they were doing. And he liked it. But there was so much more.

Stone's personality had been broken down years before. And in its place a new personality had emerged.

It had taken years.

The repetitive messages. The trigger words. The phrases. Reordering his thoughts. Before, there had just been emptiness. Now there was a pulsating array of terrifying emotions ripping through him. He liked it. And had grown to love it.

He could function in the real world. As long as he was kept apart.

The drugs kept him on edge. Steroids laced with amphetamine, he'd been told. He could go for days without sleep. He didn't know hunger. At times, though, he felt like he was going to be consumed by rage.

He would stare at himself in the mirror.

Staring back at him were his father's dead eyes. Uncaring. Blank. Terrifying. He had replaced his father. Supplanted him. And become him.

The more he thought about it, the more he felt the rage growing again.

They knew what they were doing.

Stone knew he would be returning to the familiar world of assassination. He dragged hard on his cigarette and leaned over to crush it out in the ashtray. His thoughts turned to his sister. Stuck in a mental hospital. Probably getting tucked into bed the way she used to tuck him in when he was a boy. He imagined her humming a tune. A tune he could never remember the name of. It had echoed in his mind through the years. The same one she had hummed to him when he was scared. He thought he heard a door creaking. But it was only in his head.

Then in his mind's eye he was staring at his father again. Cold black eyes looking down at him.

His cell phone vibrated on the wooden floor. The caller ID lit up in a cold blue light. He picked it up and saw it was his handler.

"Nathan, we've got a problem."

Stone's senses switched on. "What kinda problem?"

"Motion sensors have picked up movement to the rear of your property. Infrared sensors show a young woman two hundred yards away. She's crossed some fields."

Stone sat bolt upright. "What? Now? Who?"

"Fuck knows who she is. I don't like it. The nearest road is a minor road, and it's miles from here. You're in the middle of nowhere."

"You don't know who she is?"

"No idea."

"So she's lost?"

"Maybe."

Stone sighed and got to his feet. "What do you want me to do?"

"I don't know. We're still working on a response. This is a real curveball."

Stone sighed. "It's the middle of the goddamn night."

"Tell me about it. Could you ignore her?"

"Not likely. Bedside lamp is on upstairs."

"Shit."

"You think she might compromise things?"

"Shit happens. We need to roll with it."

Stone said nothing as he headed through to the rear kitchen. He peered out the window and saw the silhouetted woman, raincoat over her head, flashlight in hand. "I see her. Less than one hundred yards."

"So she knows you're there. Or that someone is. And you don't want her peeking in."

"Make the call."

A long sigh down the line. "If she knocks, you answer."

"What then?"

"I'll stay on the line. Just put your cell phone on the kitchen table. Say you're on the phone with your brother in the States."

"And then what?"

"Just do it. Then, if she wants in, you pick up the phone."

Stone placed the phone on the table. His heart was beating. Time dragged. The seconds swallowed up.

Suddenly, sharp knocking at the door. Five . . . six. Rat-tat-tat.

"Anyone home? My car's broken down! I need to make a call!"

Stone stayed still in a darkened alcove.

"Anyone in? Hello! Please, I've broken down!" She began to tap at the window.

Stone didn't move.

"I said I've broken down! Can someone help me?" Her shouting was getting louder, more urgent.

Stone stepped forward, turned the key, and opened the door. The woman had tears in her eyes.

"So sorry to wake you," the woman said. Her accent was educated, Scottish. "My car battery's dead. And I've forgotten my bloody phone. Could you help me?"

Stone cocked his head for her to come inside. "Don't worry. Get yourself out of the cold."

"You're American?" She stepped into the kitchen.

Stone shut the door behind her. "Yup. One hundred percent American. I'm actually on a call to my brother in the States just now." He handed her a dishcloth from the stove. "Here, dry yourself."

"Thanks," she said, drying her hair. "Look, I'm so sorry, but can I use your house phone to get a breakdown truck?"

"Sorry, no landline."

"What about your mobile? Can you use that to call out?"

Stone was thinking on his feet. "Sorry, only incoming calls."

"Shit. Damn. Sorry, I don't mean to sound so ungrateful."

"Can I just take this call, and maybe we can sort it out and get you back to civilization?"

"That would be great, thanks."

Stone picked up the cell phone as he smiled at the young woman. "Harry, sorry about that. Just a young lady's car broken down."

"Nathan, now listen," his handler whispered, "that was smart thinking about the phone. But it still leaves you trying to explain the truck out front and why you can't use it."

"Yeah, good point. How's the weather?"

His handler sighed. "Options are limited."

"Indeed they are." Stone smiled and shrugged at the woman.

"I got it," his handler said.

"What?"

"Say you'll contact a local cab company by email. Then I'll send over one of our guys. Say the company has a car in the area. Five minutes."

"And then what?"

"He'll pick her up and . . . you know what I'm saying?"

Stone nodded. "Excellent. Speak soon." He ended the call and smiled at the woman. "I got an idea."

The woman shrugged.

"I could email a cab company. I've got their details on my laptop upstairs."

"If you don't mind, that would be great. Thank you so much."

"Not a problem. Glad to help."

Stone headed upstairs for a couple of minutes. He paced around the room and waited for a short while. Then he headed downstairs. "You're in luck. They have a car a mile away. Be here in five minutes."

"Five minutes? That's fantastic. Thanks."

Stone nodded. "You live far?"

"Ten miles from here. Work at the local hospital. Finished just after two. Nightmare end to my day."

A few minutes later, the lights of a car swept the inside of the house. A quick toot of the horn.

"Wow," she said, "that was super quick."

"You got lucky. But glad I could help."

Stone opened the front door and waved at the driver, who nodded back as the woman got into the back of the car. They drove off into the night.

He shut and locked the front door, went through to the kitchen, and picked up the cell phone. "She's gone."

"That was a close one."

Brigadier Jack Sands ended the call with Stone. Out his office window in the facility, he saw the lights of a chopper in the distance. He stared transfixed as it came in to land. Two men got out and were escorted by the copilot into the facility. After being briefed and fed, then showering, they were shown into a conference room with Sands.

Sands knew both men well. He picked up a remote control and switched on the big-screen TV. It showed images of Nathan Stone. For the next fifteen minutes, they watched in silence.

Sands froze the final image of Stone, taken a few hours before he left. "This is the target. He's already on the mainland."

The first man to speak was Connors, who said, "Tell me more about him."

"National security risk." Sands was a master at compartmentalizing. "We believe an opportunity has arisen to neutralize him. We believe he'll be hill walking tomorrow."

The second man, Stevens, said, "Nationality?"

"European," Sands lied. "That's all I can say."

Connors sighed. "How do you want this done?"

"We're working on that. We're figuring out the best course of action."

Sands handed them each a cell phone. "You speak to me and me alone. Do you understand?"

Both men nodded.

Connors said, "How long till we're on the move?"

"Chopper'll be taking you to the mainland in exactly one hour." He pointed to the image of Stone frozen on the screen. "This man must die."

Thirty-Three

That evening, Senator Brad Crichton was pacing his room, cell phone pressed to his ear, waiting for his brother to pick up at his Dallas home. It had been ringing for a couple of minutes and didn't divert to voice mail. Just when he was about to hang up, his brother answered.

"Brad, how the hell are you?"

"You got a couple minutes, Murray?"

"Sure. What's on your mind?"

Crichton sat down and outlined the advice from the legal counsel to the intelligence committee.

"OK . . . I see why you're concerned. But I'm going to need some details."

"That's just the thing. According to Schultz, I'm not at liberty to know anything else."

"That's a crock of shit."

"Are you sure? Jack Schultz is highly regarded."

"Jack Schultz is wrong. I'm telling you, not just brother to brother but as your lawyer, that is crap. You, as chair of the intelligence committee, have a right to see materials that are marked specifically for your attention."

Crichton ran his hand through his hair. He felt exhausted. "I don't know, I'm really conflicted about this."

"I get that. But his advice is wrong. Pure and simple."

"So what do you advise?"

"I can't advise you what to do. I can advise you what I believe is either legal or potentially illegal."

Crichton sighed long and hard and sat down at the desk. "Murray, there's a guy . . ."

"A guy?"

"Yeah, a guy tried to contact me."

"What guy?"

"A blogger. Journalist. I thought he was a conspiracy nut. Said I was on some sort of hit list. Thing is, now he's dead."

A beat. "I saw that on Fox. But they were saying it was drugs or something."

"I don't know. What I do know is that this guy said my life was at risk. He wanted to pass on some details he said he was in possession of."

"The same details you are now in possession of?"

"Indeed."

"Let's get back on track with this whole thing. I need to know what that girl knows."

Crichton took a few moments to compose himself. He hated the way his brother spoke about Jessica. "*That girl* is called Jessica. Christ."

"Sorry, yeah, Jessica. Whatever. She hasn't accessed the information, I'm assuming."

"You assume wrong. She has. At least she says she has."

"Fuck. Why did she do that?"

"The blogger contacted her saying I was on a fucking kill list or something. And she says she opened the file on a USB drive. That's what she says."

"Jesus Christ." A beat. "What do you want to do?"

"I want to find out what's on the flash drive. I'm hearing second-hand what it contains. That my name is on a list. But I want to see for myself."

"Curiosity?"

"Naturally. Murray, there's something else that needs to be considered. Schultz wants to collect the flash drive in person."

"Whoa . . . Hang on, bro, are you kidding me?"

"I'm not kidding. He says not to make a copy or access it, and he'll collect it in person. He's flying over within the next twenty-four hours."

There was a heavy silence between them for what seemed to Brad like an age. His brother was notorious for imponderable silences while he mulled things in minute detail. "Now, why the hell would he want to do that?"

"That's a good question."

"Why the hell is Jack Schultz going to such extraordinary lengths? Why not ask a diplomatic attaché in Scotland to pick it up and transport it in a diplomatic bag back to DC?"

"Perhaps it's part of his job."

"But why not just send someone to pick it up? Perhaps he doesn't want you to see the contents. He's already seen what it contains. That doesn't make any sense."

"Shit."

"Indeed."

"OK, so what's my next move?"

"My advice? As long as you don't share the information with anyone else and you connect the flash drive to a computer that isn't hooked up to the Internet, and you use your highly encrypted and modified laptop, I can't see any problem."

"You think Schultz is trying to shut things down so we don't embarrass his pals at the Pentagon?"

"That's a possibility. But maybe it's the nature of the material he's concerned about."

"As the chair of the intelligence committee, I need to know any areas that are compromised or weak points or whatever. I need to know."

"I have to say—and this is just between us—I wish to God you'd kept this girl out of your life. And I'm speaking as your older brother."

"My business, Murray. Got it? Now get over it."

Murray said nothing.

"There's something else."

"What?"

"She's here. She brought the flash drive all the way to Scotland after receiving it from Patterson's lawyers. So now she's handled and accessed classified material."

"Oh shit, that doesn't look good either."

"What's that supposed to mean?"

"I don't know . . . perhaps this relationship seems a bit overfamiliar for my taste. You're married for Chrissakes, Brad. You messing around with this girl doesn't sit right with me. What about your wife and family? You considered that? I don't like it. She's a kid, let me remind you."

"Oh cut the bull, Murray."

"Your wife is a good person. A great mother. A great wife. And you're carrying on like some douchebag."

"OK, enough. Let's forget the insults."

"Fine."

"Let's say, for the sake of argument, that I access the documents on the flash drive. What then?"

"Depends what's on it. Tell me, the guy, the blogger, what did he say to you?"

"He contacted Jessica. And then he got my number and spoke to me. He said I was on a list. And then he winds up dead."

"Yeah, I got that. But what exactly did he say?"

"He mentioned the names of two people, libertarians, who'd wound up dead. Said there was a list. Said I was at risk."

"And then you're saying he wound up dead too?"

"Yup."

"Oh fuck."

"I told him to take whatever he had to the FBI."

"That was the right thing to do. Absolutely the right thing to do."

"But he never made it to them."

Murray said nothing.

"One final thing. I got a visit from someone. A pretty creepy visit."

"A visit? What kind of visit?"

"Brigadier Sands, military attaché, based at the consulate in Edinburgh. He was asking if the blogger had passed me any documents."

"You spoke to him in person?"

"He rolled up in a car."

"Christ."

"That's not good, is it?"

"I don't like this."

"No kidding."

"When're you back?"

Brad sighed. "It's late here. Tomorrow we have a free day. Sightseeing. Whatever. But I think I need to clear my head."

"That's understandable."

"The day after, there's an afternoon session, a formal dinner, and then we fly home. So I should be back in DC the day after tomorrow, late."

"Good. When you get home, we're going to talk. Do you understand? And we're going to sort this out."

"Thanks, I appreciate that."

"Hey, you all right?"

"Yeah. Just tired, I guess."

"Get some sleep. And play some golf."

Crichton smiled. "Maybe another time. I need to get out of here for the day and clear my head. Some good hiking in the mountains should hopefully do the trick."

"Let me work on this. As for you, take it easy. Love you."

"Night, Murray."

Crichton hung up. It was late. He stared out of the window over the floodlit grounds, security patrolling with dogs, feeling a long way from home.

Thirty-Four

Zero hour

Nathan Stone was floating in darkness. A black ocean washing over him. Inky dark sky, pale moon. He saw a spectral figure in the distance walking toward him. He squinted. Blurred. It looked like a ghostly woman wearing white.

He felt himself sinking, but still the figure got closer. The sound of the waves crashing off a distant shoreline.

The woman was walking on the water.

He was paralyzed with fear. Blood was dripping from the woman's fingers. She smiled a toothless smile.

The sound of ringing snapped him out of his nightmare as he struggled to get his bearings for a moment.

Stone fumbled for the phone in his jacket pocket. "Yeah."

"We're on the move."

"Already?"

"Yeah, thought he'd be making a move after breakfast. Apparently, he was up early to get a jump on the day."

"So where's he headed?"

"GPS has details already. All you have to do is follow."

Stone rubbed his eyes. "When exactly did they leave?"

"Two minutes ago, a rental car was dropped off. Pale-blue Mercedes SUV."

Stone sighed. "So what's the general direction?"

"North. That's all we know."

"Is this a go?"

"Green light, Nathan. Time to play."

That's all he needed to hear.

Stone pulled on his clothes and was out the door of the cottage and in the car, remotely tracking Crichton and his mistress.

Thirty-Five

It wasn't even 5:00 a.m. and the first pale rays of a new dawn washed over the dark mountains.

Crichton pressed his foot on the gas pedal of the high-powered SUV. Sitting in the passenger seat wearing dark glasses was his aide Jessica Friel. "Driving on the goddamn left. Whose idea was that?"

"It's a British thing, I guess."

An oncoming truck swerved tightly as it overtook them on a tight bend. "Jeez. Man, what is it with these drivers?"

Jessica grabbed her coffee out of the cup holder and gulped down some much-needed caffeine. It was strong, just the way she liked it. "Take it easy, Brad. We aren't in a hurry."

"We've got a three-hour drive ahead of us. I want to get into the hills and walk. My head's swimming."

"I know, honey."

"It'll do us both a world of good. I'm looking forward to some space to think and breathe."

"Who suggested we head northwest?"

"British diplomat I met in Washington a few months back. I told him about my Scottish trip. Mentioned in passing that I loved the outdoors. Said if we want some serious hiking and absolute peace and tranquility, he knew just the spot."

Jessica looked out the window. "It's really pretty."

"It is. And really wild. By all accounts, this place is nuts in the winter."

Friel sighed. "So . . ."

"So?" he said, interrupting her languid delivery.

"So . . . I meant to say, have you looked at what was on the flash drive?"

Crichton said nothing.

"Brad, did you hear me?"

"I heard you."

"And?"

Crichton turned and glared at her. "I shouldn't be discussing this topic."

"I see. But I'd appreciate if you didn't bite my head off, thank you very much."

"Look, if you must know, no, I haven't seen what's on it . . . yet."

"What do you mean, *yet*?"

Crichton sighed. "This is a difficult situation. I need to be very careful."

"I understand that."

"I need to be one hundred percent certain that I can access the information, first of all. As it stands, I've gotten two conflicting pieces of advice."

"I see."

Crichton felt bad he was shutting her out on this. She'd crossed the goddamn Atlantic to bring him the flash drive.

The more he thought about it, the more he wanted to see for himself what the hell it contained. It was gnawing at him.

The miles flashed past as shards of light glistened off telephone lines and huge steel transmission towers. As they drove higher into the hills, bathed in light, a lush, verdant scene greeted them. The smell of grass and pine trees drifted through the open windows.

They drove in companionable silence for nearly half an hour until they stopped for breakfast at a café beside a gas station. Crichton opted for two bacon sandwiches, while Jessica had scrambled eggs on rye. Both washed down with a mug of strong black coffee.

Crichton wiped his mouth with a napkin. "That was good."

Jessica was still eating and smiled.

"Look, I'm sorry I was a bit short with you last night."

"And today."

Crichton smiled. "Point taken." He reached across and touched the back of her hand. "I'm glad you're here. And I think what you did was remarkable. And very smart."

Jessica flushed. "Thank you." She finished up her food and took a sip of her hot coffee. "I just wanted to do the right thing. I think in hindsight I might've handled it differently. I shouldn't have opened the file. I get that now."

Crichton sighed. "We are where we are. Don't dwell on it. It's a beautiful day. We're going to get some good hiking in. Eat lunch on the hills. They've made some great sandwiches. There's a cottage I've booked, so that'll be our base camp tonight. And we'll be back in time for lunch tomorrow."

Jessica said, "Brad, I'm scared."

"Why?"

"I don't know. I just have a bad feeling about all this . . . ever since I heard about Patterson's death."

"It's going to be fine. I think, for what it's worth, that the contents of that flash drive might be confidential intelligence, and Patterson just conflated the contents with some scenario he'd dreamed up. I think it's a security breach, and this poor blogger's death is only a horrible coincidence."

Jessica didn't look so sure.

Crichton wasn't either. But he didn't want to unduly alarm her.

"Brad, before we get on the road again, there's one thing, about the flash drive."

"I thought I'd made it clear that I can't talk about that."

"You have. I just have one concern."

"A concern?"

"The flash drive . . . I'm worried about it being in the safe in your room."

Crichton leaned close and whispered, "Don't worry your pretty head. It's all in hand."

Jessica looked skeptical.

Crichton opened the second top button of his shirt and showed her the flash drive on a conference lanyard around his neck. "This isn't going anywhere."

Thirty-Six

Brigadier Jack Sands stood in the command room in the facility, watching the huge multiscreens showing a map of the Scottish Highlands and several red dots all headed north. Four operatives were scanning MacBook Pros, monitoring the SUV being driven by Crichton. As well as the car driven by Nathan Stone. But they were also keeping an eye on the position of the car being driven by the two operatives Sands had greeted in the early hours.

He could see the big picture.

Nathan Stone's GPS tracking device was highlighted on the big screens four miles behind Crichton. He was doing a steady sixty. Perfect.

Sands felt a mixture of excitement and trepidation, knowing what lay ahead. The assassination of Crichton and Friel by Nathan Stone. But also the extra dimension. The neutralization by the operatives of the man once known as Nathan Stone.

The final part of the jigsaw would be making sure the two operatives made a clean getaway.

Sands's cell phone rang, snapping him out of his train of thought. He picked up the phone. The caller ID showed it was from one of Clayton Wilson's encrypted cell phones. He was up early.

"Morning, sir."

"OK, so, are we finally under way?"

"That's affirmative, sir. The targets are en route to a location believed to be in the far northwest of Scotland. Perfect from our point of view. We knew about his plans to take a hiking trip to this specific location on this day. But we didn't expect the company of Ms. Friel. Still, it's all under control. Playing out nicely."

"Our operative nearby?"

"Four miles back, well out of sight."

"And our shadows?"

Sands cleared his throat as he looked at the tracking map. He could see they had taken the minor road to the predetermined location, a disused cottage three miles from the base of the mountains. "The shadows are headed along a parallel B road, a more scenic route, as we speak."

"I like it. Rule number one: cover all bases as near as can be."

"Exactly."

"Jack, I just got off the phone with our IT guy for the operation."

Sands nodded. He'd known Colonel Jenkins for years.

"As you know, he's monitoring not only all the electronic chatter from our facility but that within it."

Sands sighed, annoyed by the intrusion. "Yes, sir, I'm well aware of that."

"Not so fast. I'm being told a message was sent from an iPhone owned by consultant psychologist Mark Berenger, MD."

Sands wondered what Wilson was getting at. "That's impossible."

"Sadly not."

"Mark is one of us."

"I know he is."

"Are you saying . . . ?"

"I suggest we check all our footage over the last week."

"Shit."

"Get your head of security to check it out."

"This is not what I need right now."

"I want it looked into. This is a security breach."

"Mark has the highest clearance of any medical professional within the government. The very highest. And that includes National Security Council advisory roles."

"Jack, Mark has a cell phone. A specially modified cell phone that can only send or receive messages. No cellular calls are allowed in the facility, right? Those are the rules."

"That is correct."

"Check the footage. And get back to me."

Sands was worried as he headed to the security office. He scanned the banks of monitors and informed the director of security, Adrian Carson, of what he'd been told.

"Gimme half an hour," he said, "and I'll get back to you."

Sands went back to the command post, tracking the operation as Carson scoured the footage. He knew Berenger was a first-class doctor and a committed CIA operative. But he knew what he needed to do. The time dragged as Sands mulled the potential security breach. It didn't resonate with what he knew of Berenger. Just over half an hour later, Carson called Sands into his office.

"Jack, I've spliced two forty-five-second segments together," he said. "Check this out. This is real interesting."

Sands stared at the screen as the first segment unfolded. It showed Nathan Stone leaning over to crush out his cigarette in an ashtray and knocking over a mug of coffee all over the papers strewn across Berenger's desk.

"Watch Stone."

Sands watched as Stone apologized profusely and lifted up papers dripping with coffee, trying to get the excess moisture off the documents. At the same time Berenger dashed out of the room for a couple of seconds. Then Stone, seeing he was alone, crouched down behind the desk.

Carson froze the clip. It showed Stone behind the desk. "What exactly he's doing is out of the camera's view, no matter which angle we pull up."

"Cute move," Sands said.

"But we don't have any more than that. He's out of the camera's view. But I'll let it play on."

Sands stared at the screen. He watched as Berenger returned with loads of paper towels and they both mopped up the mess. "At this stage, I don't see any evidence that Nathan has the phone."

Carson nodded as the first clip finished and the second one started. "This is eight minutes later. Stone gets up and heads to the adjacent bathroom. The message is sent two minutes later, presumably from the bathroom. Then he returns to the room and the discussions continue for another couple of minutes." Eventually, Berenger leaves the room for the bathroom. "Now."

Sands looked closely. He saw Stone get up and stretch his arms before he paced the room. He stood behind Berenger's desk and bent down as if to tie his shoe. He placed the phone in a bottom drawer, then sat back down in his seat before Berenger returned.

Sands shook his head. "How the hell did we miss this?"

"Frankly, unless you have someone watching every second of every session, it's going to be missed."

"Fuck."

Carson stared at Sands dead-eyed. "Very clever."

Sands nodded, left the room, and called Wilson with the news. "Conclusively," he said, "Nathan Stone created that opportunity, got the phone, went to the bathroom, and then replaced it when Berenger left the room for a minute."

Wilson sighed. "That's settled. Stone has to be neutralized after he carries out the mission. No matter what."

Sands closed his eyes for a moment. He felt a chasm begin to open up deep down in his guts. An unbearable darkness washed over him.

Down into his soul. Burning him. He flashed back to the grainy photos of the boy on the streets of the Lower East Side. The emptiness in his eyes. The suffering he had endured. He had thought of himself all these years as Stone's wingman. The father figure he never had. A man to look up to. Sands could have stood up to Wilson. He could've fought for Nathan to live. But he hadn't. He had said nothing. Now he was powerless to stop Nathan from being deleted even if he wanted to.

Thirty-Seven

Nathan Stone was closing in. He felt exhilarated as he moved to within three miles of the senator's car as he headed northwest. The scenery was getting wilder, the peaks higher, snow topping the highest ones. He glanced at the GPS, which showed Crichton's vehicle had stopped off at another café en route. He slowed down and pulled over at an adjacent truck stop until the senator's car moved again.

He drove on. Mile after mile of deep glens, meandering trickles of water from high up in the hills and mountains, past deep lakes, woodland . . . and all the time the huge, huge sky. The glare of the light this far north, after having been confined to artificial light for so long, was something he was still adjusting to.

A deer ran across the road and he braked hard, screeching to a halt. "Goddamn fucking animal!"

Stone took a few moments to compose himself as he watched the deer disappear into the glade. He drove on and noticed the senator's car was putting some distance between them. He was five miles behind. His Bluetooth headset buzzed into life.

"Hey, buddy," his handler said on the line, "you OK?"

"Yeah, nearly had a run-in with the wildlife around here. Goddamn nearly ran over a deer."

"Take it easy. This is a slam dunk, buddy."

Stone said nothing. He didn't like to jinx operations with overconfident talk. He had gotten that from his mother. She was notoriously pessimistic and not willing to get excited about anything. Probably because she had been married to a crazy psychopath of a husband.

"You still there, Nathan?"

"Sure. Any updates?"

"Our intel indicates they're en route to a remote place on the Knoydart Peninsula in northwest Scotland."

"Are we sure?"

"One hundred percent. The details have been entered into their GPS. It was suggested by a British diplomat as a great spot for hiking."

Stone smiled at the clever trick.

"You're headed for a cove just outside a small town called Mallaig. Leave your car beside the road. A man with an RNLI badge on his Scotland hat will take you by boat to the peninsula."

"What's RNLI?"

"It's a charity that saves lives at sea."

"Tell me more about the area."

"Very, very sparsely populated. Nothing there for miles. And I mean nothing. Mountains. Streams. Isolated little houses and farms. But by and large nothing. Hikers, climbers, walkers, outdoorsy people love it, but once you're into the hills, you can go days in that part of the world and not see anyone. It's perfect."

"The method hasn't changed?"

"Proceed as per instructions. We want him to die of a heart attack."

"And her?"

"High mountains, very dangerous terrain."

Stone caught the drift of what he was saying. "Got it."

"Hang back when you get there. Observe. And track them carefully."

"I noticed the rifle in the car. Straight out of the box by the look of it."

"Absolutely. This is the exact same as the version you've been using at the facility. It's a prototype long-range Taser, except without the wires. It can immobilize an individual from up to four hundred feet. Crichton had a heart scare eighteen months ago, so this is perfect."

Stone nodded. He'd been shown earlier versions of this prototype way back at The Farm.

"Electromagnetic pulse gun. Tested extensively in Iraq. And it's brutal. You want someone down without putting a bullet in them, this is your guy. Energy directed. Imagine a Taser, but without the needles and darts and all that shit. This is clean. No direct contact."

Stone could see in his mind's eye how it was going to go down.

"You getting the picture?"

"And the female?"

"After he's down, he hasn't got long. If he's lucky, he'll be dead in five minutes."

"What about her?"

"After he goes down, she'll instinctively go toward him. That's when you step in."

"A fall?"

"Yeah, a fall. Why not? One more thing . . ."

"Sure."

A beat. "Take your time to get this right. There's no immediate hurry. Got it?"

Stone instinctively put his foot on the gas. He hadn't felt this crazy in years. "Whatever you say."

Thirty-Eight

Jessica felt a mixture of emotions as she boarded the midmorning ferry from Mallaig with Brad. They were going to be based at the tiny lakeside hamlet of Inverie for the next twenty-four hours. She felt excited and happy to be with him. All to herself. But at the same time she sensed he wanted to keep his distance.

She wondered if she should have just gone home after delivering the flash drive.

The more she thought about it, the more she realized she was like a hopeless, lovestruck teenager. What a mess. She was sticking to her boss, a married man and her lover, like a clingy girlfriend.

When she was in college, Jessica and her girlfriends—including Amy—used to groan at trophy wives and mistresses. Now here she was, in the middle of nowhere with a man who seemed to be withdrawing further into himself by the hour.

Jessica and Crichton stood on the deck of the ferry as the cold air buffeted them. She linked arms with him.

"I think some time away from it all will do both of us a world of good," she said.

Crichton smiled but said nothing.

Jessica felt a wide gap open up between them. She didn't want that. It was the first time she'd felt that atmosphere with Brad, his manner distinctly chillier than usual. She wondered if this was a portent of things to come.

The journey lasted just over one and half hours. The mountains appeared to rise out of the cold waters of the lake as they approached the whitewashed cottages of Inverie on the shore.

As they disembarked, the silence was deafening.

After stopping at the luxury lakeside accommodation Brad had booked online a month earlier, Jessica made him a coffee and served up a platter of smoked salmon sandwiches. He looked in the huge refrigerator and saw it was stuffed with milk, cheese, bottled water, champagne, numerous savory snacks. It felt good to have a base, away from everyone else.

Crichton ate in silence as he studied a walking guide. It indicated a path behind the cottages that led out onto the mountain trail. When they finished their sandwiches, they put on their walking gear and backpacks and began the hike.

The sun glinted off the craggy rocks as they started the steep climb. Crichton felt his breathing becoming more labored. This wasn't going to be a gentle workout at an air-conditioned gym in DC. They walked higher and higher, the trail getting narrower. They were walking in single file. About a mile along the trail, he stopped for a swig from the bottle of chilled water. He handed it to Jessica, who was squinting against the glare.

She took a sip and handed it back.

Crichton headed up the dirt track with Jessica now by his side. It felt good to be out and about and away from the hectic back-to-back meetings. His head needed clearing after days of six- and seven-hour briefings on security in the Middle East, and why foreign intervention with boots on the ground was inevitable. He saw the logic. But he also saw the hell that had engulfed Iraq with direct US intervention. The withdrawal had only made it worse. There was no easy choice. It was the least bad option they were talking about. But he had steadfastly refused to countenance the US becoming involved in more wars. He could see that it was just a cover for Western nations to access the immense natural resources of Iraq while also providing America with a launchpad into and around Iran, a country the neocons were desperate to get embroiled in.

He breathed in the crystal-clear air and felt himself relax.

The more he thought of his day away from the business agenda and remembered the unsettling death of the blogger and Jessica turning up unexpectedly, the more he realized he needed to look at how he was leading his life.

He didn't love Jessica. He never had. She was nice. A kind heart who just was there. With a listening ear.

So why was he now with this young woman on his day off in the glorious, isolated Scottish Highlands? This didn't sit well. He felt bad. He was cheating. No way around it. He began to wonder if he shouldn't have just told her to head back to the States. He had been looking forward to this day away from everything and everybody. But her presence was a constant reminder of how he needed to change the way he was behaving.

"You OK?" Jessica asked, smiling at Crichton.

"Yeah, just a bit distracted. But the fresh air'll do me good. Haven't been hiking in weeks."

Jessica nodded as she hitched up her backpack. "What's wrong, Brad? You don't seem yourself."

"What do you mean? I'm fine."

"Brad, I can look into your eyes and see something's bothering you. Eating away at you. You don't want me here, do you?"

Crichton strode on and blew out his cheeks as he and Jessica began to ascend a narrow, winding path up the side of the mountain. "Jessica, let's not rehash whether you should or shouldn't have come here. Let's enjoy the day, the scenery, and our time together."

They walked in silence for the next hour. Crichton felt tightness in the back of his calves as they headed higher into the mountains. He was feeling his age. By contrast, Jessica was bounding ahead, lithe and fit.

The craggy cliff faces loomed over them as they negotiated the narrowing mountain paths. His heart was pumping faster as the hike wore on. Slowly he felt the endorphins begin to kick in. Washing through his body. He felt lighter. Happier. Sharper.

Crichton turned and looked down over the magnificent landscape all the way below. He drank some water, sat down, and Jessica joined him. They opened packets of fresh smoked salmon sandwiches. "One heck of a view. I never seem to find the time to enjoy this sort of thing anymore."

Jessica smiled. "Me neither."

When they'd finished eating, they continued their ascent along the winding, precarious path for another hour until they reached an overhanging ledge. They sat down and contemplated the view.

This time they said nothing.

Jessica offered her hand.

Crichton reluctantly took it. It felt soft.

Jessica squeezed his hand.

Crichton stared out over the rugged landscape and sighed. Soon the clouds began to roll in. The wind started to pick up, whipping his face.

It was then, in a terrible split second, that Crichton had a terrible sense of foreboding like he'd never felt before.

Thirty-Nine

A little after 2:00 p.m. Nathan Stone stepped onto dry land. He saw the cove outside the town. He walked over and found an unmarked trail, just as he'd been told. He pulled on his huge backpack and headed up through a gorge. Then through a wooded area. Higher and higher, till he was shrouded by the deep summer foliage.

Stone found a rocky outcrop and switched on the tracking device. His handler would have cyberexperts remotely accessing the senator's cell phone, pinpointing the GPS location. Then the position would be sent to Stone's device. It showed that Crichton was more than two miles away. Stone checked the Ordnance Survey map, located the coordinates, and set off due east into the mountains.

They had a head start. But that was fine.

Stone checked his watch. It was time to phone in. He pressed his earpiece into his right ear. Three minutes later, it buzzed to life.

"OK, Nathan, good to see you're up and running. Once you're through this stretch of woods, you'll be on a high trail. The same one the target and his lady are on."

"I'm not far from them. But I need to be a bit closer."

"Your current range is twenty-four-hundred yards, but you're right, get in closer. A mile will be perfect, but with line of sight. You should be able to hear them within the next fifteen minutes with a feed we're working on."

Stone nodded.

"One last thing."

"What?"

"Once this is done, get off the island."

"Got it."

"Good luck."

Stone began to climb. He could see this was going to be a tough workout. But he was prepared for anything. He pushed through the undergrowth and branches and saw a minor trail developing. He checked the map and the compass. He was on course. He followed the trail for a half mile until he reached another outcrop of rock, with views of the surrounding mountains and rocky summits.

Away in the far distance, an imposing peak rose ominously out of the moorland.

Stone was in awe of his surroundings. He felt at one with the terrifying wilderness he was now part of. A land of ever-changing colors, weather, skies altering by the second, clouds rolling in low, the sun flooding the area with a heavenly glow.

He pressed on, up the rockier mountain trail, one eye on the cell phone GPS tracking Crichton and Friel. He was getting closer. A mile. Within range, certainly. But he still couldn't see them.

Stone crunched through the scree and loose rocks as he ascended. He felt the wind whip up off the water down below, buffeting him high up on the steep crags.

Then he saw something in the far distance. Spectral figures.

Stone lay down flat on the ground and took out his binoculars. He trained the range finder on the highest ridges. And there on an impossibly craggy peak, he saw two figures. Senator Brad Crichton and Jessica Friel. They were sitting on a cliff edge, talking. He watched them, transfixed.

Suddenly, his earpiece crackled to life with their conversation. He listened to them talk about their secret affair.

"I'm sensing a coldness I haven't felt from you before, Brad."

"This isn't easy. My wife is a good person. And I'm concerned that when . . . if . . . this comes out, what it would do to her. I don't want to hurt her."

"Brad, you started this affair. Isn't it a bit late to start thinking about what might hurt your wife?"

"I need space to think things through. You coming over here, this kill list, Patterson's death, my mind is swimming with it all."

"I love you and want to spend the rest of my life with you. I want to have children with you."

"Let's not get ahead of ourselves. I'm worried this is happening too quickly. I think we need to slow it down."

Stone couldn't abide such talk. They were wrapped up in themselves and their own disgraceful behavior. It reminded him of his own crazed father, leering at barmaids, drunk, psychotic, grabbing these innocent women as he, just a boy, watched from a corner booth. He remembered the embarrassed expressions of the young women trying to fend off his father's unwanted attention.

Then his father would drag him home . . . and punishment from a broken loser was meted out on him and his sister.

Stone refocused the binoculars. He saw Friel now had her arm around the senator's shoulder. But he wasn't reciprocating. The senator talked of feeling trapped and needing more space.

Something inside Stone lit up. It was like a light had been switched on. He was now in the zone. He put down the binoculars and looked around. No one for miles. Not a soul. Apart from him and the senator and his mistress.

Stone took off his huge backpack and carefully removed the specially calibrated hunting rifle and assorted military devices: knives, compass, map, and his specially encrypted cell phone.

He drank in the surroundings for a few moments.

He picked up the rifle and stared through the crosshairs. He had Friel in his sights, partially concealing the senator. He waited for a few moments. He had to be sure. But there wasn't a clear shot. Yet.

He waited and held his breath, finger on the trigger.

Forty

Brigadier Jack Sands paced the command room within the facility, a Bluetooth headset on. He stared up at the screens showing the real-time video footage from the pinhole camera disguised as a North Face logo on the collar of the fleece Nathan Stone was wearing. He watched as the couple disappeared up a further rocky incline. He clenched his fists as the slim chance of a long-range shot disappeared.

Get it right.

Sands knew Stone would be frustrated. He felt the same. But he also knew Nathan Stone was a man of infinite patience.

He slumped in his seat and stared at the screens. Watching and waiting. He heard the deeper breathing as Stone headed up the mountain. He checked the Ordnance Survey map showing tight contours, illustrating the steepness of the hills and mountains all around Stone's location.

"OK, Nathan, coordinates are perfect and you're right on the timescale we anticipated," Sands said. "Don't sweat it. Plenty of time."

"Copy that."

Sands was transfixed, watching the bird's-eye view of the mountains as Stone headed higher up the trail after the couple. "I estimate you're fifteen minutes behind them. And we believe they're heading for the highest peak. Ordinarily, they'd get there by around 1700 hours. But there's a huge plateau farther down from the summit. They should be there by 1730 or thereabouts. Concealed throughout at that point. So that would be a natural opening for you."

"Copy that, sir."

Sands ended the conversation and began to pace the room again, arms folded. He took off the headset and switched it off-line for a few moments. He took a deep breath. Then he put on the red Bluetooth headset for the two shadows and switched them online. "How far now?"

A voice said, "We're in the cottage you designated."

"Excellent. No radio contact from now. Are we clear?"

"Got it, over."

Sands took off the headset and sat down. He put on the white headset for Nathan and switched it back online. He stared at the footage of Nathan Stone ascending the path around the mountainous terrain. He wondered, knowing how devoted Stone was to his sister's welfare, why he had risked contacting her. He must have known that was a no-no. She believed he was dead, after all.

Sands had pushed aside his personal feelings for Nathan. This was business. He could see where Clayton Wilson was coming from. It couldn't be allowed. The whole mission would be inadvertently jeopardized. *Fuck*. Why hadn't he seen it coming? He was the one who'd put Stone's name forward. But he also knew Stone was dispensable. That was the long and short of it.

Deep down in the darkest recesses of his soul, he did feel some compassion, even love, for Stone. Sure, he was a machine. He was ferocious. Smart. And ruthless. But he did have some semblance of humanity: he cared about his sister.

Sands had lost count of the times that Stone had asked him over the years, *How's my sister?* A small part of Sands cared for Stone. It had taken multiple operations on Stone's face to create a new person. He remembered watching Stone's reaction through a one-way mirror when he was shown his new face. The way he touched the new skin. Felt around the folds at the eyes. The way he touched his new nose.

It was eerie.

Stone had been reborn. A new man. A man who everyone thought was dead.

From the corner of his eye, Sands saw movement on a facility surveillance monitor. Security guards were escorting former CIA psychologist Dr. Mark Berenger to a waiting chopper.

What the hell was going on? No one moved into or out of the facility without his knowledge.

Sands stared at the monitor and dialed the direct line to the facility's director of security. "This is Sands. Where the hell is Dr. Berenger going?"

"His work is done."

"What the fuck are you talking about? Who's in charge here?"

"You are, sir."

"So . . . why the hell is Berenger leaving? This hasn't been authorized."

"Sir, with respect, authorization just came through in the last few minutes from General Wilson."

"Clayton Wilson?"

"Yes, sir."

"No one gets in or out without my say-so. That's the rules. So there's no goddamn authorization."

"Sir, General Wilson said he wanted Dr. Berenger back in the US with immediate effect for a debriefing."

Sands stared at the monitor as the chopper door slammed shut and it took off into the slate-gray skies as he ended the call.

His mind began to race. An operation was under way. A complex, sensitive operation. So why the hell was a highly experienced psychologist being withdrawn from his facility right now? And why would General Wilson do so without going through him first? He weighed the options. Do nothing and be left in the dark. Do something, and try and find out what was going on.

He dialed General Wilson's direct number. Three rings and he answered.

"Everything OK, Jack?" he said.

"Sir, I just saw Berenger leave the facility without my permission. I've just been told you OK'd this."

"I did."

Sands closed his eyes for a moment. He was struggling to contain his anger. "You mind explaining the rationale, sir?"

"He compromised the mission."

"Sir, Nathan used a classic diversionary tactic. It might've fooled just about anybody."

"The doctor is an experienced man. He should have seen the signs."

"Even so, surely with an operation under way as we speak, this could have come after the targets have been dispatched. This is most irregular, sir."

"Jack, can I be frank?"

"Why not?"

"We can't afford the tiniest slip. We've already had problems we've had to deal with."

Sands knew he was talking about the blogger. "Mark is an honorable man."

"He fucked up."

"Sir, we shouldn't be having this discussion now."

"We have to act."

"You mind explaining the thinking behind shipping him out right now and without my permission? I'm in charge. I'm the lead on the ground."

"I apologize for not alerting you. But you have enough on your plate already." Sands detected a cold edge in Wilson's tone. "I can't have any more problems."

Sands glanced at the monitor showing Stone's progress up the hill.

"Once this is over, we'll be debriefing everyone to see what we can learn about this operation and the lessons we need to take on board."

Sands could see he wasn't going to win this exchange with Wilson.

"Now, if that's all, I want you to focus on the task at hand. Good day, Jack. And I'll be waiting on your call later with the news."

Forty-One

Senator Crichton was lagging a few yards behind Jessica as they climbed higher. She stopped and turned around.

"Tough going, huh?" she said.

"No kidding. What was I thinking?"

Jessica unzipped a side pocket of her backpack and took out a chocolate bar, which she handed to Crichton. "Here, take this for energy, old-timer."

Crichton smiled. "Hey, less of the 'old,' would you?" He opened the wrapper and bit into the dark chocolate. It tasted good.

His cell phone began to vibrate in his backpack. He groaned. "Gimme a goddamn break. Just when I was enjoying some peace."

"Just let it go," Jessica said.

Crichton shook his head. It wasn't his way to let anything go. He took out his phone. The caller ID showed his brother's name. "Hey, Murray, you're up early. I'm halfway up a mountain in Scotland, for what it's worth."

Murray ignored the small talk. "Brad, is it OK to chat?"

Crichton said, "Jessica's here." She looked puzzled.

"So is it OK to talk?"

"Yeah, sure."

Murray sighed.

"Bad news?"

"Brad, last night you mentioned you had a chat with Jack Schultz, the legal counsel for the committee, am I right?"

"Sure."

"I don't know how to explain this."

Crichton wondered what was bothering Murray. His brother was no shrinking violet.

"Brad, I just turned on the news. It's all over the place here. Hasn't anyone told you?"

The line began to break up. "Told me what?"

"It's breaking news. Fox and CNN are both reporting that Schultz was found floating in the pool at the sports club he's a member of, three blocks from the White House."

"Jack Schultz?"

"Brad, listen to me. This is bad, bad news. Do you understand what I'm getting at?"

Crichton closed his eyes as the wind buffeted them on the mountain. "Fuck."

"Think about it. Only a matter of hours after he spoke to you, Schultz is floating facedown in his club's pool. Reporters are saying they suspect a heart attack."

"Murray, he was the one who told me not to open the files on the flash drive. But he saw what was on it."

"We can't jump to conclusions."

"Damn straight I can jump to conclusions. The blogger. Now Schultz. There's a list."

"Brad, you need to hand it in to the FBI."

"I intend to."

"How about I reach out to the FBI legal counsel in London?"

Crichton felt empty inside. "I think that would be wise. Thank you."

"Let me see what I can do. I'll get back to you within the hour."

Crichton sighed. “Shit.”

“Get your ass out of wherever you are. Back to your base. And catch the next flight to London unless I say otherwise.”

“Murray?”

“Yeah?”

“Appreciate the heads-up. I owe you one.”

“Take care, man.”

Crichton ended the call.

“That wasn’t good news, was it?”

Crichton bowed his head for a moment. “We need to get back.”

“What’s happened?”

Crichton relayed the story. “Very fit guy. Swam a hundred laps each and every day. Jogged. And he dies of a heart attack?”

“It happens.”

“It happened a few hours after he read the file and warned me not to access it.”

“Oh shit, what have I done? That’s awful.”

“Jessica, this has nothing to do with you.”

“But it does.”

“You were just the messenger. How would you know?”

Jessica bowed her head and began to cry. “I’m scared. Really scared.”

Crichton took off his backpack and hugged her tight. “Listen to me. I’m here. You’re fine, OK?”

“Nothing’s fine, though, that’s just the thing.”

Crichton wiped the tears from her eyes with the back of his hand. “What do you want to do?”

“I don’t know. We won’t get back in time for the ferry.”

“I could get us choppered out.”

“Imagine if that got out, though,” she said. “Senator Crichton and his female aide helicoptered off mountain. Media firestorm.”

Crichton knew that would be the end of him. “You think we should get the first ferry out tomorrow morning?”

Jessica dabbed her eyes. "I think that's for the best. Do you want to head down now? I don't have the stomach to carry on."

Crichton nodded. "My heart's not in it now."

Jessica stared out at the endless horizon and the lake down below.

"I need to formulate a media response."

"The team will be working on that. I guarantee it."

Crichton nodded, knowing she was right. "I feel sick."

"About what happened?"

"Yeah . . . and what's coming. I don't know if this is a destabilization strategy to derail my plans."

"Pretty elaborate."

"If they link my name, no matter how tenuously, with the deaths of some blogger and the legal counsel for the intelligence committee, nothing will help us."

Jessica brushed her hair off her face. "What else?"

"What do you mean?"

"Brad, I can look into your eyes and see everything there is to know about you. You're pulling away."

"Jessica, now is not the time."

"Do you still care for me?"

"I just really need some time to think about all of this."

Jessica nodded. "I see."

Crichton looked up toward the top of the mountain as the clouds began to drift in, smothering the vista. "You understand that, don't you?"

Jessica said nothing.

"I'm undergoing a bit of a crisis. I'm torn. I'm married. And here I am with you. This is just getting too complicated."

"You don't have to explain."

"I want to talk about us. And about our future," he lied. He realized at that moment he had already mentally cut ties with her. "But not now. Is that clear?"

Jessica forced a smile. "So it's not over?"

Crichton couldn't say the words. "Let's talk about it when we get back to DC." He tried to find the right phrase. "This Patterson business is weighing on my mind too. You understand that, right?"

Jessica gave a wan smile. Her eyes filled with tears. She looked around. "That's fair."

Crichton wanted to change the subject. "I can't think straight right now. I was really looking forward to this hike. Have been for weeks."

"Look, Brad, I figure we're only twenty minutes, maybe half an hour, from the summit. I know this is bad news. And I can see you're not yourself right now. But we probably won't be back here, right? Let's finish this hike. Besides, we can't leave till tomorrow morning, anyway."

Crichton ran a hand across his face.

"What do you think?"

Crichton sighed. His heart wasn't in it. He just wanted to call it quits there and then. The call had him spooked. "Can't really face it after that news, Jessica."

Jessica sighed. "Look, I've come all this way. Why don't you just head down, and I'll finish the hike myself?"

Crichton groaned. The last thing he wanted was for his young assistant to be out in the wilds by herself. He wondered for a moment if he shouldn't just pull rank and tell her to get the hell off the mountain. "Can I be frank? You're stubborn and silly. I want to get the hell out of here."

"Brad, yes, I am stubborn. But we can't leave until tomorrow morning. Look, I'll be fine. I'll return well before sunset."

"This is crazy."

Jessica had already turned and was headed back up the mountain trail.

"What the hell do you think you're doing?! Goddamn!" He pulled on his backpack and shielded his eyes from the sun. "The summit and then straight back down, you hear me?"

Forty-Two

Stone crunched the scree on the trail underfoot as he closed in on the senator and his mistress. He checked the GPS tracking device. He was within seven hundred yards of his prey. They had again stopped for a rest close to the summit of the mountain. He was looking for a clean shot. But he also needed to stay out of their line of sight.

He came to a sharp drop and stopped, heart pounding, scree falling away below. "Fuck," he said, startled by the sudden cliff edge.

Stone's gaze wandered across the ridge. In the distance, he thought he saw something. He crouched down and looked through the binoculars. The senator and his girlfriend were drinking water. They both looked animated, as if arguing. He unzipped his backpack and assembled the specially modified rifle.

He pressed his eye up to the sights. He saw the couple through the crosshairs. Then he used the range finder to pull Crichton into the middle of his sights. This was the one he wanted. He stared, wanting to get a direct shot to the chest.

Stone felt excited. He was about to test the Venus Technique Shooter, an electromagnetic pulse gun used in its original form to counter jamming technology. Now he had in his hands the modified version: an assassination tool.

He locked on to the target, needing a clear shot for this to work. The seconds dragged and the senator was still in his sights.

Stone was breathing hard. He needed to calm down. Focus. And relax. He held his breath and moved his finger to the trigger.

Forty-Three

Jessica Friel opened the wrapper of a granola bar and gave it to Brad. "Look, if you don't want to finish this hike, it's fine."

Crichton took the bar and began to nibble.

Jessica could see he was angry. She wondered if she shouldn't have just headed down when he had told her to. "Look, maybe I was hasty. What if we just called it quits? Would that make you happy?"

Crichton forced a smile.

"It would, wouldn't it?"

Crichton nodded. "My head's full of a thousand things I've got to do. My head's not in the right place. I'm sorry."

Jessica took out a flask and poured a cup of black coffee for each of them in two plastic cups. "Caffeine, and then we get back to the cabin and you can make some calls, OK?"

Crichton took a gulp and smiled. "Sounds like a plan."

"I'm sorry about everything."

Crichton drank the rest of his coffee and handed the cup back to her. "Jessica, when we get home, we need to talk a few things over."

Jessica sensed it wasn't going to be good news. "I see."

"I don't want to hurt my wife. You know that."

"Do you love her?"

Crichton blew out his cheeks. "She's the mother of my children."

"Do you love her?"

"Jessica, yes, I do love her. I'm sorry, but I do. I care about her very much. And I don't want to hurt her."

Jessica nodded, curling her windblown hair behind her ear. She ate the rest of the granola bar and put the empty wrapper back in her pack. She turned and looked up at the summit. "Looks like I've come a long way just to get dumped."

"It's not like that. Please don't make it like that."

Jessica felt stupid and empty. She couldn't believe she hadn't seen this coming. He was brushing her aside. And being nice as he said it. "I thought we had something."

Crichton groaned.

Jessica turned around. His eyes were closed, as if he was in pain.

"Brad, you OK?"

Brad fell to his knees and clutched his chest as he vomited and his eyes rolled back in his head.

Jessica felt a wave of panic wash over her. "Oh Christ!" She took off her backpack and kneeled beside Brad on the rocky, windswept ledge as the color drained from his face. She checked his wrist for a sign of life. A faint pulse. "Brad, listen to me, you need to hang in there, do you understand? I think you're having a heart attack."

Crichton's eyes opened wide for a few moments. Then they began to roll back into his head. He garbled something.

Jessica leaned in close. "Brad, please . . . What is it?"

"Not gonna . . . Not gonna . . ."

"Tell me, Brad!"

"Not gonna make it."

Jessica was gripped by a growing sense of panic. She was alone with him, stuck up some goddamn mountain in a foreign land in the middle of nowhere. "Oh Christ, Brad! What do I do? I don't have any aspirin or anything!"

Brad clutched his chest tighter and clenched his teeth. He grabbed Friel close. "Take it!"

"What?"

Crichton was gripping the lanyard with the lip-balm flash drive around his neck. "Take it to the Feds! Do you hear me?"

Jessica held the lanyard. "This?"

"Take it!"

Jessica shook her head. She cursed herself for not bringing aspirin. She knew Brad had had a heart scare not long ago. "I'll get you out of here, Brad. Don't worry about the flash drive."

Crichton began to shudder.

Jessica watched her lover spasm and started to sob. She felt helpless as the shock began to take hold of her. But she was also angry with herself.

"Think, goddammit! Do something!" She reached over and pulled her phone out of her backpack. She punched in 999, the number for UK emergency services. There was no signal. "Gimme a break!"

It seemed like the whole scene was playing out in slow motion.

Jessica dialed the number again. Still no signal. "Bullshit." She looked and saw Brad was turning blue. She kneeled beside him and wiped his mouth with the back of her hand. "Goddamn you, Brad." She felt tears spill down her face. She clasped her lips around his and began to give him mouth-to-mouth, breathing in hard, then compressing his chest. Breathing out, compressing his chest. "Wake up, goddammit, Brad—do you hear me?"

Jessica could see he wasn't responding. She began to hyperventilate, slipping into a blind panic. "Think, goddammit! Do something!"

She checked his pulse. There was nothing.

"Oh come on, think!"

She began to thump his chest harder. Harder. Harder. Bone-crunching punches around his heart. "Come on, you bastard! Don't do this to me!"

Brad's lips were gray.

Jessica pressed her lips against his cold mouth and breathed hard. "Please," she wailed, punching down onto his chest. "You! Will! Not! Fucking! Die!"

No sign of life.

She dialed 999 again. Still no signal.

Jessica rifled through Brad's pocket and pulled out his cell phone. She tried 999. Still no signal, no ringing, no connection. Dead. She began to scream as if she were losing her mind.

Forty-Four

The sound of the young woman's screaming was arousing Nathan Stone. He was watching the whole scene through the military binoculars. Transfixed by her helplessness. It stirred deep emotions. He felt exhilarated. And realized he was smiling broadly.

Stone pulled on his backpack as he crouched behind the crevice, out of sight. The sound of her frantic voice in his earpiece cut right through him as she desperately tried to call the 999 dispatcher again. But he knew there was no connection. Not on that frequency.

Time to play, Nathan.

The phrase was echoing around in his mind.

Stone doubled back for fifty yards and climbed over the outcrop above him. Then he headed over the ledge in the direction of the young woman.

The more he thought of what was about to happen, the crazier he felt.

He was back in the zone.

It felt good. The air got colder as he climbed higher. The air bit into his skin. He felt alive. Invigorated. Vital.

In his ear, the woman was muttering, frantic, moaning, desperate for Crichton to come back to life. For someone to help her.

His earpiece crackled into life. "Nathan, five hundred yards as the crow flies, we estimate."

"Yeah, sounds about right. I just have to get over the next ridge and she'll be in sight. Fifteen minutes. We still good?"

"We're very good. You've got a clean run at this. Crichton appears to be either unconscious or dead. He's done."

"The girl . . . She next?"

"She's . . ."

"She's what?"

"Fuck. We believe she's got Crichton's phone. She's using it to try and call out."

"It's jammed though, right?"

"Yeah . . . but it'll be US government-issue and might have some work-arounds in place."

"Got it."

"Let's pick up the pace. And get this over with."

The line went dead.

Forty-Five

Jessica Friel was crouched by the senator's body, weeping, head in her hands. She knew she needed to get Brad off the mountain. But the fact of the matter was they were on an isolated mountain range in goddamn northwest Scotland. A place only accessible to most people by a huge trek around the mountains. Or by boat. And she was stuck two thousand yards up on an overhang, with her lover, an American senator, not breathing.

"Think, you fucker!"

She racked her brain.

Friel began to hit her head with the palm of her hand. "Think, for Chrissakes! Help!"

She broke down and sobbed. She felt like she was losing her mind.

Friel beat hard on his chest. She restarted mouth-to-mouth in between sobs. Cold lips. Purple.

"No! Don't do this to me!" She held his cold face in her hands. "Please, God, please."

She dialed 999 again and again, but still no goddamn signal.

She stared at Brad's phone. All the numerous apps.

Her mind began to race. She flicked through the apps. And then she saw it.

FireChat.

She didn't have that particular app on her phone, though she had heard about it. She remembered a conversation with her friend Amy, who said it was possible to send a message even without a signal or Wi-Fi connection. It worked by connecting to any cell phones in the area via Bluetooth.

"Goddamn," she said.

Friel wondered exactly what she should do. She clicked on FireChat. She saw Brad's chief of staff as one of the contacts. She took a photo of Brad lying motionless on the ledge. Then sent a message:

SOS! Medical emergency! Brad not responding! Help! Stuck on mountain in Knoydart Peninsula, Scotland! No signal! PLEASE CALL 999 in UK. Can't get through! Jessica

Friel began to shake after sending the message. She knelt down and touched his neck. It was cold. No pulse. She gave him the kiss of life again and again.

Suddenly, she detected a pulse in his neck.

She pounded hard on his chest. Again and again. Then again.

"Do *not* die on me, do you hear me?"

Forty-Six

Brigadier Jack Sands was watching the multiple screens with interest. He took off the headset connecting him to Nathan Stone and leaned back in his seat. He checked Friel's GPS and saw that Stone wasn't far away. A matter of minutes.

He wondered why the jamming technology emitting from Stone's phone hadn't jammed the signals. It should have created a dead zone for cell phone use via base stations in that tiny area of northwest Scotland. But Friel's smart thinking had circumvented that.

How the hell hadn't they anticipated that possibility?

He dialed the number for the operation's chief technology officer, Matt Clamerson. "Matt, a message was sent, you see that?"

A long sigh. "The jamming should've worked."

"But it didn't. It fucking did *not*!"

"Jack, you know FireChat isn't connected to a centralized service. So we've got cell phones within a few kilometers theoretically running, the app acting as a node in a mesh network, passing messages, and this helped the message get through, unbelievably. That's why it's very, very difficult to block."

"Should we have foreseen this?"

"Perhaps we should have . . . Fuck."

Sands gathered his thoughts. "What's done is done. I need to find a solution. And fast."

"I'm trying to get into the recipient's messaging system and delete the message."

"How long?"

A pause. "We have a problem."

"What?"

"The message has now been copied to every contact in Crichton's team."

"By who?"

"I'm checking the recipient's cell phone settings as we speak." A beat. "Yup. As I thought, anything sent from the senator's phone to his chief of staff automatically goes to the whole team."

"Everyone knows?"

"Yup. And two have opened it."

"Fuck! Fuck! Fuck!" Sands began to pace the room. "Can we stop them sending those messages?"

"Already done that."

"Good, so those two can't make calls from those cell phones."

The sound of tapping down the line. "Precisely. And I've now deleted the unread messages too."

"So technically the two people could still contact police or the Feds or whoever."

"Yeah. But they'll have to call from another cell or landline."

"Gimme a fucking break, someone."

Sands ended the call and stared up at the screens as Stone edged closer to his prey.

Forty-Seven

Nathan Stone figured he was less than five hundred yards away. But still out of sight. His earpiece crackled into life. "We estimate you are about six minutes away on that terrain," the voice said.

"Copy that."

"Bit of information. She just managed to send a message via FireChat calling in an emergency."

"You kidding me? Any response?"

"None so far. But it's just a matter of time till this is picked up."

"Are we a go?"

"This is green. I repeat, we are green. Proceed to destination. And let's complete the task."

Stone scaled a rocky outcrop and climbed over a ledge. Farther along the ridge, he finally caught sight of the young American woman. "I see her!"

"Now listen, Nathan, you have the time. Scrambling a chopper to where you are we estimate, at the earliest, forty minutes. The target is down. Not moving. So you have a clear run. Get to it."

Stone climbed down a ridge. Closer and closer. His senses were switched to max. Then he stared down the well-trodden trail and saw in the distance the mistress crouched over the senator.

Forty-Eight

Out of her peripheral vision, Jessica Friel saw a tiny figure in the distance. She turned and stood up, flapping her arms frantically.

"Help!" she screamed. "Please help!" She groaned as the hiker walked toward her, unaware of her predicament. Her desperation. "Please help me! Hurry!"

The hiker was of a muscular build, carrying a huge backpack.

"Hurry, please!" she shouted.

The man began to jog toward them, as if realizing she was in trouble. He took off his sunglasses. "Jeez, what happened?"

Friel felt relieved at the familiar accent. "Oh my God, thank you. An American. He's my boss. He's a senator. Please, we have to do something."

"Don't panic, ma'am. It's important not to panic."

"He's collapsed. Heart attack, I think. I can't contact 999 on my cell, but I managed to send a message to some folks back in the States."

The stranger took off his backpack and bent down beside Brad, pressing his neck. "There's still a pulse. Real weak, though."

"He's alive?"

"Barely."

Friel felt euphoric. "Thank you so much. Thank you."

The man began hitting Crichton's chest, like she had been doing.

Friel looked around and saw a rocky outcrop about two hundred yards from the ledge they were on. "I'll just be a minute."

"Where are you going?"

"I'm gonna try and call for help again. See if I can get a better signal up there."

The man nodded. "Let me work on him. Quick!"

Friel began to cry as she climbed higher up the rock face. She had the senator's cell phone in her pocket. But as she climbed up, she wondered if she was doing the right thing leaving Brad with a total stranger, fighting for his life.

Forty-Nine

Nathan Stone waited for a couple of minutes until she was out of sight. He hadn't felt a pulse at all. He opened the senator's closed eyes and shone a penlight in them. Nothing. No pupil reaction. He checked for a pulse in the neck. And then in the wrist.

Nothing.

He let out a long sigh and whispered into his concealed microphone, "Arlington." It was the code word alluding to the military cemetery. His earpiece crackled into life. "Copy that. You need to close this down real quick and get out of there."

Stone rifled through Crichton's pockets. "There's no cell in his pockets. I think target two has them both."

"They must be retrieved. And search for the flash drive too."

"Copy that."

Stone crouched by the body for a few moments. He leaned in close and pressed his face against the cold skin of the American senator. He closed his eyes, feeling the dead flesh on his. Like cold wax. Inert.

It was then he saw something tucked inside the senator's collar. A lanyard. He pulled it out and saw what was fixed to it: a tube of lip balm. He pulled off the top to reveal . . . a metal flash drive.

Stone carefully took it off the senator's neck. Then he slid it into a zipped side pocket of his backpack, which he closed immediately.

He felt aroused.

"Got what we were looking for."

"You do?"

"I've got this."

Stone rose to his feet and stared up at the young woman climbing to the next peak. He would wait for her return. Then kill her.

Fifty

Jessica Friel was panting hard. The wind howled as she ascended the final peak. She was willing herself to stay focused. Her heart was pounding. Almost out of control. She felt sick. Insides knotted tight with tension.

She desperately wanted to get a signal. Didn't know if she would. But she had to try.

Fuck.

She felt tears rise up and spill down her cheeks. "Get it together, Jessica, do you hear me?" She willed herself to climb higher. She was scared. So scared. But she had to dig deep and get to the next peak.

It was within sight.

Slowly doubts began to crowd her thoughts. She wondered again if she should have stayed with Brad. She was caught in a cross fire of emotions.

Shouldn't she have asked the fellow hiker to go and get help? But that could've taken hours. They didn't have hours.

They were out of time.

Friel gritted her teeth. "You can do this! Come on!"

She climbed higher, her face at times pressed against the cold rock face of the ancient Scottish mountain. She began to think of death. Brad's death. She could see it all before her.

The more the questions piled up in her head, the crazier she felt. She plowed on, nearing the summit, blood dripping from her broken fingernails.

She had never felt so alone.

She had no one.

She imagined her mother, angry and resentful about her illicit affair with a married senator. She'd been told by her mother that she would come to regret it. Now she was regretting it.

But not in the way she, or anyone else, had imagined.

This was worse. Far, far worse.

This wasn't in her plans.

She had imagined Brad quietly divorcing his wife after a few years and then marrying her. But now here she was, scrambling about on a remote Scottish mountain range thousands of miles from home as Brad lay close to death . . . If he wasn't dead already.

Friel pushed those thoughts to one side as she drove herself on. Clawing at the rock face. She was calling on every ounce of strength she had to get to the top. She was close. She got onto a new trail that would take her to the summit.

She moved on. Fear gnawed at her. She climbed and climbed. Then she felt her legs give way on the rocky scree. The pain shot through her right ankle like a hot knife. She groaned in agony. "Goddamn!" She limped on. Eventually, it was too sore.

So she got down on her knees on the trail and began to claw her way up. Yard by goddamn yard. Her knees were on the hard rock and scree, which bit into her skin, as she felt herself going into shock.

Her hands were shaking. Down below was a thousand-foot sheer drop.

Eventually, she clambered to the top and sat there whimpering as the wind howled. She pulled out both cell phones. There was still no reception. No signal. She dialed 999 in the hope she might get lucky. But the line was dead.

She closed her eyes for a few moments and began to cry.

"Don't give up!" she implored herself. "Try again, goddammit!"

She tried again and waited. "Please . . . please. Please, someone. Anyone. Please answer. I'm begging you."

A terrible silence answered her.

Then the phone crackled to life. "Operator," a woman's voice said, "which service do you require?"

Friel began to shake with joy. "Ma'am, ambulance, paramedics . . ."

"I'm sorry, I didn't catch that . . . It's a bad line."

"Ambulance, paramedics, please. Emergency."

Suddenly the signal dropped out.

"No! Goddamn!"

She pulled out Brad's phone and saw there was a message on the FireChat app. She opened it up.

Help is on the way. US Embassy, London. Sit tight.

Friel began to cry.

She composed herself. She had to get it together.

She wiped her eyes, a mixture of fear and relief washing over her.

Would they get there in time?

She turned and gingerly made her way back down the trail, feeling sick and slightly manic.

She wondered how they would get Brad off the mountain. How long would they take?

The more she thought about it, the more weepy she got.

"Christ," she said, blinking away the tears.

She descended faster as the scree gave way to a firmer dirt trail. She began to remember the words of a prayer deep within her and buried since she was a child. A prayer she had learned as a girl at church. She felt the tears spilling down her face again as the wind whipped dust up into the air.

Darkening skies in the distance rolled in across the sea.

Friel slipped on her backside and began to slide down the path. Her hiking boots slowed her. She traversed down to a lower ledge. Then she looked below and saw the stranger sitting beside Brad, head bowed.

She scrambled down.

"No, no," she said, the words out before she could even stop herself. "Please, no!"

Friel scrambled down the last fifty yards to the ledge where Brad was lying, not moving, as the stranger sat. She edged closer to Brad before she kneeled and wrapped her arms around him.

He was cold.

"No, this can't be!" she wailed.

The stranger sat in silence.

Friel clasped Brad's cold face in her hands and kissed his lifeless lips. She felt a terrible chasm open up inside her. A blackness. A nothingness. "Brad, please don't leave me," she said. She felt herself begin to sob and pulled his head to her breast. "Brad, please don't do this. Please."

The stranger shifted on the ground and got to his feet. "I'm sorry, ma'am. He's gone."

Friel held Brad tight, her face pressed to his cheek. She began to hum a favorite song of her mother's. "Moonlight in Vermont." She felt herself in free fall. As if someone had taken the wind out of her sails. She had been hollowed out. She was a shell.

She dabbed her eyes. "I'm sorry I couldn't save you, darling," she whispered. "Will you ever be able to forgive me?" She ran her hand through his hair. His eyes were shut. Mouth open a fraction, as if it had frozen where he had gasped his last breath.

She placed his head back down on the ground. She stroked his face. It was then she noticed something. Two buttons were undone on his shirt.

Brad was a one-button guy if he wasn't wearing a tie. She wondered if maybe she was mistaken.

The more she thought about it, the more she knew that Brad would never unbutton more than one button on a casual shirt. He was virtually OCD about it.

Her mind flashed back to him showing her the lanyard around his neck.

She surreptitiously pulled back his collar and saw there was nothing there. No lip balm.

Friel's blood ran cold. She felt paralyzed. He had wanted her to have it. But it wasn't there. He hadn't been able to move when he had spoken those words. She hadn't taken it from him. And then it began to dawn on her.

She sensed the stranger watching her.

She turned around and saw he was now standing over her, eyes dead.

"When I left him, he was still breathing."

The stranger said nothing.

"You said he was definitely breathing."

"There was a faint pulse."

Friel blinked away tears. "But he was breathing, right?"

The man stared at her long and hard.

Friel's mind was free-falling. She knew something was wrong. She felt like screaming. But she couldn't.

She composed herself, got to her feet, and lunged straight at the man, pushing him backward over the edge and into the void.

The stranger was caught unawares and plunged down, crashing fifty feet below onto a rocky outcrop with a sickening thud.

Friel held her breath. She looked down through a film of tears. The man wasn't moving.

Fifty-One

Brigadier Jack Sands stared transfixed at the images on the big screens. Blood-specked rocks. He was seeing what Nathan Stone's camera had captured. But there was no movement. "Nathan," he said, "respond!"

Silence.

"Nathan, cough, groan. Do something to let me know in some way you're still alive, goddammit!"

Nothing.

Sands began to pace the room. "Nathan, I repeat, give me a signal or something to show you're still with us."

Still no response.

Sands was in charge of the operation. He had the authority to do whatever it took to complete the mission. It had been partially completed. Crichton had been neutralized. But the staffer, Crichton's mistress, had taken a course of action he hadn't foreseen.

And now their guy, Nathan, had been taken out. Or, at best, immobilized. This wasn't the method of their choosing. They had their own plans to deal with Nathan Stone. Sands couldn't understand why Nathan hadn't just picked her up and thrown her over the edge.

The more he thought about it, the more it seemed like a nightmare. An operation jinxed from the start. He needed to focus.

Sands put on the red headphones and made the call to the backup team. "Change of plan. Head straight to locale. Emergency."

"Copy that, sir."

"Two things. First, take care of the female target, who has not been neutralized. Do it right. And afterwards, retrieve the flash drive device contained within a lip balm, which is now either in a pale-blue backpack or on female target's person. Also, collect any cell phones on her or in the backpack."

"Got it. Second thing?"

"What's your ETA?"

"We can be there in fifteen minutes and get to work."

Sands stared at the screen, which showed no movement from Stone's pinhole camera.

"Sir, the second thing?"

Sands stared long and hard, and then sighed. "You are also to neutralize Nathan Stone with immediate effect, as previously discussed. Make it look like a fall. And retrieve any cell phones, devices, cameras, etc. We believe he may already have fallen on the mountain. So he may be injured. Proceed with extreme caution."

"Copy that, sir."

Sands ended the conversation, called Clayton Wilson, and gave him the update.

"Jesus H. Christ" was all Wilson could say after a long silence.

"Sir, we have a credible backup plan."

A long sigh echoed down the line. "We need to get that goddamn flash drive."

"We're on it, sir. We have more than enough time."

"You'd better. Or we'll all be out of fucking time."

Fifty-Two

Nathan Stone was floating in a black lagoon, the sky white. He felt himself drifting on the water. Then he felt himself beginning to submerge, unable to breathe.

The sound of a woman crying in the distance roused him. Slowly, he came to and tasted blood and dirt.

He spat it out. Didn't know if he could move. His eyes were shut tight. Forced himself to open them. Blurred vision. Blood dripping from a head wound. Using his hands and arms to support himself, he got to his knees and stared into the distance. Tried to focus. His vision was blurred for nearly a minute. Eventually, it cleared. He got to his feet unsteadily and grimaced as shocks of pain from his ribs reverberated through his body.

"Goddamn!" he said, clenching his teeth.

Stone felt a craziness begin to engulf him. He wasn't used to anyone getting the better of him. Especially some fucking Capitol Hill staffer.

"Fuck!"

He turned and looked up at the ledge, fifty feet above, from where he'd been pushed.

Think, goddamn it, think.

He needed to alert his handler. First things first.

"Sir, can you hear me?"

Stone hunched over, hands resting on his thighs, wincing at the pain. "Sir, can you hear me, urgent?"

He waited and waited for a response.

"Sir, please respond immediately if you can hear me."

Nothing. Silence.

Stone checked his lapel and saw the pinhole camera cum microphone had been lost in the fall. He scrambled around on the rocks and scree, frantically searching for the tiny device.

He realized the search was futile. It was gone.

He was out of radio contact.

Stone took in a deep breath and winced. Ribs broken. He reached into his pocket and pulled out a dissolvable emergency sachet. High-strength amphetamine and morphine mix. He felt the drugs race into his bloodstream in moments. The morphine killed most of the pain, while the huge quantity of amphetamine gave him energy.

He took a few deep breaths. Searing pain still there in his ribs. "Goddamn."

He negotiated a few rocks and boulders and climbed back up onto the path. Stopped to check he still had the 9mm strapped to his right ankle, which fired dissolvable poisoned darts. Good for a two-hundred-yard range.

He felt his senses working again. He went across to the senator's body. He stared down at it for a fleeting moment before stepping over it. Then he turned and headed down the trail.

Stone felt the pain digging into him, erupting across his body. The minutes were eaten up as he descended the rough ground, and he began to feel stronger, the pain nullified.

He tasted the residue of the amphetamine on his tongue and swallowed hard.

He stopped and stared off into the distance. Saw, about a mile away, a figure carrying a backpack, heading into the forest. This was Friel. The bitch was on the move.

He estimated she was ten minutes ahead of him.

Time was running out.

His gaze wandered around the mountainside. Stone's twenty-twenty vision included a secondary trail parallel to the main one, but far more treacherous.

Stone considered his options as he headed down the mountainside. The pain had subsided. But in its place was a putrid black anger, burning deep within him. He wondered whether he would catch her by sticking straight behind her. He decided to get onto the minor trail and cut across the mountain ridge.

The beauty of it was it would be out of sight.

A few minutes later, he was on the secondary trail, unbeknownst to anyone but him, running parallel to Friel's route to freedom.

Fifty-Three

Jessica Friel stopped and looked at her watch, tears streaming down her face, beside herself. Driven by fear, anxiety, terror, wondering what the hell was going on. She retched. But nothing came up.

She was traumatized, having left the body of Brad high up on the mountainous ridge. But she didn't have any options.

She'd checked the backpack and found the lanyard with the flash drive still there. The hiker who appeared had obviously taken it off Brad.

Friel was willing herself to be strong. She strode on as the foliage thickened, trees and bushes overhanging the trail, brushing her face in the wind. She reached into her pocket and pulled out Brad's phone. No more messages from the US consulate. Did they have people on the way? Friel dialed 999 on Brad's cell phone again and pressed the green button, and waited. No ringtone. Nothing. No signal.

She needed to get back to civilization, down to the small hamlet by the lake.

She felt so very alone. Trapped, almost.

She was in an environment she knew nothing about. And as evening fell, the sky darkening, she knew she had to get down the mountain soon.

Her heart rate was quickening.

Friel hiked on for another mile, getting eaten by midges in the moist undergrowth. She checked her watch. Where the hell was everyone? Where was the help? "Goddamn."

Her mind flashed back to the moment she had pushed the mysterious American hiker off the ridge. She wondered if she'd gone mad and imagined it all. It was ridiculous. This didn't happen to normal people. She was from DC. She didn't belong here.

Whatever this was, it had nothing to do with her.

But the sad truth was, it had everything to do with her.

She'd ignored the warnings from the dead blogger. And, being headstrong, she'd flown across the Atlantic with the goddamn flash drive disguised by the lip balm to give to Brad in person. She should have implored him to head back home. She should have told him to cancel his appearance at the conference. But she hadn't. Now he was dead.

The more she thought about it, the more frantic she felt.

One of the two cell phones began to vibrate. She saw it was Brad's. A message.

Friel opened the message. It was from the US consulate.

Important. Stay exactly where you are, Jessica. Help on the way. Mountain rescue/paramedic experts very close. Minutes from your current position. Will get you to safety. Do not move. Chopper with team landing to pick up Senator Crichton in eight minutes. FBI from London and armed Scottish police en route. More to follow.

Friel sank to her knees and began to cry. "Thank you. Thank you, Lord."

Fifty-Four

Nathan Stone was hurting bad and bleeding as he crouched in the woods. He rubbed his hands in the dirt and mud. Smeared it across his face and ears and through his hair to blend into the surroundings. Then he headed farther up the rocky single track winding around the mountain, going higher and higher. The track edged away from the main path and diverged, heading over a rocky outcrop, where it continued out of sight on the other side of the hills.

He checked the angle of the sun as he got his bearings. A burning twinge in his sides. His breathing was labored. But he was relatively uninhibited, despite the bitch pushing him off the ledge.

Stone gritted his teeth and strode on. He picked up the pace and began to jog as the path wound its way higher along the hidden side of the ridge. It went on like that for half a mile and then zigzagged back over the ridge.

Stone crouched down. He sensed a presence. A sixth sense. He heard sobbing. A woman's sobbing.

He closed his eyes and realized it was coming from a couple hundred yards west of where he was, down below.

Stone moved with stealth along the path. He took out the 9mm dart gun strapped to his ankle and put it in his waistband. He always had a backup plan. Always had a weapon within easy reach.

Such preparation had served him well.

He had lost count of the times plans had gone awry over the years. But his planning, and his training back at The Farm all those years ago, had been drummed into him.

What happens if it all goes to fuck during the operation? What happens if plan A is blown out of the water?

The answer was always the same.

Have a plan B. And a plan C, D, and E if need be.

But usually a plan B was more than enough.

Stone quickened his pace as he headed along the ridge, hidden by the foliage and trees, his rubber-soled Timberlands hardly making a sound on the earth. Only the occasional twig or loose rock gave a soft crunch underfoot.

The sobbing was getting closer. A lot closer.

Stone got down on his stomach and crawled for a hundred yards, maybe more, his ribs burning, blood still dripping from a head wound. He was panting heavily. The pain was gnawing at his sides. But the morphine was taking the edge off just enough, the amphetamines giving him the energy he needed.

He moved forward as the sobs drifted up the mountainside, beyond the tree line. And then he looked down. Through a gap in the trees, he saw her.

Jessica Friel was sitting and crying as she sat on his backpack, head in her hands.

Stone held his breath. He took out the 9mm and pointed the gun with the telescopic sights at the target. He closed one eye as he got her in the crosshairs. He flicked off the safety, finger on the trigger.

Fifty-Five

Jessica Friel heard voices coming toward her. "I'm here!" She felt weepy. Overcome. She knew they were there for her. The rustle of the waterproof coats and the trudging steps on the scree path. Broken twigs, branches cracking. She heard some water in the distance, perhaps a mountain stream running wild down the hills.

She waited as her instructions had told her.

Her emotions were tearing her to pieces. She felt sick. Elated. Scared. But most of all, she felt empty over Brad's death.

The more she thought about it all, the strange American on the hills, the colder she felt. She wondered if she was going into shock.

"Hi!" a man's voice shouted from up ahead.

Friel saw two guys with huge backpacks outfitted for the elements. She began to sob uncontrollably.

The smaller of the two men took off his backpack and shook her hand. "Hi!" he said.

"Thank you for finding me. Thank you. I think there's a guy out there trying to hurt me. I'm an American."

The man who shook her hand nodded but didn't say anything.

"My partner is on the hill. They said the chopper was coming for him."

The man nodded, took out a penlight, and shone it in her eyes. He nodded. "Yeah . . . extreme shock." His accent didn't sound Scottish.

"Are you from the mountain rescue?"

The man nodded as he took out a pill and handed it to her with a bottle of water. "It'll counter the shock before we get you to the hospital."

Friel nodded and knocked back the pill. She washed it down with the water. It felt good.

The second man smiled. "You're gonna be fine now."

When he spoke those words, Friel was gripped by a strange fear. The man's accent was definitely American. Midwest. She tried to open her mouth to speak but couldn't. She was paralyzed. She felt her body go limp as the foliage and towering trees began to spin.

She was falling.

She felt her eyes rolling back in her head.

"Just fall asleep, Jessica. Time for a long, long sleep. Then you'll feel better."

Friel fought to stay awake as the drug overwhelmed her. Staring down at her were two men, both smiling.

Suddenly, she was lying on her back, then engulfed in darkness.

Fifty-Six

Nathan Stone saw everything through the sights of the military-grade 9mm handgun. It was clear what was going down. First, his target was supposed to be neutralized by him. But when his handler thought he was indisposed, a two-man team flew in from the wings to deal with it.

He watched as she willingly swallowed the pill. They'd convinced her they were there to help, maybe paramedics. And that's why she'd taken the drug.

It was a fast-acting anesthetic. That's what they would have used.

Friel wouldn't be able to move.

Stone watched, transfixed. One man took out what looked like a pen but probably had a syringe tip, which would administer the deadly, virtually untraceable drug to paralyze her. She wouldn't be able to fight back. Then the drug would stop her heart. She would be dead within three minutes.

The two men didn't speak. One watched and one acted.

Stone spied through gaps in the trees. One of the men pulled out a cell phone. Stone heard the words "job done." The men dragged Friel's body through the woods. They each took out small shovels from their backpacks and began to dig a shallow pit. Her grave.

Five minutes later, they'd finished the job, and they carefully lifted her body into the grave. Then they filled in the grave with all the soil, covered it up with branches and twigs, and used another branch covered with leaves to sweep away their footprints.

The two men inspected the area, photographed it, then made another call.

Stone could hear the voice, a southern drawl. He smelled the moss and earth pressed against his face. He felt himself begin to dissociate. He could disengage from any situation. This prevented fear from informing his physical actions.

He raised his head barely an inch. It was clear this was a top-grade operation. He assumed they were working under orders for the same handler. His handler. Had to be. This was no coincidence.

This was compartmentalization. It was a well-known concept in intelligence. The fewer people who knew the full details of an operation, the better, to reduce the chances that the mission might be compromised.

He wondered if the two-man team had been on standby in case of problems.

Nathan began to think through the possibilities. He pondered another scenario. What if the two guys had been brought in for another part of the mission? Not to kill the woman. Not to be the backup. But to neutralize Nathan after he'd finished off the woman and the senator.

Was that it?

Were they ghosts waiting to take him out when he made his way back off the mountain?

The more he considered the scenario racing around his head, the more he began to see it as a credible explanation.

The decision to neutralize the triggerman, the only link back to the organizers, would make sense. The job gets done, but all trace is erased. It would point to a lone wolf. A bad seed.

Stone was indeed a lone wolf. And a bad seed. An assassin. But he was never, ever acting alone. He was always following orders.

For his handler, if Stone was indeed dead, he couldn't be left out there.

The call ended and the two men headed back onto the trail in the direction of where they had emerged. Like ghosts.

Stone held his breath for nearly a minute.

Were there others? Were others scouring for him? For his body?

Stone's killer instincts had been roused as he watched the men coldly neutralize the aide. He wondered if the same fate awaited him.

Was that it?

Were they going to be waiting for him when he returned to the facility?

It was then that the germ of an idea began to form.

Slowly, a plan was taking shape in his head. A plan to get him out of here.

Stone waited, watching and listening for a few moments, before he continued along the path across the high ridge. Then he was behind the tree line, out of sight and out of mind.

Fifty-Seven

Brigadier Jack Sands was transfixed. Watching the real-time footage from a hidden camera on one of the shadow operatives as they made their way down the mountain. They were headed along a two-mile trail as the light faded. He looked at the other monitor, which showed the frozen image of rocks and boulders where the device had landed when Nathan Stone was pushed over the edge.

The more he thought of Nathan's untimely demise, the harder he took it. Stone, for all his coldheartedness, had never once let Sands down. A small part of Sands hoped Stone was dead, if only so he wasn't suffering in agony, like a wounded animal.

Sands had been told by two doctors within the facility that it was "highly probable" that Stone was either dead or incapacitated. To be pushed backward from such a height in such terrain would have meant fracturing either his back or his neck, losing pints of blood, and being unable to get back to base.

The one consolation for Sands was that he knew they had a recovery team in place to get the body of Stone off the mountain.

The missing aide wouldn't be mentioned by anyone. At least not now.

Eventually, awkward questions would be asked when it emerged that Crichton's aide had arrived in Scotland too and was missing.

Sands knew countless people died on remote, dangerous, and wild Scottish mountains each and every year. Sometimes discovered days after they'd disappeared.

But he knew that the grave of the aide was highly unlikely to be found. No one would be looking for her there. They might eventually. But it would be local mountain rescue, and they'd be looking closer to where the senator was found.

Not some wooded area in the foothills of the mountain.

And if they did happen upon it and dig it up days later, perhaps weeks or months, it wouldn't show anything. The drugs used to kill the aide would not be in her body.

Investigators might speculate that the senator had killed his mistress and then killed himself.

The possibilities were endless.

His phone rang, and he instinctively sighed as he picked up.

"Sands."

"Jack, it's Clayton."

"Sir."

"So we got a man down?"

"I believe so, sir."

"Dead?"

"Maybe."

"Are we sending in a full team to retrieve him?"

"Not a full team. I don't think that's wise, sir. That would alert Scottish police and God knows who else."

"So what's the contingency?"

"We have two operatives en route. They will deal with the girl."

"What if our operative is still alive?" Wilson said. "He knows too much."

Sands closed his eyes. "He will be neutralized."

"Once this is done, I want them out of the UK as soon as possible."

"Chopper already waiting for them."

"Hell of a way for Stone to leave us."

"It is what it is, sir. Besides, he's Tom McMasters now."

Fifty-Eight

Nathan Stone was tracking the two men as he headed through a high trail on the mountain. He'd caught sight of them fifteen minutes after they'd dispatched Jessica Friel. He had tracked them from afar. The pain was gnawing at him. But he could deal with pain.

Stone watched through binoculars until they reached an isolated whitewashed cottage, curtains drawn, smoke from the chimney. He crouched low as they headed inside. He watched and waited. A light went on inside.

Stone weighed his options. He decided to double back for a quarter of a mile before he traversed down a loop trail for more than a mile. Then through the woods. Eventually, he stopped. Through the trees and foliage, he saw the rear of the cottage.

Logs piled high in a woodshed adjacent.

He crouched low and retreated deeper into the woods, maintaining his line of sight.

Stone found a dip on the forest floor and lay facedown. Branches crunched and he grimaced. He stared through the trees at the small, unassuming stone house. It might've been an old abandoned woodcutter's house from decades earlier. Maybe a small farmhouse. Maybe even a bothy, a respite for hikers if they encountered harsh conditions on the mountains and needed a place of safety. Then again, maybe it was a cottage rented for the job.

Stone knew his handler would be wondering where the hell he was. He might even have assumed he'd met his end on the mountain. A jolt of pain like a sudden electric shock in his sides reminded him of his ugly fall. He wondered if his handler had factored in him being taken out by a fall.

His instincts told him to get back to the facility by hook or by crook. But the two operatives holed up in the cottage cast a further shadow over the day.

Stone had seen the expert way they'd gained the young American woman's trust, drugged her, and then dug her grave. There was a meticulous quality to it.

He began to run some endgame scenarios through his head. He could do one of three things. First, he could make his way directly back to the facility and ignore the two operatives. That had simplicity and was probably what the textbook would call for, as well as what his handler would expect. Second, he could hunker down and sit tight for the next twenty-four hours, concealed by the vast woods and immense mountains all around him. He knew no mountain rescue team would find him without tracker dogs. Even if they did, he was just an American hiker who was in an unfamiliar landscape and had gotten disorientated. Third, there was an option no one would probably imagine except Stone.

In the distance, he heard the drone of a chopper. He lay still. Then he closed his eyes.

Stone felt the morphine begin to overpower the amphetamines in his system. He felt himself falling into a dark space. Flashing before him was the face of Jessica Friel as she took the drug, unaware that within a minute she'd be in her grave. His mind began to drift. He felt himself falling. He closed his eyes.

Stone was floating on a stagnant black river, the sky on fire.

Fifty-Nine

Brigadier Jack Sands put on the red headset and began speaking to the more senior of the two-man backup team. "Very clean," he said. "Compliments on a neat bit of work."

The operative said, "Mr. Clark, here, sir. Copy that."

"Ah, Mr. Clark . . . slight change of plan. The original deliveryman got held up. He needs to be shown the way home, do you copy that?"

"Coordinates?"

"I'll send these through in a few minutes. But we believe it will be very close to where the original delivery was made."

"Yeah, we've got those coordinates."

"We believe he has compromised the operation. Needs a long sleep to help him recover, if he's injured or incapacitated in some way."

"Copy that, sir. *Long sleep*?"

"You know the drill, Mr. Clark. And I want your friend Mr. Thomas to proceed with that side of things. He will then make his way back to base, but without returning to your current location."

"Very well."

"Mr. Thomas will be responsible."

"And me?"

"Wait till nightfall. I believe it's late in such northern latitudes. So after midnight the chopper will find you. And you should be home in time for breakfast, Mr. Clark. I believe you have fresh documentation at your location, am I right?"

"Looking it over just now, sir. Anything else?"

"No, that's all."

Sixty

Nathan Stone was roused by lights and a searing pain in his sides. He winced as he adjusted his position, deep in the woods. His gaze was drawn to one of the men with a flashlight headed out of the cottage and down the trail adjacent to the woods. It led straight back onto the mountain. He had a backpack on, huge, as if it was filled with equipment. He wondered if the guy, one of the two operatives who had neutralized Friel a few hours earlier, was going to do some recon and see what was happening.

Stone had watched two choppers overhead earlier, perhaps winching down a crew to retrieve the senator. He knew it was only a matter of time before mountain rescue teams and police with dogs began scanning the hills at daybreak. He wondered if the operative was going to retrieve what he thought was Nathan Stone's injured or lifeless body.

The more he thought about it, the more he realized the operation had now gone into "neutralize Nathan" mode. It was possible the operative was going to recover his body and take it off the mountain. But that would be risky.

So what was the purpose if it wasn't to find a seriously injured Nathan Stone and dispatch him for good?

Then again, once the operative saw there was no Nathan Stone to be found, it would be clear that he'd made it off the mountain. And that in itself would set alarm bells ringing back at the facility.

The minutes dragged by as Nathan wondered what his next move should be. Pain burst in his back like electric shocks. He felt throbbing waves of agony wash over him.

Stone ripped open the second pack of amphetamine and morphine mix and washed it down with water. He felt the drugs kick in after a few minutes. The pain was subsiding. He felt alive again. He pressed the LCD digital display on his watch. It showed 11:30 p.m. The hours had dragged. And now he was still hunkered down.

Just after 11:45 p.m. the back door opened and the second operative emerged with a smaller backpack.

Stone looked through the sights at the silhouette of the man outside the cottage. His mind slowed as he began to focus. He held his breath. Then he pulled the trigger of the dart gun. A near-silent *phut* was the only sound as he fired.

The man grabbed his shoulder blade where the dart had entered.

Stone watched as he fell to his knees and began to groan. He waited as the spectral figure on the ground emitted heavy breathing noises. The man had minutes to live.

Stone lifted his head and pushed aside a branch to get a better look. His senses were all switched on. He knew they were alone.

He got to his feet and walked out of the woods toward the man on the ground. Stood over him for a few moments. The man's eyes were shut, mouth slightly open, as he gasped for breath. He was seconds from death and he knew it.

Stone bent down and dragged the dying man inside the cottage. Shut the door. A corner lamp bathed the room in light. TV in the corner. Digital radio. He went through to the kitchen. Nothing out of the ordinary. Or upstairs.

Stone took off the man's backpack and looked inside. He pulled out a penlight and a 9mm Glock, an unassembled sniper rifle, night sights, and night-vision goggles. In the man's pocket was an iPhone. He scrolled through the messages. Only one sender. Clearly a onetime-issue phone for a one-off job.

The only sender was known by a moniker. The Sandman.

Then he saw the message.

Neutralize NS and the girl.

A smiley face beside it.

NS could only mean one person. The message was telling this guy and his fellow operative to take down Stone as well as the girl. They'd managed to kill the girl.

But it was the final message, sent just thirty-two minutes ago, which resonated. *Ferry. Then make your way back to the facility.*

Debrief thereafter. The Sandman.

Stone paced the cottage. He felt sick as the full realization of the extent of the betrayal hit him. This was the command of the Brigadier. His handler. The man he had always looked up to. The man he had trusted. The man whom he thought looked out for his interests. He thought of him standing in the rain at the facility, smiling. His exterior exuded calm, authority, and confidence. But he was cutting Stone loose, leaving him to die. Nathan was expendable, just like the senator.

The more he thought about the deception, the more isolated he felt. He had trusted this man. It was then that a burning anger began to build deep within him. A gut-wrenching anger, threatening to explode.

Stone took a deep breath, knowing he needed to focus.

He switched on the penlight and swept the kitchen with it. He saw a metal cellar hatch and pulled it back. He shone the penlight down. Chopped logs for the winter.

He put the penlight between his teeth and dragged the man to the opening. Stared at the man's closed eyes and pushed him down onto the logs in the darkness.

Stone shut the hatch, knowing the man would be dead before he was found. Not a trace of what had happened to him. Except the tiny pinprick on his shoulder blade.

He put on the backpack and winced at the pain. He went over to the side window and stared into the darkness. He made sure all the lights were off. Then he headed out the rear door, into the woods, and onto the trail leading back to the mountain.

Sixty-One

Brigadier Jack Sands's headset buzzed into life as he stood in the control room. "Talk to me, Mr. Thomas."

The operative said, "I've checked the GPS coordinates where he was and rechecked, and there's nothing."

"Gimme a break. No sign of anything?"

"There's no sign of him. I have, however, retrieved the pinhole camera he was wearing. Scanner picked it up."

"That's something. Good."

"I've been over it and around it. No sign of life. But I can confirm that target one is off mountain."

Sands knew the operative was referring to Crichton. "Chopper picked him up."

"Copy that."

"Body's at a UK military base in Scotland, before repatriation."

The operative sighed. "A few hours until the place is crawling."

"Get yourself back to your base camp."

"Copy that."

Sands pressed a button on the headset and removed it, ending the communication. He began to run the scenarios in his mind. He wondered if Stone had managed to crawl off the mountain and was headed back to base. Was he badly injured somewhere nearby?

"Fuck a duck," he said, shaking his head.

Sands picked up the phone and dialed Clayton Wilson's encrypted line. He answered on the fourth ring. "Sorry to bother you, sir. We have another problem."

Wilson said, "I'm listening."

Sands outlined the situation to Wilson, who listened in rapt silence.

"You're saying you don't know where he is?"

"Sir, you know better than anyone that in this game shit happens."

"Shit does indeed happen. OK, give me some possibilities."

"Possibilities? Let's look at what happened. Stone neutralized Senator Brad Crichton as planned. Perfect. He then moved in to be seen as a helpful Good Samaritan hiker. What I believe transpired is Nathan got the flash drive from around the senator's neck while the girl tried to get a cell phone signal a couple hundred feet up the mountain. Remember they were near the top, on an overhanging ledge. He then placed the flash drive in his own backpack when she was out of sight."

"Go on."

"I've looked at the footage again from Stone's camera and it showed her coming down the mountain, then going across to Crichton. She held him, cradling him. I'm wondering if this was when she noticed the flash drive was gone and freaked out, knowing Nathan was the only one who could've taken it."

A long sigh down the line. "Possible. And plausible."

"She then spun around, realizing this stranger is a danger to her, and Stone was sent flying down onto a lower overhang. The pinhole camera became dislodged during the fall. And Nathan was clearly injured. How bad? We just don't know."

"If he is injured, was it a head injury? If so, how bad? But there is plausible deniability. He's an American student in Scotland hiking."

"I have to say, sir, with all due respect I don't like loose ends."

Wilson sighed. "There are aspects of this operation that just aren't gelling. I can't ever remember so many things going so wrong."

"I think the first sign was that Stone contacted, or tried to contact, his sister."

"You think that might be preying on his mind?"

"No idea, sir, but we really need to neutralize him. The fact we can't even goddamn locate him concerns me."

"Jack, we have an operative missing in action. We gotta fix this shit."

"I intend to, sir."

"We've got to find him. And kill him. Do you understand?"

"Absolutely. Leave it to me, sir."

Sixty-Two

Nathan Stone headed through the woods, backpack on, weapons hidden, at least for now. He hiked up again onto the upper trail that skirted the mountain edge. He edged higher until he came to the isolated spot where he'd watched the two operatives kill the young woman.

He took off his jacket and laid it on the bracken and stones beside the ledge. He knelt down, quickly assembled the sniper rifle, and attached the night sights. He stared through into an algae-green world, midges darting in the night air around him.

He trained the sights on the lower trail, two hundred yards from his position, scanning it for any sign of life.

He wondered when the second operative would return. He knew there was a high probability he would go back to the base camp and pass along the same trail.

Stone wondered if the man would head up onto the high plateau trail he had accessed. It was a possibility, but he knew it was less likely.

The more he thought about it, the more he could see what was happening. The second man had been dispatched to clean up any loose ends. And that included Nathan Stone.

Stone checked his watch. It showed 0249. The man had been gone for a while. But since it would soon be light, he would want to get off the Knoydart Peninsula before the news of the senator's sudden death was reported. He didn't know if it was in the public domain yet. But he knew it would be only a matter of time.

He knew his handler would want all elements out of the locale before dawn.

It might be hours before news seeped out. But seep out it would.

Stone spread himself flat on the ground. Perfect line of sight of the trail. He could hear his breathing. Feel the cool air on his skin. A twinge on the back of his head. He touched the spot. Blood on his hands. He rubbed them on the bracken.

He replayed the day's events over in his mind. The prey. The hunt. The kill. He moved his night sights again to the area where the two operatives had killed Jessica Friel.

He wondered how he had gotten it so wrong. He wondered if he was getting sloppy. Had his enforced idleness made him soft? Had he made a critical mistake in his approach?

Thoughts filled his head as he ran through the scenarios. Would he have done anything differently?

He thought he would.

The instruction he'd been given to kill the senator from a distance was fine. Shouldn't she have been killed the same way? Then again, should he have just killed her as she knelt at the senator's side? Pushed her off the mountain? Perhaps those should have been the instructions from his handler.

It would have made perfect sense.

But to be fair to his handler, he probably hadn't envisioned the extraordinary reaction the girl had. The realization that the flash drive was gone from around the senator's neck had sparked fury in Friel. And instead of wondering where it had gone, or even asking Nathan if he had taken it, she'd reverted to primeval survival mode.

The more he thought of it, the more he realized Friel must have known her life was under acute threat and deduced that the Good Samaritan American hiker was the assassin.

His thoughts turned to the contents of the flash drive.

What the hell did it contain?

It was strange. Usually, he would just carry out the mission. But now he was beginning to question things. Critical thinking.

The sound of bats swooping low carried on the breeze.

Time dragged. Seconds. Minutes.

Then all of a sudden, through the night sights Stone saw a figure. Carrying the large backpack, moving quickly along the trail back to base.

He stared through the display. It showed the target about four hundred yards away. He clicked off the safety and watched.

It was the second operative. Stone knew from how the man walked, his build. He picked out the Berghaus logo.

It was him.

Stone held his breath. He felt his finger on the trigger. He had the operative in the crosshairs. The middle of his chest. He tracked the man. Then he squeezed the trigger. The muffled *phut* sound. The man slumped to the ground face-first. Some birds flew from the trees in the inky black sky.

Stone didn't move. He waited and waited. Still the man didn't move. He took aim again, crosshairs on the back of the man's neck. He squeezed the trigger. Another *phut* sound. A few birds rustled.

The man still wasn't moving.

Stone had made two shots. He waited a few moments. Packed his gear away, headed down onto the lower trail. His heart was racing as he approached the body. He knelt down and felt the man's neck. Skin warm to touch. No pulse.

Stone looked around. He needed to move fast. Dragged the body into the thick woods for nearly a hundred yards, then dumped it. He took the backpack off the dead man.

Stone's mind was racing. Where to dispose of the body? He headed deeper into the woods. Trudged for fifty yards through muddy ground, moss, and water.

He felt himself sinking in. "Fuck!"

He'd walked into a bog. After a struggle, he extricated himself. Relieved to be back on solid ground. He retraced his steps and returned to where the body was lying. Rifled through the man's pockets and took out the flash drive and cell phone, putting them in his zipped back pocket. Saw a familiar fake ID. American, studying international politics at the University of St Andrews. He looked down at the man one final time. Pulled the body toward the bog and rolled it in. The body disappeared under the moss, thick mud, peat, and water.

He was breathing heavily from the exertion.

Stone looked at the dead man's cell phone and scrolled through the messages. The same one from the same person. The same handler the first operative was dealing with.

His mind began to race, and an idea was beginning to form.

Sixty-Three

For more than an hour, Brigadier Jack Sands hadn't received a message from either of the two operatives on their whereabouts. He leaned back in his seat in the command room, along with Major Frank Drenge, an ex–Special Forces adviser to the Pentagon.

"Frank, something feels wrong about this," Sands said.

Drenge leaned forward in his seat, hands clasped. "I know these two guys. They'll be on their way. They did a perfect job on Friel."

"But we have Nathan fucking Stone on the loose."

"Jack, he's almost certainly seriously injured or dead. Maybe crawled off part of the mountain. Maybe dead. Either way, he won't see the night out."

Sands closed his eyes for a few moments. He felt bad about how things had worked out for Stone. He was a tough, resilient warrior. A killer. An assassin. An American ghost. And a cold-blooded machine who had served his country and the intelligence agencies for well over a decade.

"Look, the guys are well versed in communications. I suspect they'll have things well in hand. If I know the operative who's out on the mountain, he'll find Nathan."

"What a fuck-up."

"It is what it is, Jack, you know that. Nothing's ever clean. Perfect. This is messy. A lot of shit to clean up. But the bottom line? We neutralized the two targets, end of story."

"I don't like messy. I like order. I like clean kills. Clear exits. No sign we were ever there. No trace. No fuck-ups."

"Nothing will be traced back to this facility. We've compartmentalized the whole operation on that basis. The two guys on the mountain? Bare minimum."

Sands nodded. "You know what worries me?"

Drenge shrugged.

"If one or both of them is detained. And then Nathan's discovered dead on the hill. And they start asking questions. And the press gets wind of it."

"That's why we've got guys like you who work in consulates and embassies across the world, Jack."

Sands sensed things were going terribly wrong. "You know when we get problems? When some smart-ass, like the blogger—"

"The libertarian kid? Jeff Patterson?"

"Yeah, Patterson. When they start messing around in things, life tends to get complicated for everyone involved."

"Hey, Jack, you know how it is. Innocent people get hurt. It's the name of the game sometimes. Fallout."

Sands nodded.

"The good thing is we'll have the flash drive back here within hours."

Sands's cell phone vibrated. He flipped it open and saw there was a message from the second operative, code-named Mr. Thomas, who'd been out on the mountain hunting for Stone. The message said *Delivery complete. Returning to HQ*. A photo was attached. He opened it up. It showed a close-up picture of Nathan Stone's upper body, lying on heavy undergrowth, shrouded by trees. He turned and showed the image to Drenge.

"Good and gone," Drenge said. "That clears that up."

Sands called Clayton Wilson and stared at the image of Stone's face, eyes closed, and felt a mixture of relief and sadness wash over him. "Poor fuck."

Drenge nodded. "It is what it is, Jack. We all go the same way in the end."

Sixty-Four

Nathan Stone ditched his own phone in the bog, along with one of the others, and kept a spare one. He knew the facility would be tracking the phones. They'd wonder why only one of the signals was being picked up. The first assumption they'd work on was a technical glitch. The second assumption they might make was that only one of the operatives was headed back to base. But either assumption would work in Stone's favor.

He mulled that as he headed back onto the high trail for another few miles, then descended hundreds of yards from the usual entry point for the mountain. Then he climbed a stone wall and walked through a field of Highland cattle grazing under the dark sky.

Stone wanted to get off the mountain and away from any early-morning hikers or rescue teams. His detour took him through boggy ground, so he was glad of his sturdy leather hiking boots.

Just after 4:00 a.m. the sky lightened enough to allow him to read the map and check the compass. He got his bearings and doubled back along little-used paths and trails to the outskirts of the village as the land flattened out by the lakeside. He took out the night-vision glasses from his backpack and saw in the cove a small, empty boat intended to take the two operatives back to the mainland.

Stone climbed in, started the motor, checked the sea maps, and set a course.

Just over an hour later, the sun edging over the horizon, he pulled the small boat onto an isolated sandy cove three miles from Mallaig.

He walked across a country road to a woodcutter's shed he'd seen marked on the map. Inside were two high-powered BMW motorbikes. Two small backpacks with biker gear. He took off his dirty clothes and put them in one of the backpacks. The shed had a sink, and he washed off the mud and blood and filth from his face and head the best he could. He opened the pannier of one of the bikes and found a comprehensive first-aid kit. He pulled out some antibacterial spray and liberally applied it to his wounds. Then with a needle and thread, and using one of the motorbike mirrors, he carefully sewed up his head wound. He popped the last of the amphetamine and morphine sachets and swallowed the pills with water from the tap. Then he pulled on the gear.

Stone saw two sets of keys hanging from a nail. He took one set and put on a helmet, flipping down the visor. He opened the shed doors and wheeled out one of the BMWs, locked the door, pulled on the backpack, and fired up the bike.

He gave it a couple of revs. It sounded strong. Powerful. He cranked it into first gear and pulled away, heading down the isolated country lane. The sun was now flooding a dark-orange sparkle over the water of the lake and a gentle glow across the distant hills and mountains.

He sped on faster and faster. It wasn't even 6:00 a.m., and Nathan Stone was back on the mainland.

Sixty-Five

Brigadier Jack Sands was watching Fox News coverage of the death of Senator Crichton on a hiking trip in Scotland. A solemn female reporter with blond hair stood outside Crichton's home, which was located in an affluent gated community. She described him in hushed tones as a great American, a great believer in free enterprise, free choice, and small government. But a man of principle. Victim of a tragic accident. Speculation, fed by Pentagon sources, suggested the accident might have been caused by a heart attack after a series of stressful meetings.

Sands folded his arms. He'd heard all that bullshit a thousand times before.

His cell phone rang.

"Jack, it's Dr. Brian Foster." Sands had known the CIA doctor for nearly two decades. He was based at the embassy in London and was medical liaison with the CIA.

"What's going on?"

"Sorry to bother you, Jack. Just wanted to let you know I've arrived at Campbeltown Airport." Sands knew the former NATO airfield was still mostly run by the British Ministry of Defence, although the eastern side was used for civilian flights. "I've signed for the body of the senator, and he's now on board a US government Gulfstream."

"Very good work. Tell me, was there any medical examination?"

"No. He was in the hospital morgue in Inverness and removed by British military personnel while I was there."

"So the diplomatic niceties have been taken care of."

"They're fine. Good people."

"And he was helicoptered off the hills?"

"RAF Mountain Rescue helicopter picked him up, and he was taken to Raigmore Hospital, in Inverness. Jack, do I now have your permission to give the all clear for the flight to take off for the States?"

"Absolutely."

"I'll be accompanying the flight before the formal handover."

"Very good work, Doc. I owe you one."

The line went dead.

Sands felt happy with the news. Crichton was dead, with an autopsy carried out by a CIA-approved medical examiner. His mistress, Jessica Friel, was lying dead in an unmarked shallow grave. And Nathan Stone had been disposed of. But despite everything, Sands still had a gnawing feeling of doubt in his gut.

Why was that?

He pondered that point. Two operatives still out in the field. One hadn't been in contact for three hours, and the other hadn't replied to any message in the last hour.

A hard knock at his door snapped Sands out of his reverie. It was Major Frank Drenge, his face drawn and lined.

"Frank, what's the latest?"

"We're looking very good. I'm hearing through diplomatic channels that there's no formal police investigation, and the procurator fiscal will not be launching a fatal accident inquiry. No suspicious cause of death, and we're home and dry on that front."

"My only concern is the one signal we're getting," Sands said. "Operative B is en route as we speak."

A tracker of Operative B's cell phone buzzed as a red dot on the big screen. But this wasn't the approved route.

Sands stared at the screen showing the GPS location. "Shit."

Drenge said, "What?"

"He's not taking the agreed route home."

"Maybe things changed. You know how it is."

"He's not on the right road."

"There's probably a perfectly suitable explanation," answered Drenge.

What was happening slowly began to dawn on Sands. He ran the scenarios in his head. And then he got it. "Son of a bitch!"

"What?"

"Things aren't what they seem, Frank."

Drenge shrugged.

"We've been blindsided. All of us. Right down the line. Your guys have been deleted."

"What the hell are you talking about, Jack?"

Sands pointed to the screen showing the moving red dot. "This is not Operative B."

"What are you talking about?"

"This is Nathan Stone. The photo was a setup. Very cute. I get it."

Drenge rubbed his hands across his face.

"We need to intercept."

"How can you be sure it's him?"

"Trust me, it's him."

"But are you sure?"

"Damn right I'm sure. I trained the fucker. That's what I'd do."

"You don't know that for sure."

"Trust me on this one. The guys we sent in are gone. Nathan Stone is on his way back."

"To do what?"

Sands stared at the moving red dot on the big screen with a growing understanding of what they now faced.

Sixty-Six

The rain was falling as Nathan Stone negotiated a winding Highland road on the high-powered motorbike. He checked his rearview mirror and overtook a slow-moving trailer. Sped on for nearly fifty grueling miles. Stopped off for gas and a bite to eat at a roadside café. Fried eggs and toast washed down with black coffee.

The waitress poured him a refill. "Bit of a bad one coming in today," she said.

Stone nodded.

"Deepening low, according to my husband. He listens to the weather forecast night and day."

"Is that right?"

The woman smiled. "You from America, if you don't mind me asking?"

"Yes, ma'am. Doing some hiking and climbing."

"Well, probably not the best day for it. Get yourself into a nice wee B&B and get warmed up. You look frozen."

Stone grinned. "Appreciate your concern."

The woman returned to her post behind the counter.

Stone pulled out the map from his pocket and checked his location. He was about seventy-five miles from the grounds of a private estate in northwest Scotland, where a chopper was waiting. But that wasn't an option for him now.

He began to run escape scenarios through his head. What he was going to do. How he was going to do it.

The more he thought of it, the crazier he felt.

Stone was being engulfed by a fury almost unquenchable. He loved that feeling.

The rain rattled the café's metal roof. Stone went to the bathroom, wiped his visor, and left. He fired up the bike and sped off through the horizontal rain, riding hard. The rain was slashing at him. And the bike was sliding around bends on the slick asphalt. He pressed on. Farther and farther north. The miles being eaten up. Fifteen miles away from the café, he saw lights in his rain-streaked mirror. A fast-moving car. He slowed down, giving the driver time to pass. He glanced back and saw the driver staring back at him. He indicated for the car to pass. The driver just sat on his tail for a mile. He sensed in that moment that something was wrong. He wondered if the guy was just driving cautiously on the isolated narrow road. But if that were the case, why the hell was he driving so close?

He again signaled for the man to overtake him.

The driver just hung back, maybe ten yards behind him. Way too close for comfort.

Stone looked back as the driver continued to stare at him. What the hell was the guy playing at?

He opened the accelerator and lifted the speed of the bike, revving hard. Hitting eighty, ninety, keen to put some distance between the bike and the tailgating driver.

Stone glanced back and didn't see any lights. He slowed down to sixty and rode on. Just a couple of minutes later, the lights of the car came into view at high speed. But this time Stone sensed the driver wanted to run him off the road. Kill him.

He revved the bike hard and moved through the gears as the car rushed toward the bike.

The car was coming right at him, but he accelerated hard and fast, and sped away from the oncoming car.

Stone's heart was pounding. He accelerated again and again. Hitting one hundred in the driving rain as the car began to catch him. He drove faster as the rain lashed off his visor, his visibility now only peripheral.

He looked back, the car nearly upon him.

Stone could see the car was aiming to ram him off the road at high speed in the next bend. He needed to do something. Fast. He couldn't outpace the driver on the bike. He'd tried, but the car had quickly made up ground.

His options were pretty much zero.

Kill or be killed.

Who was this guy?

Was this another operative unleashed from the facility?

Stone sped on at max, reaching well over one hundred miles per hour. He was squeezing every bit of speed out of the bike. Glancing in the mirror, he saw the car was only six feet behind him. Up ahead in the far distance, he saw the lights of a huge truck, winding its way slowly down the hill.

Stone's mind was flipping through ideas. He rode on harder and harder. Then he switched off his lights, chest tight to the gas tank. Around a bend over a stone bridge. Then a sharp right.

He glanced up ahead through the rain. The truck was within sight.

Stone swerved and skirted the huge truck with only a yard to spare as it braked hard. Screeching on the slick asphalt. Then behind him an almighty explosion as the truck plowed straight into the high-speed oncoming vehicle.

Sixty-Seven

Brigadier Jack Sands was watching as a live Sky News chopper feed showed the smoldering remains of the truck and the car. Firefighters were hosing white foam over the blackened metal. Police cars nearby, forensics wearing white full-body suits taking pictures of the burning wreckage. Investigators discussing on the sidelines.

Sands kicked over a chair, sending papers flying onto the floor. "Are you fucking kidding me?!"

Drenge was blowing on a cup of hot coffee.

"What in God's name is he doing?"

"This, Jack, is what is known in the trade as going rogue."

"No fucking kidding!"

"Indeed."

Sands folded his arms and stared at the images. He could see that what had been a little local difficulty had dramatically escalated. "Two missing operatives."

"Consider them gone."

"This is not the game plan. This is not the fucking game plan."

"This is Nathan Stone we're talking about, Jack. You said so yourself. We made that crazy fuck. We built him as he is. Molded him. Trained him. He's our guy."

Sands sighed. "My boss, the US ambassador to the UK, was on the phone to me a few minutes ago."

"Oh shit, what did he want?"

"Asked what the hell was going on."

Drenge sipped some coffee. "What did you say?"

"One of our guys got hit by an oncoming truck."

"And that's it?"

Sands nodded.

"What else did he say?"

"He said he wanted a full report on why he was speeding. What was his role?"

"Give him the usual spiel. Our guy was stressed, drinking too much, maybe wasn't concentrating, that kind of thing. The last thing he needs to hear is we're running a shadow operation."

Sands ran his hands through his hair. "Ben is not a stupid man."

"Does he know anything about this operation?"

"Not a thing. He thinks I'm hanging out in Scotland with some British diplomats, drinking whisky with NATO planners and doing all that schmoozing crap."

"Jack, I don't have to tell you we have a problem."

Sands nodded.

"Nathan Stone is a bad-to-the-bone motherfucker. He's gone rogue. And this has all the makings of a diplomatic incident."

Sands began to pace the room as he tried to gather his thoughts. "The cell phone signal of Operative B is still live."

"Question is, what's his next move? Is he going to make a jump for freedom?"

"Back home?"

"Yeah, that's where his sister is."

Sands bit his lower lip. "This seems like something else."

"Something else? Like what?"

Sands said nothing.

"Worst-case scenario you can envisage?"

Sands stopped and stared at the red dot on the screen, still on the move. "Nathan Stone is going to try and kill each and every one of us for double-crossing him."

Sixty-Eight

The weather began to abate, and Nathan Stone was thinking of stopping for a break. Farther up the road, he spotted a man standing beside an RV with binoculars, scanning the deep gorge below. He slowed down as he considered his options. The man was wearing a burgundy polo shirt and pale-blue shorts, white socks, and sandals.

Stone parked beside the RV on the gravel overlook. He noticed the expensive mountain bike on the rear rack and the German license plates. He took off his helmet and jacket as the sun came out.

The guy with the binoculars turned and smiled at Nathan. He had a mug of coffee on the ground next to him. "What a view, no?"

Stone wiped his brow and nodded as he scanned the forests and mountains and the river down below as the vista opened up. "Helluva place."

"That accent . . . Are you American, yes?"

Stone nodded. "Yes, sir, I am."

The man stepped forward and shook Stone's hand, looking admiringly at the motorbike. "BMW, huh? Very nice. German."

Stone said, "You got it."

The man spoke. "Gerdhard."

Stone smiled. "Gerdhard, nice to meet you. I'm Tom McMasters."

"You on holiday, Tom?"

"No, I'm a student at Edinburgh University. Just taking a few days off."

"Interesting."

"Can I ask a favor, Gerdhard?"

"Sure, why not?"

"Have you got any coffee? I've just had a bit of a nightmare ride in the rain. Need some warming up."

The German looked concerned. "Of course. I've just made some coffee. How do you take it?"

"Just black, that'd be great."

Gerdhard blushed. "My pleasure." He headed into the RV and returned with a piping-hot mug of coffee, the way Nathan liked it.

Stone took a few gulps, feeling the warmth in his stomach. "That's mighty decent of you. Great coffee, thank you very much."

The German picked up his mug sitting on the ground. "Are you visiting anywhere in particular?"

"Just traveling around. Catching a few sights. A few castles, that kind of thing."

"I was down in Edinburgh a couple of days ago. At the castle. My God, it's fantastic. Utterly amazing. In the middle of the city. Breathtaking."

Stone looked at the RV again, the door ajar. "Where's your family?"

"My two sons are back in Munich. Doctors. Always working."

Stone nodded. "Tell me about it. What about your wife?"

The man went a bit quiet. "I lost my wife, sadly, exactly a year ago. She always wanted to make the trip to Scotland."

"I'm sorry."

"Time heals, trust me. Slowly. But this is what she would have wanted me to do. And she'd have been doing this trip with me, so it was a way of remembering her."

Stone gulped the rest of the coffee and sighed.

"Your family back in the States?"

"I'm not married. But I have a sister."

The man smiled.

"Cool RV you've got."

The man smiled proudly. "It took up a small chunk of my retirement income, but it allows me to get out and about, explore, go hiking, camping. Germany, Austria, France. And now Scotland."

"I've always loved the thought of getting an RV just like that. Beautiful."

"Very spacious too." The German cocked his head. "It's ideal for a single guy but has enough space for a couple if you wish. Check it out yourself."

Stone followed the man inside and looked around. Saw the leather upholstery, large-screen TV, expensive hi-fi equipment. German newspapers neatly piled on the table with glossy magazines. "Oh yeah, this is more like it. What a beautiful interior."

The man picked up a remote control and pressed a button. The TV came on, showing English soccer. "What do you think?"

"I could get used to this, my friend. Wow!"

The German looked pleased.

Stone pulled out the silenced 9mm, pressed the nose to Gerdhard's head, and pulled the trigger. Blood splattered off the interior as the German, dead already, collapsed in a heap on the floor.

Stone shut the door and drew the curtains. Wrapped the body in a duvet and stuffed it into a closet, upstanding. Then he locked the door.

He looked under the faucet and found antibacterial wipes, cotton cloths, and a bucket. He filled it with bleach and warm water and wiped down the surfaces. Then he went over the same area with the lemon-scented antibacterial wipes.

He put all the dirty, blood-spattered cloths in a trash can under the sink, then went outside. He picked up the binoculars and scanned the roads in both directions as far as he could see. No cars. And he hadn't seen a car, truck, or bike for the last fifteen minutes.

Desolate.

Stone walked up to the cliff edge and stared down into the gorge. He went across to the motorcycle, kicked the stand away, and maneuvered it to the precipice. Then he pushed it over and watched it disappear hundreds of feet below into the mud, trees, and foliage. He waited for a couple of minutes. No explosion.

The dampness had its upsides.

Stone went back to the RV and slid into the driver's seat. He began to laugh as he turned the ignition, then pulled away.

Sixty-Nine

When Brigadier Jack Sands saw the face of Clayton Wilson appear on one of the big screens in the command room, his heart sank.

"Jack, what in God's name is going on?"

Sands took a few moments to compose himself. "We're still trying to establish what has happened. But . . . we believe he's dropped off our radar, that's what's happened."

A deep sigh. "Any updates?"

"I sent a three-man extraction team in to see what the hell's going on. We can say for sure that one operative is now missing, and another we found just fifteen minutes ago in the cellar of the cottage."

"Fuck."

"Indeed."

"Flash drive gone?"

"We're working on the assumption that Nathan Stone has it."

"Are you kidding me? This is a mess."

"Sir, we haven't used up all our options."

"Maybe not, but you have, Jack."

"What does that mean?"

"It means you're being relieved of your duties, effective immediately."

"Clayton, sir, that's crazy. We've got an ongoing operation."

"It should've been wound up by now. But instead we've got a full-blown crisis. He's gone rogue, hasn't he?"

"Sir, we don't know that."

"What we do know is that things have gone wrong. On your watch, Sands. Maybe the truth of the matter is that Nathan Stone was the wrong man at the wrong time."

"I don't accept that, sir."

"This has all gone to shit. We have that fuck on the loose in a friendly country, one operative missing, and another deceased."

"Sir, if I can interject here."

"What is it?"

"The two main targets have been neutralized."

"But the fallout is potentially catastrophic. The documents on the flash drive. Are you kidding? This is so ridiculous it's hard to know where to start."

"Sir, I'm asking for a chance to put this right."

"Jack, we go back a long way. You know how it works."

"Sir, I can fix this situation. Gimme a chance."

"You're out of chances. Drenge is taking over."

"What? When?"

"Now. You're relieved of duties. You'll be shipped out within the next twenty-four hours by chopper, then taken to the air base, where you will be flown back to London to be with your family."

Sands stared up at the face on the screen. "Is that your final word?"

"The damage has been done. We need to make things right. Frank is now officially in charge. Dismissed."

The screen went blank.

Seventy

It was dark when Nathan Stone pulled up at the near-deserted trailer park in the stolen RV. He parked and slept for a couple of hours. When he woke, the first thing he did was check that the flash drive was still in his pocket. He took it out and looked at it for a few moments before putting it back.

His mind replayed the events of the previous crazy day. He looked at the locked cupboard that hid the body of the German tourist. He knew it was in the early stages of decomposition. But it wouldn't be long before it would start to smell something awful.

Stone checked his watch. It showed 0119.

He shut the curtains and sat down on the sofa bed.

Stone held his head in his hands as he wondered what his next move should be. He clenched his fists tight into balls. He felt deceived. They thought he was dispensable. He didn't think so. He'd never questioned orders before. But it stuck in his throat, the thought that the man who had overseen his recruitment into the CIA from the US Army, then as a freelance military contractor, had turned on him. The mask had slipped, allowing him to see with terrible clarity that he was just a cog. A mere fucking cog. A man who had outlived his usefulness.

A man who could be killed as easily as he could kill.

The more he considered it, the angrier he got.

The sound of a cell phone vibrating snapped him out of his dark thoughts.

Stone couldn't understand. He'd gotten rid of the two operatives' cell phones. There was nothing to explain the ringing.

The sound seemed to be coming from a drawer adjacent to the RV sink. He opened the top drawer and saw a large-screen Samsung Galaxy Note with a message in German. It had been sent by someone named Claudia.

Was this from the man's girlfriend? Sister? Were they asking how his vacation was going?

Stone looked at the phone. He had been out of circulation for more than a year. The cell phone looked brand-new. Big screen.

He toyed with it for a while as he gathered his thoughts. Should he move now or wait?

Stone ran his thumb across the screen and accessed the menu. It was then he noticed, down the side of the phone, a USB port. He'd never seen a USB port on a phone before.

"Son of a bitch," he said.

He leaned over and picked up the flash drive.

Then he slid it into the phone. The screen filled with encrypted gobbledygook, but slowly it began to populate with words, sentences, and then pages. He had before him an eight-page document stamped *Top Security Clearance*, code-named Sundowner Winds.

Stone felt as if he were in free fall. He was no longer moored to reality. He was floating in some surreal parallel universe. The document listed several people in alphabetical order by last name. It also gave a rationale for killing each one.

Top of the list was *CRICHTON, Senator Brad William*.

Stone read the details. He didn't know most people on the list, although one or two newspaper writers he'd heard of. A right-wing talk-show host. An industrialist.

When he'd finished reading the document, he saw there was a five-man distribution list. Generals, admirals, in addition to Brigadier Jack Sands, the man he knew so well.

He felt sick. Conflicted.

He'd been tasked to carry out the targeted assassination of one man. But this was a whole goddamn list, with reasons given for executing them.

The questions were piling up. Had someone passed on this information who had then subsequently decrypted it? Was that it? Was it Jessica Friel? Was she the one who had brought it from the States? Was that why she had to die too?

The more he thought about it, the more his burning rage gnawed away. Eating him alive.

So this was what they wanted so badly.

Stone knew the information would be dynamite. He didn't know if it was legitimate. But the tone sounded military. Like an intelligence briefing, professionally assembled.

He began to wonder what he should do. If he kept it, what if he was apprehended before he could act? What if it was retrieved by another operative, who might at that moment be trying to track him down?

Stone made a snap judgment. He clicked on the Google icon and keyed in *Tor*. A moment later, he was staring at the screen for an anonymous but highly secure router of information. It was used by WikiLeaks, among others.

He navigated his way through Tor to a part of the site, where he uploaded the document and keyed in a short message to accompany it:

This is what I found around the neck of the man I was hired to kill, Senator Brad Crichton. He had clearly been passed this information. It appears to be a top-secret military document. I have no way of verifying if this is authentic. But what I can say, categorically, is that I was tasked with assassinating Senator Brad Crichton, along with Jessica Friel. Weapon used: long-range electro-pulse rifle to initiate a heart attack. Friel I did not kill. That hit was carried out by two operatives whom I did not know. They buried her body in the woods at the base of mountains in Knoydart, northwest Scotland.

My name is Nathan Stone. I did not drown in a car accident. I was saved. And I was disappeared. The records show I died. But I did not die.

Do with this what you will.

Stone pressed the "Send" button, and the document and his message were uploaded to the secret site. But he knew that his own location would now also have been geotagged, and his security was therefore compromised.

He had to move.

Stone walked over to the small kitchenette and ran the cold faucet. He splashed water on his face and felt refreshed. Dried himself with a towel, which he dropped on the floor.

He knew he had crossed a line. He knew they were going to kill him whether he liked it or not. He couldn't hide. It wasn't his way.

It was time.

He picked up the backpack, with all the guns and night sights, and two knives.

Stone peeked out of the window. No one around. He climbed into the RV driver's seat, switched on the lights, and started up the engine. Then he pulled away. The headlights picked out the road ahead. He drove until he saw streetlights in the distance. He noticed a sign for the harbor and turned toward it. Through deserted streets, not a soul around. At the harbor, he switched off the lights and the engine of the RV.

He picked up the backpack with all the equipment. But something made him stop.

He checked the phone and saw that the document and message had been uploaded.

Stone was taught that it was better to double up to be safe. A double tap to the head was better than one bullet. Certainty. He pulled up the website of the *New York Times*.

Mark Mahoney's name jumped out at him. The journalist had been embedded with the US Marines in Baghdad. He'd won a Pulitzer. And the name flashed through Stone's head. He'd once had to get him from one building in the Green Zone to another during an attack. They had spoken briefly.

Stone dialed the *Times*'s main number. "Mark Mahoney," he said.

A man's voice said, "Mr. Mahoney is not working out of this building. He works from home."

"I need to speak to him."

"I'm sorry, sir, I can't give out his number."

"Fair enough. Get him to call me on this cell phone within the next five minutes. I have a document."

"Sir—"

"Shut the fuck up and do what I said, you understand?"

The line went dead.

Three minutes later the cell phone vibrated.

"Mark Mahoney. I was asked to call this number."

"Yeah. Gimme your private email address."

"I don't usually—"

"Be quiet. I'm genuine. I met you once in Baghdad, in the Green Zone."

"You gotta name?"

"It's on the document I want to send you. They think I'm dead."

Silence.

"Can I have your email, please?"

Mahoney sighed before giving the details, which Stone entered into an email. Then he sent the document and message.

A few moments of silence.

"You got it?"

Mahoney said, "Nathan Stone? What the hell is this?"

Stone said nothing.

"So who are you?"

"I kill people."

Mahoney said nothing.

"Senator Brad Crichton is dead. I killed him. Did you hear what I said?"

A long silence opened up. "That's not correct. He died of a heart attack."

"Negative. Made to look like a heart attack."

Mahoney began to read the details of the list. "Christ."

"What?"

"Where did you get this?"

"It was around Crichton's neck. Someone passed it to him."

"This doesn't make sense. I deal with military and intelligence people day in and day out. What the hell is this?"

"Names at the bottom are behind this. Sands is my boss."

"You're kidding me."

Stone sighed. "Do I sound like a guy who kids around?"

"Who else has this?"

"It's been uploaded to Tor for WikiLeaks."

"And that's it?"

"Yup."

"Where are you?"

"Not far from where Senator Crichton was killed. They've already tried to kill me twice."

"This is bullshit."

Stone was getting bored with the tone of the conversation. "If you say so."

"Listen, it appears, with just a cursory glance, to jibe with something I heard a few weeks back. Intelligence chatter from a couple of sources but never firmed up."

"That would make sense."

The journalist whistled down the line, as if finally grasping the significance of the document. "This does indeed look like a log of an intercepted message retrieved by the NSA that was stolen by a contractor. It was meant to be deleted, but it wasn't. That's what I heard."

Stone said nothing.

"Nathan . . . I've just googled your name. It says you drowned. Nathan Stone."

"It's a lie. I was reborn. But I haven't got long."

"Give me your date of birth."

"Listen, do me a favor and do what you have to do with it."

"I've got questions for you."

"Maybe another time."

Stone ended the call. Took out the battery and dropped it on the floor. He got the flash drive and prized open the dead German's right hand. He placed the flash drive in it, closing the fingers and fist tight around it. He knew rigor mortis would set in and keep it closed until he was taken to the mortuary. This would be a third way to get the information out.

He took a few moments to compose himself. He got up, put on the backpack, opened the door, and locked it quietly behind him.

Then he took the short walk to the harbor's edge. Boats bobbing in an eerie darkness.

Stone spotted a small boat, lobster traps piled high in the stern. He jumped on board and cut the rope. He switched on the engine, and the radar monitor lit up. He maneuvered the boat out of the harbor with the aid of GPS. Then out into dark, choppy waters.

An idea that had been forming in his head for hours was going to play out.

Stone negotiated the tight harbor entrance and steered a path clear of the rocky outcrops several hundred yards out. He was then in open water. No obstacles. He plugged in the coordinates for the island eight miles northwest of his position.

The small boat was moving slowly, but he was happy. While he used one hand to steer, he used the other to pick up the night-vision binoculars. In the far distance, he saw a few lights on the island. Twinkling, innocent, and unassuming in the murky darkness.

The boat sped out into the dark waters. He was at cruising speed, bouncing off the waves, salt water in the air, seagulls swooping low. Thoughts racing with what lay ahead.

Half an hour later, as he approached the island from the northwest, Stone cut the engine. He dropped anchor two miles offshore. The night-vision binoculars picked out tiny figures on the cliff edge. Two men smoking cigarettes, chatting.

Stone wondered if he could land at that location without being observed. He realized that wasn't the best option. He switched on the engine and sailed around the island, approaching from the southeast this time. When he dropped anchor again, he didn't see any figures. He didn't see any lights. Just darkness. And a small sandy cove.

He dropped a small inflatable over the side and climbed down, bringing the backpack.

Stone began to row toward the shore.

Seventy-One

It was the dead of the night in the command room, and Brigadier Jack Sands was stifling a yawn as he leaned back in his seat. He looked across at Drenge. "Look, I don't hold any ill will toward you. You're calling the shots. And whatever you want, if I can help you in any way, you just need to ask."

Drenge said, "Appreciate that. OK, we've lost two good operatives, with one still missing. We haven't got the flash drive. And we have Nathan Stone unaccounted for. It ain't good."

Sands nodded.

"Look, you know Nathan Stone better than anyone. We find him, we clear this whole goddamn thing up."

"What do you want to know?"

"File says he worked for you the best part of a decade. American ghost."

"Nathan Stone is possibly the most dangerous person I've ever worked with. Not so much what he can do but what he won't. He doesn't do boundaries. And he follows orders to the letter. Always has. But something has changed."

"Got to admit, this doesn't look good."

Sands felt a cold knot in his stomach.

"We gotta kill him."

"You gotta find him first."

Drenge rubbed his face with his hands. "Yeah . . . you know how it works. We train these guys. They can do anything. No compunction about neutralizing anyone. But we also teach these bastards how to disappear, drop off the grid. We haven't gotten any signals from our original two operatives. The body of one has already been found."

"Know what I can't get out of my head? That bizarre death shot of him using one of the other operative's phones. Got to say he fooled me."

"Misdirection. Very clever."

"The question is, where do we go from here?"

Drenge sighed. "We don't know where he is. We don't know if he's alive. He might be dead for all we know."

"We blew it by trying to get him on the road."

"The direction he was traveling said one thing."

Sands nodded. "I know exactly what it means."

"You think he's become enraged that two operatives were tasked to take him out?"

"One hundred percent."

"What the hell does he think he'll accomplish?"

Sands sighed. "Nathan Stone has a very disturbed background. Which makes him ideal for our purposes. He is cold. Focused. Deadly. But also a brilliant critical thinker. You think you understand him. You think you know him. But no one does."

"He's got a sister, right?"

"Been in an institution since she was a young woman. Killed her father with a pair of scissors. Nathan was there. But over the years he's visited her on numerous occasions. That was the old Nathan. He'd look out for her. I made sure she had what she needed. And I used that as leverage. She's the thing we can truly say he cares about. He doesn't give a shit about anything apart from his sister."

Drenge got quiet before he spoke. "You think he's coming here to try and kill or be killed in the process?"

"That's what I'd do."

Seventy-Two

Nathan Stone landed in the sandy cove, pulled the dinghy high up the beach, and buried it. He was wearing night-vision goggles. Then he began the tough climb up the cliff face as a howling gale barreled in off the sea. It wasn't long before his fingers were bleeding from the sharp edge of the cliffs. He was panting hard, climbing his way to the top, backpack heavy. Heart pounding. Working at the outer limits of his physical ability. He clawed his way higher and higher, the winds whipping in hard, almost losing his footing.

His stomach churned as he considered the scale of the task ahead.

The more he thought about it, the more he wondered why he was undertaking such a crazy mission. Wouldn't it have been easier to just take care of the two operatives sent to kill him and then disappear, like any ghost would have?

It would've made sense. He could get himself out of Scotland. Out of the UK. Maybe get to France on the Eurostar.

He had his Tom McMasters's documentation, but he couldn't use that now. They would find him almost immediately. It would make things tricky. But not insurmountable. It was common knowledge that, since the former Eastern Bloc countries joined the European Union, hundreds of thousands of Poles, Czechs, and Lithuanians had been free to work legally across EU countries, including the UK. And there was a black market in getting forged passports from these countries for people from non-EU neighboring countries.

Stone knew that in Warsaw he could get a Polish passport for 300 euros. He knew the name of the bar where people got them.

So he could disappear back to the US on a fake Polish passport without any trouble.

His mind drifted as he climbed. He thought of his sister, stuck in a psychiatric unit in Florida. He wanted to see her. To talk to her. But he knew they would be waiting for him to do that.

He wanted to hear her voice. That was why he'd called her.

He wanted to be back home. He missed being on the move in the States. The ability to jump on a Greyhound bus or train, or get in a car, and go anywhere at will as and when he was needed.

But he knew those days were over, and he was going to die before her.

Stone felt a sharp pain in his leg as he scraped his shin against the sharp rock face. "Fuck!" he said through gritted teeth.

He scrambled up the final fifty or so feet of near-sheer rock, clinging onto the cliff for dear life. Inching his way to the top. Closer to his fate.

The mission was madness.

What was he trying to prove? What was the point?

Stone edged his way to the top. He pulled himself up to the cliff edge. Then he peeked over some rough grass. Through the green hue of the night-vision goggles he saw harsh light and movement. Maybe five or six hundred yards away, a man driving a golf cart with high-powered lights illuminating everything in its path. But it was being driven away from Stone's position.

He saw a rabbit bounding into view. It was no more than twenty yards from him, its body highlighted through the goggles. His breathing was more settled after the exertion of the climb. He was getting his bearings.

He scanned the surrounding area. Mile upon mile of bleak fields as far as the eye could see. He had no idea how big, wide, or long the island was. But it was clear the facility was situated at the far end of the island.

Stone checked his watch. It showed 3:32 a.m. He wondered if he had just caught the tail end of a three-thirty inspection. That would make sense. Were they once an hour? Once every four hours? Once a day?

Then again, maybe inspections were ad hoc. Guys patrolling the island night and day.

Suddenly, in the distance the drone of a chopper. Then lights scouring the open fields.

Stone pressed himself close to the cliff face. His breathing was fast. The rotor blades were getting louder. But still he could hear his heartbeat. The roar got louder as the chopper swooped in. Lights searching for any sign of life.

His fingers gripped the cliff edge tight as the downdraft shook the ground. Stone held on for dear life as the chopper banked hard and turned back inland. The seconds seemed like hours as he clung on, fingernails bleeding.

Stone didn't move for a few moments. He waited until the downdraft had subsided. He pulled himself up a few inches and dared to look over the edge. The only movement through the night-vision goggles was from a few rabbits.

He scrambled to the surface and opened up the backpack. He pulled out the night-vision rifle parts and assembled the weapon in seconds. He took off his goggles, placed them in the backpack, and zipped it up.

Then he lay spread-eagled on the ground, rifle locked and loaded as he used the range finder to get his bearings.

He sensed he didn't have long. He knew it was just a matter of time before the patrol returned. It could be seconds. Minutes. Maybe an hour if he was lucky. But he knew there were only two options.

The first option was to get up and get on the move. That would be the natural reaction. But it would make him a much easier target.

The second option was to sit and wait. Hunker down. That left him badly exposed.

It did, though, offer one advantage. He wasn't a moving target.

The night-vision goggles used by helicopter pilots would kick in from a couple hundred yards away. That gave him a slight advantage with his long-range sniper rifle and night sights.

Stone scoped out the green-hued landscape. It had no cover to mention. He ran through in his mind some scenarios that might evolve. Mapped out a series of plans.

He thought of the weeks and months over the last two years when he'd been confined in the facility.

He rationalized that he was lucky to have been saved in the first place. He was glad they had let him live. And he had no compunction about the mission.

What he did have a problem with was being neutralized.

Stone knew the final decision to neutralize him would have been made within the facility. By his handler. *He* was pulling the strings. At least within the facility.

He could see now that he was being drawn back. It was almost as if events were unraveling and taking on a life of their own. He was no longer in control of his actions.

Stone peered through the crosshairs and saw a spectral figure in the far distance, partially concealed by a small vehicle. The night-vision optics showed the person was slightly more than a thousand yards away. The man's body heat was revealing his location. Stone stared. It looked like the man was taking a piss. He turned around and climbed into what looked like a golf cart. The lights came on. And the cart began to move in Stone's direction.

Stone felt time slow down. He felt his finger on the cold steel of the trigger. The man was in the crosshairs. Closer and closer. Eight hundred yards. Seven. Six.

Stone held his breath. His heart beating . . . he could hear it. The man was five hundred yards away. Then four hundred yards. He squeezed the trigger. The silenced rifle went *phut.* And the man slumped in the cart, which came to a grinding halt, his foot having come off the accelerator.

Stone stayed crouched for a few moments. The wind was buffeting hard up the cliff face behind him. The grass before him was cold and wet.

He got to his feet and ran toward the cart. Panting. Breathing hard. His heart pounding mercilessly. He was aware he was on open ground. He had broken cover.

But it was too late now.

As he approached the cart, his senses were on fire. He stepped forward and touched the man's neck. Felt for a pulse. Nothing.

The dead man was wearing a uniform. Stone pulled it off until he had stripped the man down to his underwear. He took off his own clothes and pulled on the uniform. Then he pulled back the tarp over the rear of the buggy. He shoved the man's body in beside flashlights, night-vision goggles, flares, CS gas canisters, and two gas masks. He took three flares, the CS gas, and a gas mask and placed them in the backpack. He put on a pair of the facility's night goggles. Then he carefully took the lanyard with the ID that was hanging around the man's neck and placed it around his own.

He covered up the body with the tarp, then pressed the ignition switch. The electric cart lurched forward.

Stone turned it around and headed toward the faint lights in the distance. The facility was no more than a mile away.

Seventy-Three

Brigadier Jack Sands stared at the real-time images from the facility's cameras scanning the perimeter of the three-mile-square site and over various points across the ten-square-mile island. He watched the images from the night-vision cameras of the security patrols. Also images from the chopper's thermal imaging cameras scouring the island, the facility on high alert for any intrusion.

He sensed something wasn't right. He turned and stared across at Major Frank Drenge. "He's on his way."

"Jack, there is no evidence of that."

"Trust me. I know Nathan Stone. The whole operation is being turned inside out. By him. He's calling the shots. Except we haven't fully realized it yet."

"I don't know Nathan Stone, Jack, that's true. But I do know what guys like him are capable of. And he sure as hell cannot penetrate us here."

"You're not listening, Frank. Stone is not only disturbed. He's smart. Analytical. And very dangerous."

"I'm not buying it. I say his destination will be the States. He'll be on his way to see his sister. Remember the call. I'm telling you, Nathan Stone will be trying to get the hell out of Scotland if he isn't out already."

Sands sat down in his seat and stared up at the images. "I feel it." He pressed his fist against his heart. "I feel it in here."

"That doesn't mean anything."

"You need to read his psychiatric evaluations. I've studied them all. Retribution. Revenge. Bloodlust. Rage. This is what propels him. This is what drives him. And believe me, he's coming here, if I know him at all. Just got a bad fucking feeling about this."

"Trust me. We'll pick him up at a port."

"And if we don't?"

The ringing of Sands's phone interrupted the conversation. He reached over and picked it up. "Yeah?"

"Sir, we have a problem." It was the voice of IT systems expert Frederick Parsons, an ex-NSA contractor, who monitored the operation's systems.

"Freddy, I'm kinda busy just now. Besides, Major Drenge is in charge."

"Sir, I'm monitoring cell phone traffic into US servers, and the name Nathan Stone has popped up twice in conversations."

"You have got to be kidding me."

"Sir, we've done voice analysis. The voice was that of Nathan Stone calling the *New York Times*."

"Now you *are* fucking kidding me."

"Sadly not. And someone uploaded documents to WikiLeaks using the same cell phone."

"Where was it sent from?"

"The port just eight miles from here in mainland Scotland."

Sands ended the call and stared at the screens showing no movement from any of the twenty-four cameras around the floodlit facility.

A sense of foreboding like he'd never felt before was washing over him.

Seventy-Four

Nathan Stone adjusted his night-vision goggles as he drove the golf cart toward a barrier at the facility's east gate. He spotted a hooded man sporting a semiautomatic rifle and slowed down. But he was waved through immediately.

The barrier rose and Stone drove on through, giving a thumbs-up to the guy. He pulled up in an outer parking lot. He jumped off the cart and threw on the backpack.

Still wearing the goggles, he went up to a scanner beside a huge steel door. He ran the bar code on the lanyard through the scanner. A green light, and the steel door clicked open.

Stone pushed it wider, and suddenly he was inside a cavernous concrete space. He saw what looked like a security checkpoint with an airport-style scanner. He walked forward and smiled.

"Josh," one of the two guards shouted toward him, "where the hell have you been? I've been calling you. The boss wants updates!"

Stone walked toward them and stopped. He pulled out the 9mm silenced handgun, then double-tapped both guards in the forehead before they had time to understand what was happening.

He picked up one of their radios and headed for an elevator. He was getting his bearings. He felt crazy. Euphoric. Out of control.

Stone took off the backpack and pulled out the gas mask and two gas canisters. He took off his night-vision goggles and put on the mask. Then he punched Level 2 on the elevator. The doors opened and he dropped in the containers just before the doors slammed shut.

Stone's mind was racing. He headed to the stairwell and bounded up to the next level two steps at a time. He passed a fire alarm buzzer and smashed the glass with his handgun. Then he pressed the red button.

Deafening alarms began to blare and the noise echoed around the concrete and stone walls of the building.

Stone was on Level 1. He swiped his ID card through the security reader. The door clicked open as the alarms grew louder. A burly guard stood nearby on a cell phone, one finger in his ear. "Make your way to the exit, people!" Stone shouted through the mask's voicemitter. His voice sounded amplified and distorted through the device.

"On whose orders?"

"Brigadier Sands. This is not a drill, soldier. We have smoke and fire reported on the upper levels."

The man ended the call. Stone walked up to him.

"Who the hell are you?"

Stone pressed the gun to his head and pulled the trigger. Blood and brain splattered onto the whitewashed wall and floor. He stepped over the mess and swiped the card as he went through to a large, empty gymnasium. He shut the door and took the stairs to the second level.

The alarms were nearly deafening.

Stone was heading up as people were going down, choking, vomiting, and gasping for breath, eyes streaming. He brushed past them. Headed through the open doors to the empty security station, monitors unattended. He switched on a microphone and spoke. "Please evacuate the facility. I repeat, please evacuate the facility immediately."

Stone pushed a red button to cut the power. Lights flickered as the backup generators kicked in. But the monitors stayed off.

He headed through some more doors and down a long corridor. He knew where he was. He pulled out the radio. "Is anyone there?" he said. "Copy, I have Nathan Stone. I repeat, I have Nathan Stone."

A brief pause before a familiar voice was heard. "This is Brigadier Jack Sands, soldier. What's your location?"

"I have him, sir. Where do you want him?"

There was a long silence before Sands spoke. "Good man. Safe Room 2, Level 2. Got it?"

"On my way, sir."

Stone dropped the radio as the sirens got louder and red lights flashed on and off. He saw a door marked "Off-Limits." He shot off the lock and pushed the door open. Inside was a huge storeroom. He headed down a row. A man came into view, arms outstretched as if wondering what was going on.

Stone gunned him down. The man dropped to the ground face-first. Blood spilled across the aisle. He stepped over the man and saw pallets of uniforms and boots. Pallets of radios and boxes of cell phones. Rows of 40mm riot guns. Then he saw pallets of tin containers with hundreds of CS gas canisters. His gaze was drawn to another adjacent pallet with "Danger" emblazoned in red across the front. Underneath was stenciled "Anesthetic Grenades."

Weaponized fentanyl.

Stone picked up a riot gun and loaded it with the fentanyl grenades. He picked up a pair of size 10 boots and a black uniform with a matching cap that read "Security" and pushed them into his backpack. Then he left the storeroom. His mind was racing as fast as his hard-pounding heart. He headed along a deserted corridor, the alarms still blaring, lights still flashing.

He knew the safe room was at the end of the building, directly above the psychologist's interview room.

Stone spotted a guard on a radio approaching and shot him once in the head. The man dropped like a stone as the blood gushed from his wound, pooling on the ceramic floor.

Stone lay down on the floor and stared through the sights of the riot gun. He aimed it at the far end of the corridor, where the safe room was. He fired twice, and the grenades landed eighty or ninety yards away, exploding gas and smoke everywhere.

The gas filled the corridor rapidly. It dispersed under doors and through the air-conditioning system.

He put down the riot gun and took out the scoped night-vision rifle. The seconds passed. Then the sound of screaming and choking.

Doors were flung open as operatives ran for their lives.

Stone mowed them down. One at a time. Tap. Tap. Tap. They dropped. Blood flowed. The gas cloud was coming toward him.

Then he saw Brigadier Jack Sands emerging from the cloud of gas, eyes bulging, handgun pointed toward Stone. "Nathan!"

Stone held his breath. He squeezed the trigger. And Sands collapsed, blood oozing out of a shoulder wound as the gas continued to envelop the space.

Stone moved toward him and stared down at his face. He saw the fear in Sands's eyes. The man who'd trained him. Mouth open, bug-eyed, white foam coming out of his mouth, blood dripping onto the floor. Seconds from death. "You betrayed me!" The voice was distorted and harsh. His breathing was fast. "You betrayed me! Why?"

"I didn't want to," he gasped.

"I trusted you! I always trusted you!"

"I had no choice."

"We always have a choice. Wasn't that what you told me? But you chose to betray me. Me! I have always been loyal. I would've gone to the ends of the earth for you."

Sands's eyes were streaming from the gas. "I didn't have a choice! Please don't do this. I have a family. They need me."

"*I* needed you! I don't have a family! My sister. That's my family. She thinks I'm dead. I trusted you. Like a father."

"They made the choice."

"Who?"

"The Commission. Trust me, it was them."

"You sacrificed me. You wanted to sacrifice me. I would've laid down my life for you."

Sands's arms were outstretched, trying to reach Stone. His eyes rolled back in his head. "Please forgive me. Nathan, please forgive me. Spare me. As God is my witness, I didn't want to hurt you. Ever."

Stone stared down and down. The seconds passed as the gas did its work. He waited until Sands ceased moving. He felt nothing for his mentor. A man he had trusted with his own life for years. But that was then. Now the rules had changed. His job was done.

Stone turned and headed down the nearest stairwell for the basement. He pushed through a door to another stairwell and down into a subbasement below.

Stone ripped off his clothes and changed into the black security uniform and put on the cap, pulling it low. He put on a pair of dark glasses. He kept a 9mm on him and left via a fire exit.

The alarms were still blaring as he saw the helicopter's rotor blades start up on the helipad.

Stone strode toward it and tapped on the pilot's window. "Open up!"

The pilot opened the cockpit door. "Waiting for evacuation signal."

Stone pressed the gun to his head, slid into the seat, and slammed the door shut. "Mainland! Now!"

The pilot nodded slowly. "Anything you want, sir. I don't want no trouble." He pushed a few buttons and pulled back the joystick. The helicopter took off into the suffocating darkness, lights sweeping the facility.

Gathering height.

Then a sudden climb and a turn and they were heading back to the mainland.

Stone looked down and saw the bodies of operatives lying at the far end of the facility, overcome by the chemical agent. Some of them were crawling, some were retching, on all fours.

The yellow sulfurous lights faded into the distance.

Stone was free.

Seventy-Five

The days that followed were like a crazy dream for Nathan Stone. He knew that every major port, airport, and train station would be on high alert, the CIA or some such body having leaked the details that he was wanted for a fictitious crime in the US. And that was why Stone, after being dropped off, hitched a lift in a truck to the small fishing town of Fraserburgh on the northeast coast of Scotland.

He paid cash for a basement room for a month. He disguised his appearance, growing out his hair and a beard, and wearing a tattered old beanie hat. Then one night, over a few drinks in a bar, he was hired by the skipper of a fishing trawler. Cash in hand for the job. The way he liked it. No papers needed. Just hard work pulling in the fish, mending nets, cooking for the fishermen.

It was tough. Three weeks on the North Sea was like three years anywhere else. Crazy, rough, mountainous seas, storms blowing in out of nowhere. When he was finished, he got dropped off in the small port of Dunbar, further down the east coast.

The skipper contacted a trucking firm he knew. And with money in his pocket, Stone caught a ride in a freezer truck across the border, down to Manchester. Then another lift from a white stoner in a pickup truck, all the way down the M6 freeway to southern England. The outskirts of London.

Stone knew it was easy to disappear in London. He met up with some Roma criminals at a Soho nightclub. Seventy-two hours later, he had a brand-new Polish passport for £1,000. Pretty steep. But they delivered.

He caught a ride with a Polish plumber who wanted to share the cost of the long journey back to Warsaw. Stone gladly obliged. They drove down to the South Coast, to Folkestone, and onto Le Shuttle train, which took them across to Calais. It was a breeze.

Forty-eight hours later, Stone was in Poland. He was even driven to the international airport, and caught a flight from Warsaw to Málaga. Then to JFK.

Stone flashed his Polish passport and was ushered through. He could barely keep the smile off his face. Just over two months after he disappeared on the trawler, he was back in the States. He caught a Greyhound down to Florida. And then he got a room in a crummy motel close to a psychiatric facility on the edge of the Everglades.

Stone did the same thing every night. Opened a bottle of cold beer, sat down on his upper-level balcony, just over a mile from where his sister exercised in the yard, as the evening sun went down.

The sky was bloodred. Then he would take out the military-grade binoculars and watch his sister from afar.

During the day, she would invariably sit on the same bench and sketch. Occasionally, a nurse would fill her glass with orange juice. She sat, smoked, and stared up at the perfect blue sky, not realizing her younger brother had kept the promise he'd made all those years ago.

He would never leave her. She had received the call from him. She recognized his voice. The voice of the brother she had saved all those years back in the Bowery. It echoed in her head over the weeks and months. For him, it felt good to be so close to her.

"God bless you," he said.

Stone put down the binoculars, picked up his cold beer, and closed his eyes.

Epilogue

Three weeks after Stone arrived in Florida, at a closed session of the Senate Intelligence Committee, Retired Major Frank Drenge gave evidence.

"Was there an official element to this program?" the chair asked.

Drenge leaned forward in his seat, hands clasped. "This was no program. This was a wholly privately funded exercise."

"Tell me about the Pentagon involvement, Major. You do work for the Department of Defense, I believe."

"It's complicated, sir. I have worked for the Pentagon in the past."

"Was this an officially sanctioned facility? A black site, if you like?"

"No."

"Are you saying this was an unacknowledged program then, on Scottish soil? Was the UK government aware of this facility?"

"I don't believe so, sir. This was a private research facility."

"Backed by the Pentagon?"

Drenge shifted in his seat as his gaze wandered, examining the stern faces of the politicians he despised. "We were aware of the research that was under way."

"What kind of research?"

"Research into psychological pressures on soldiers. Alienation. Psychological tests. Evaluations."

"Major Drenge, was the use of this facility connected in any way to the death of Senator Brad Crichton or his assistant?"

"Absolutely not."

"Do you currently work for the CIA, Major?"

Drenge sighed long and hard. "Mostly on a consultancy basis since I retired, sir."

"Does the name Nathan Stone mean anything to you?"

Drenge leaned back in his seat for a moment as his legal counsel whispered in his ear, "Say nothing."

"No, can't say it does."

The chair picked up black-and-white photos. "These surveillance photographs taken inside the facility were only discovered by chance by a computer forensics expert we hired. Said it was on a private cloud server. This is Nathan Stone, isn't it?"

"I couldn't tell you, sir. I've never met him, whoever that man is."

"What if I told you that this operative died and then was officially disappeared before he was resurrected again for one final mission? Then he went rogue. Isn't this what this is all about, Major? That's what some people are saying."

Drenge stared at the chairman and sighed. "I have no knowledge of this man, sir."

The chair stared back at Drenge before glancing at his notes. "Were you ever stationed within this facility?"

"I visited it once, I believe."

"A man who identified himself as Nathan Stone sent highly classified documents via WikiLeaks and to a *New York Times* reporter relating to a so-called assassination list." The chairman lifted up a stapled set of papers. "Have you ever seen this list?"

Drenge sighed. "What in God's name is this? Am I on trial?"

"No, Major Drenge, you are not on trial. Please answer the question. On this list is the name of Senator Brad Crichton. This list was compiled by a group of individuals—military and business—with the aim of eliminating anyone they viewed as off message with regards to government military spending or foreign intervention or foreign wars, am I right?"

Drenge said nothing.

The committee grilled Major Frank Drenge for more than six hours in a series of tense exchanges. When it came to revealing the group of individuals who had compiled the list, he refused to comment, citing the Fifth Amendment.

Afterward, in his suite at the Ritz-Carlton in DC, as he nursed his third single malt of the evening his cell phone rang. He picked up. He didn't recognize the number.

"Drenge, very well played," the voice said. It was Clayton Wilson.

"Thank you, sir."

"Frank, we go back a long way."

"Sir?"

Wilson sighed long and hard. "We have a problem."

"What kind of problem, sir?"

"Your daughter. She's at Columbia, I hear."

Drenge felt a cold chill. "What the hell has she got to do with this?"

"I'm being told she's been under surveillance for the last week. At this moment, she's under surveillance by two operatives. That's what I'm hearing."

"What the fuck?"

"I know how to get rid of these guys."

"What are you talking about?"

"I know the only way they'll leave her alone."

Drenge felt paralyzed.

"There has to be a fall guy, Frank. There always has to be a fall guy. At least for the record. And that's why you have to do the honorable thing, Frank. If you love your daughter, you have to sacrifice yourself."

Drenge knew Wilson was serious. He thought of his daughter. He weighed his options. And he realized that if he didn't die, she would. "And if I don't?"

"You know how this works, Frank."

Within the hour, Major Frank Drenge finished two bottles of single-malt whisky. Slit his neck. Tears in his eyes, he slipped away into the darkness, TV on loud in the background. Left a suicide note for his wife and family. Telling them he loved them but couldn't go on.

They found his body late the next morning.

Acknowledgments

I would like to thank my editors, Jack Butler, Jane Snelgrove, and everyone at Amazon Publishing for their enthusiasm, hard work, and belief in the new American Ghost thriller series. I'd also like to thank my loyal readers. Also Faith Black Ross for her terrific work on this book. Special thanks to my agent, Mark Gottlieb, of Trident Media Group, in New York.

Last but by no means least, my family and friends for their encouragement and support. None more so than my wife, Susan.

About the Author

Photo © 2013 John Need

J. B. Turner is the author of the Jon Reznick series of conspiracy action thrillers (*Hard Road*, *Hard Kill*, *Hard Wired*, *Hard Way*, and *Hard Fall*), as well as the Deborah Jones political thrillers (*Miami Requiem* and *Dark Waters*). He loves music, from Beethoven to the Beatles, and watching good films, from *Manhattan* to *The Deer Hunter*. He has a keen interest in geopolitics. He lives in Scotland with his wife and two children.